The Not So Nice Girl

Skye McDonald

For Ava,

Rock on, rad chick!
(I hear y'uke @Clemson. While I'm
a Tennessee Vol for life, I wish you
all the very best! ♡ :)

Cheers,
Skye McDonald

Also by Skye McDonald

The Anti-Belle Series:
Not Suitable for Work
Off the Record
Nemesis

The Unlikely Pairings Series:
(co-authored as Sarah Skye)
Sips & Strokes
Vibes & Feels
Whiskers & Sunshine

Writers Inspiring Writers: What I Wish I'd Known
(Contributor)

Cover Illustration by: Sara Valente

https://saravalente33.wixsite.com/valentes

Library of Congress Control Number: 2023935969

For information please contact:

Small Town Girl Publishing

www.smalltowngirlpublishing.com

ISBN: 978-1-960226-01-3 Paperback
ISBN: 978-1-960226-05-1 Ebook

For Every Woman Who Ever Had to Make a Choice.

1

ELEANOR

May 1986

Her mixed tape was two years old, and her Walkman had seen too many miles and too much outdoor exposure. So "The Killing Moon" by Echo & the Bunnymen faded in and out of her headphones as she took a deep breath and made herself step off the plane.

Eleanor had a three-hour layover in Atlanta on her way to Nashville. When the flight from Lima touched down, she wandered into the terminal with her heart skipping as badly as her music. Technically, she reasoned, an airport was its own little city. If she didn't exit the sliding glass doors, it didn't count. If her bags never touched her hands, she wasn't in Atlanta. She was in transition.

Transition was a much better place to be than the affluent Atlanta suburb of Buckhead, that was for damn sure. Transition didn't include expectations, or parties, or late nights in the backseat of...

Transition was a much better place than Buckhead.

But her layover got extended by twelve hours thanks to storms in Boston that logjammed flights across the East Coast. Eleanor had already been traveling since the day before. She was dusty from the tiny bus that took her into Lima and achy from carrying most of her possessions in her backpack. The last shower she could remember had been a couple days ago, and that had lasted about 60 seconds in the failing hot water at camp.

There was hot water aplenty in Atlanta. There were fluffy towels with monograms and pale blue sheets that were soft and cozy from so many washings. From her mother's insistence that the housekeepers use Downy fabric softener. There was her father's booming voice. There was food.

There were memories. There was shame.

She stayed in the airport.

Eleanor filled her time flipping through culinary magazines in the bookstore until the clerk began to clear his throat to let her know she'd best buy or move on. Then, she curled into a hard plastic booth in the food court with a cup of Sprite and some French fries, trying to pretend it was enough to satisfy her hunger. Her hands were still covered in tiny cuts from hours of work and not giving a damn about being dainty. Her hair was so dirty that it didn't quite fall back in place if she pushed a hand through it.

She didn't care. She might've had a layover in Atlanta, but she was still in transition. No sleep till Nashville.

Eleanor bent her head over the waxed paper littered with burnt fry ends. "No boys. No drama. Nothing complicated. I'm going for the summer to be me. Whatever that means. I swear, right now, this is my reinvention. I'll do it right this time. I'll do it smart."

She collected the trash and smiled. Her vow made the businessman in the booth across from her stare. Eleanor didn't care. She knew what she wanted.

2

SAM

Celebrating my breakup by downing a pitcher of beer might not have been the best idea. Sam Greene bobbed his head to the music, unsure where to look. Twenty feet in front of him, two girls writhed on the dance floor. "West End Girls," blared through the club, and Sam wondered if they did, in fact, live in Nashville's West End.

"Dude. Dude, listen up. Are you listening?" Sam's friend, Dylan, shouted against his temple.

If they lived in the West End, would that be irony or coincidence?

"Dude!"

Dylan's second shout shattered that train of nonsensical thought. Sam looked around again. Brian was locked at the mouth with a blonde on the bench to his left. His brother's hand was quickly working into her gold lamé handkerchief of a shirt, but he caught Sam's eye and winked.

Sam laughed. *Maybe she lives in the West End, too. Oh, shit, I'm wasted.*

"Dammit, Sam, are you going to listen to me or not?"

He shoved Dylan away. "You're screaming at my head, so yeah. What is it?"

"Fuck Trish, man." He declared it so loudly that Sam winced and jerked away—and promptly fell over onto the bench.

The room became a Tilt-A-Whirl as he tried to sit up. When he was mostly upright, he shook his head. "No, that's the point—I'm not fucking Trish. Ever again," he decreed.

"Well, yeah, that's what I meant," Dylan grumbled, then raised his beer pitcher in cheers. They'd abandoned glasses long ago. There was nothing but foam left in the bottom, but Sam drank it down anyway and burped so loud that he drew scowls from Brian and his make-out partner.

"Let's get out of here," Dylan said. But then, he grinned suddenly. "Unless you want to go dance with those chicks over there because damn, dude, I kind of wish I was single to get in on that action."

Sam watched the girls again and shook his head. It was official: he was single for good this time. After years of an off-then-on relationship, his ex-girlfriend, Trish, had dumped him a few days ago, just before she left for Spain for the summer.

He had been ready to propose.

But being "tied down" was super uncool, apparently. A heinous blight on her summer, not to mention her future. She called it off before he could officially ask.

Sam had been relieved from the moment she shut the door.

He expected that, eventually, there would be a period of mourning, but it never came. After so many breakups and makeups, there was a sense of finality that he welcomed. It was time for a new chapter.

Despite his newfound freedom, Sam knew he wasn't going to hit on those women. Brian would have been between them in a heartbeat with no hesitation. Even if Sam wasn't slurring drunk from downing a personal pitcher of beer, there was no way two girls like that would ever want to dance with a guy like him. If he had the nerve to go over, the best he knew he could hope for was a couple of smiles and an acceptance of an offer to buy a round. "Aren't you sweet" would probably be cooed at least once.

He shoved Dylan out of the booth and waved at Brian. His brother lifted a hand from the girl's hair in farewell.

The night was warm, and the fresh air was nice, but it also intensified the reality that Sam was hammered. Dylan seemed to be feeling it, too. He swayed on his feet and squinted hard, clearly trying to remember the right direction to walk.

Sam clapped a hand on his shoulder, and it almost toppled him. He pointed. "That way. I think."

"Thank god for the girls," Dylan sighed. "I'm serious, though. You better be really done with her this time because I don't… think… I can take…"

Sam looked over as Dylan's sentences crumbled. Even in the orange streetlight, his friend was an alarming shade of green. Dylan stumbled to a stop, holding his sides, and finished the point he'd been making by falling to his knees and retching into the storm drain.

Sam watched him, eyes burning, bile creeping up his throat. He tried to promise his doneness with Trish again, but it ended with him on his knees beside Dylan, puking his brains out.

When they were both empty, they slouched onto the pavement and leaned on each other's shoulders. "Shit," Sam wheezed.

Dylan nodded. "Fuck Trish, man."

"No."

"Exactly."

They looked at each other and laughed.

The only way to get up once the world quit spinning was in the lamest way possible: by crawling to their hands and knees. Once the guys were on their feet, they traded a slightly more sober frown.

"No one saw that," Dylan muttered.

Sam bumped his fist against his in agreement.

Dylan's girlfriend, Monica, lived only five blocks from the bar. A little of the alcohol had worn off by the time they got there, leaving them quiet and tired. Monica and her roommate, Jennifer, were sitting out on the front porch. Monica took one look at them and began to giggle. Jennifer sprang up and returned seconds later with two glasses of water.

"I always liked you best," Dylan said gratefully, getting a tongue poke from his lady.

"How was Trish's farewell party?" Monica asked with an eye roll as they all settled in on the porch.

Sam rubbed his forehead. "I think we drank enough beer for her to sail to Spain on. So, pretty damn good."

"Poor little Sammy," Monica cooed. She ruffled his hair, and Sam smiled.

"He is not," Dylan said. "He's better this way."

No one argued, and Sam looked around.

"What? Y'all didn't like her?"

"No, it's not that," Monica hurried to say. "She was part of the group for sure—kind of. She was alright—I guess. It's just…" She shrugged the end of her thought. Sam was too tired to press.

"Where's Brian?" Jennifer asked in the quiet that fell.

Dylan and Sam traded a look. "He was still at the bar," Sam said, carefully casual.

Jennifer inspected her nails and nodded, but he knew it wasn't what she wanted to hear. He shifted the topic away from his brother's evening plans by rising and rubbing his face. "Is it cool if I stay over?"

"Yup, but you have to sleep in the den." Monica grinned. "Front room's occupied."

By then, Sam was barely conscious. He nodded and waved goodnight, leaving his friends chatting softly in the summer night. When the screen door clicked behind him, a rustling sound to his left caught his attention. He leaned in the doorway to the living room and tried to focus his bleary eyes.

Occupied.

A girl slept on the couch. She squirmed, rolled to her side, and sighed peacefully. His eyes opened a little wider. The haze of alcohol receded fast.

Moonlight poured in from the front window and painted the room in a silvery blue glow. The mystical light caught on her fair hair and made it shimmer. She was wrapped in a white sheet, her hand under her cheek on the pillow. A little smile curved her lips.

She hummed a tiny sound of sleep, and Sam forgot to breathe.

He realized he was staring at her so hard that his eyes burned. He realized that made no sense at all and was definitely creepy. But her porcelain skin in the light was so soothing. She somehow took the edge off his drunk and his relationship angst.

Who is this? Had Monica mentioned a friend coming to stay? Maybe? He couldn't remember any details if she had.

He also couldn't bring himself to move.

Through the open window, Sam heard the others shuffle. Chairs scraped the concrete. Standing there gawking at a stranger was the height of weird, so he took a deep breath and hightailed it to the bathroom.

When he stretched out on the couch in the little den, Sam wished for morning, just so he could figure out who the beautiful stranger was.

* * *

Except he slept until eleven, and by the time he woke, he was the only one left in the house. His head was cotton and dust, reducing the whole of the last night to tumbleweeds and blurry memories that were too much trouble to recall. The beautiful stranger was nothing more than a hazy dream that dissipated by the time he got back to his apartment.

* * *

Four of the crew—Dylan, Brian, Jennifer, and Sam—had thrown their mortarboards together just days before Trish dumped him. She had elected to take an extra year for the study abroad and internship opportunities she'd wanted. Monica was a year younger than the rest.

Only Sam was going straight to grad school. Jennifer already had a teaching job lined up for the fall. Dylan and Brian were working construction for the summer and generally intending to have the time of their lives. Meanwhile, Sam picked up two lab courses and a job as an assistant to the head of the chemistry department that kept him on campus all day twice a week. Since he was there, he also held on to his DJ gig for WRVU, the school's radio station.

They let him spin The Smiths and Depeche Mode all he wanted on the late shift, and the cash came in handy.

By the time they were a week into June, Sam was well into his summer routine. Campus days were long, but anything was manageable with five days free and money in his wallet.

The Saturday after he downed a pitcher of beer and barfed in a storm drain, Sam and Brian reported for their monthly dinner with their parents.

Over meatloaf, Brian glanced at Sam. "Last weekend was fun."

"You said it," he snorted, recalling the position Brian had been in when he and Dylan left the bar.

Brian just grinned into his tea glass.

"Hey, uh, have you seen the girls since then?" Sam asked casually. He'd not seen or talked to anyone in over a week, but suddenly he remembered the girl on the sofa that night. That beautiful blonde hair slammed into his brain.

"Nah. Dylan and I have been too wiped after work to do anything but crash."

Before Sam could try a different track, their mother jumped in. "Have you heard from Trish?"

Her smile froze when both her sons winced. "What? I wasn't supposed to say that?"

Sam shrugged. "No, it's just—Trish and I broke up."

"Again?" Dad grumbled, stabbing peas.

"For good," Brian chimed in.

That got their attention.

"How did she take it?" Mom asked.

"She asked for it." Sam saw no reason to lie.

"For good?" Mom echoed.

Sam understood her doubt. Trish's father died the spring of her senior year of high school, just months into their relationship. She had leaned heavily on Sam for security, and he'd let her. But Trish had asked for "breaks" from the relationship with growing frequency over the last three years. The first one had been rough, but he'd adjusted. She'd come back, crying and begging, each time.

Sam pushed his hair away and traded a look with Brian. "For good. And that's okay. I'm fine, really. It was time for something new. I thought I'd be sad, but really. I'm not."

Dad pinned his shrewd eyes on Sam. His lips curled into an unexpected, smug grin that stunned them all. "Damn right, my boy," he chuckled, lifting his glass. "That's damn right."

Mom hummed a gentle scold at him. Brian laughed and hoisted his glass, too.

Sam would've rather sat through one of his dad's vacation slideshows than keep talking about Trish. Photos of his parents in swimsuits were more fun than this conversation, but Mom wasn't done. As she dished out homemade peach ice cream, she said, "Well, with Trish gone, I just hope both of you boys can find some nice girls. Now that you're graduated and are going out into the world, it's time to settle down." She cast a glance at Brian, too. "Grandchildren would be lovely one of these days."

Brian groaned. "Bogus. Uh, I mean, come on, Mom. We totally just graduated. We turned twenty-three two months ago. There's time."

Sam hid a smile. Brian had been declaring that he wouldn't get married until he was thirty-five for the past three years. He'd never say it to their mother, though.

Mom groaned right back. "Bogus? Totally? Are you one of those surfer dudes now, young man?"

Brian grinned and continued. "Anyway, I don't want Sam going out and finding a nice girl. Trish was nice enough. Look where that got him: practically married since high school. I want Sam to enjoy being single and meet every kind of girl he can, including some wild ones."

Their father's chuckle rumbled underneath their mother's loud protestation. Brian and Sam both laughed.

"You don't need any wild girls, either of you," Mom tried to declare, but the point was lost, and she knew it.

Sam thought the conversation was over at last. He helped clear the dishes and followed everyone into the living room. The family settled in to watch *Barney Miller* on their brand-new, remote-controlled TV.

When the show went off, Dad clinked the ice in his scotch glass and said: "What you really want, Sam, is a girl who the world sees as nice."

We're still talking about this? Sam nodded.

Dad cocked a brow. "But with you? She knows how to let herself be completely wild. That, son, is the perfect woman."

Brian choked on his tea while Mom blushed to her toes at his pointed stare. Sam gaped, then laughed because he didn't know what the hell else to do. Dad didn't react to any of them. He just wiggled his brows at Sam and nodded resolutely. Soon after, the brothers headed out, promising to come for dinner again soon.

As he got ready for bed, Sam kept thinking about his dad's words. He'd never heard something so bold and frank from either of his parents, but he liked the idea.

Not a nice girl. A woman. The kind who's a little bit of every-thing when you really get to know her. Damn, that does sound perfect. He stared at his reflection in the bathroom mirror and grinned around the toothbrush stuck in his mouth.

That grin faded fast, though. Sam rolled his eyes. *As if the perfect woman would fall into your lap. Dream on, doofus.*

3

SAM

The following Thursday, with cash in his wallet and *Born in the USA* on the tape deck, Sam cruised around Nashville with no real purpose. As always, though, he ended up near campus at Stacked Records, aka Mac's Joint.

The bell chimed when he pushed open the door. He took a moment to inhale the signature scent of his favorite haunt: paper and vinyl, with patchouli underneath, thanks to the incense frequently burning at the register.

"Woof!"

Sam grinned when Myrtle, the Golden Retriever mascot of the store, bounded up to greet him. He paid the entry fee—a good, long scratch behind her ears—and made his way to the back counter, calling hello in the empty space.

Mac appeared, carrying two boxes stacked haphazardly on top of each other. He might've grinned, but it was hard to tell with the box cutter between his teeth. Sam rushed to grab the top box before it toppled, and Mac dropped the knife onto the counter.

"I had it, buddy, but thank you. How's it been, man? Whatcha think of Lou Reed's new stuff?"

Mac was one of those guys who never ended a conversation. He just picked up where he'd left off whenever anyone walked into the store again. He and Sam fell into discussing new record releases, bashing everything New Wave, and arguing the merits of The Smiths.

"It's all about Dire Straits right now," Mac said with a shake of his head. "That's the stuff out of England you want to hear."

By then, Sam was leaning on the counter, flipping through the latest edition of *Now Playing* magazine. He snorted and said, "England's got so much going on, I'm not even going to dignify that with a response."

Mac laughed and finished breaking down the boxes. He eyed the mountain of records he'd created, then looked around the empty store. "I'm gonna smoke a joint. Want to join? I'll lock up."

Sam grinned. "Won't your boss be pissed?"

Mac laughed again. "I am the boss, Sam. I own this store."

Sam's startled expression elicited another laugh before Mac wandered into the back room.

"Back in ten. Keep an eye on the place, okay? Somebody steals something—shoot 'em," Mac called over his shoulder.

"Yes, boss." Sam saluted his disappearing form.

The mess on the counter was ridiculous. Sam had no idea how to catalogue or inventory anything, so he left it alone and sat on the stool by the register. *Dark Side of the Moon* started playing. He shouted his approval at Mac's music choice, whistled for Myrtle to come keep him company, and went back to reading.

When the door chimed, Sam was absorbed in an article about Berlin and the music of a divided country. "We're closed," he muttered without looking up. "Come back in an hour."

"I called about an album—"

"Closed," he insisted, flipping the page.

"You're definitely open. Door: unlocked. Register: manned."

Her voice got a lot more insistent—and a lot closer. A small hand with dirty fingernails spread across the magazine. Slowly, Sam looked up.

Sea glass. Emeralds. My undoing.

Sam found himself gazing into the most unreal green eyes he'd ever seen. Half a second later, everything got worse. The face that held those eyes was the same one he'd seen on Monica's couch two weeks ago. That fair skin and golden-blonde hair which had glowed in the moonlight were impossibly better in the light of day.

A heartbeat after that, things got even worse. She smiled at him.

At first, it was just a little curve of her full, pink mouth. But while he watched, dumbfounded, her nose wrinkled. Sam noticed the faint dusting of freckles there. Then her smile deepened, flashing perfect white teeth before she reigned it in and tried to put on a serious face.

All of this couldn't have taken more than thirty seconds, but Sam felt every moment in his pounding pulse. He knew his brows were lifted in surprise, but he had no idea what message his expression conveyed.

She cleared her throat. "Well?"

"Well?" he echoed.

Another smile twitched her lips. "Well, I'm right, right? Open?"

"Oh, uh, well." Sam fell over himself, running a hand through his hair and looking toward the back room. "Uh, it's," he fumbled again.

Myrtle saved him by shuffling around the counter to greet the new customer.

"Ooh, what a cutie!" the girl exclaimed.

Thanks, girl. Sam thanked the dog for the double bonus of distraction and the flash of cleavage in the V-neck tee he caught when she bent to pet her.

"That's Myrtle," he said, semi-coherent at last. "She is pretty cute."

"I wasn't talking about the dog," she murmured. The teasing flash of green eyes through her bangs did something almost painful to his lungs.

Sam's jaw hit the counter.

She straightened and threw her head back with a de-lighted laugh. "I always wanted to have the setup to use that line. Read it in *Cosmo* years ago. What did you think?"

"Extremely… smooth?" Sam reached for the right adjective, beginning to smile at last.

She leaned elbows on the counter across from him so they could regard each other. Her dark blonde brows drew together. "Smooth? Are chicks supposed to be smooth?"

"What were you going for? Alluring? Surprising? Flattering?"

She struck a deep-thinking pose with her chin in her hand. Sam furrowed his brows in mock commiseration, relieved to at least be verbal again. Finally, she said, "I think I hoped it'd be—"

"It was. Absolutely," he assured her with a nod before she could finish. She laughed again, and Sam was tempted to punch the air in triumph.

"Look, I've got places to be. Are you going to help me

or not?"

"Do you?" he asked.

"What?"

"Have places to be."

She made a show of studying the magazine's cover. "Not really," she admitted, tucking her hair behind her ear and revealing a streak of dirt below her lobe. Sam was struck by how unappealing it wasn't as she spoke again. "But I want my album. You promised it would be in today, and—"

Sam stood up straight and shook his head. "I really don't work here. Mac's… busy… but—"

"Busy doing what? Burning one? Because it reeks in here."

Sam smirked and shrugged. "But, um, what album are you looking for? Maybe it's in this pile."

"Red Hot Chili Peppers." She began to examine the mountain of LPs.

"What? Is that the album or the band?"

"Both." She lifted the top record. "Madonna. Not my bag," she grunted, setting it aside.

Sam moved behind the stack. It was so high that he couldn't see her anymore as they began switch-hitting, pulling titles off to create two new piles. When they'd moved enough of them that she reappeared, he was treated to another smile as their eyes locked.

The happiness this girl radiated made it very damn hard for Sam to not look like a total fool in front of her.

To be fair, he thought he usually looked like a total fool in front of distractingly gorgeous women. That was Brian's area of expertise. But this girl was something else. And, for once in his life, nothing about her demeanor seemed to be pushing him into the "aren't you sweet" zone Sam was accustomed to. She really seemed to be flirting with him. That knowledge sent even more adrenaline through his system as he did all he could to keep it going.

"What's your name?" he blurted. *Smooth, Greene.*

"This is it!" she cried, eyes on the album in her hands. She did a little shimmying dance that made Myrtle's tail wag and Sam's pants tighter.

"Can I check it out? Ring me up first if you want." She dug her wallet out of her jeans. It was a snap-shut men's trifold with a The Cure sticker on it.

Sam nearly swooned. *She likes The Cure? I might be in love.*

Mac appeared with a yawn and a cough. "What it be, y'all? Totally dozed off for a sec." He looked at the girl and the album, and then coughed again and laughed. "You're the one who's been busting my chops to get this in."

"Yep. You're Mac?"

"The original." He held out his hand, and she shook it.

"I'm Len."

Sam's brows knitted. *Len? Leonard? Leonardo? What kind of a name is Len for this woman?*

Mac nodded. "Far out. What's with this holy grail of albums, Len?"

"They're a group out of California with a cult following. This album came out a couple years ago. My friend had it on tape, and I got obsessed."

"California, huh? Bunch of hippie crap, then." Mac eyed her. "Figured with how you've been calling every couple days, you'd be all into something uptight and electronic. Now I don't know what to think, between this and that wallet you're holding."

She bubbled another laugh. This one was just for Mac, who grinned right back. "Not hippie crap, pothead Joe. Gah, and The Cure is where it's at—what do you listen to? Country?"

Mac pointed to the door. "Out. Get out," he commanded, absolutely kidding. "Or else I'll sic Myrtle on you."

"Ooh, shaking in my sneakers," she shot back with a shudder, sliding bills his way.

Mac glanced down at the cash and winked at her. "Or maybe I won't tell you my surprise."

She leaned on the counter again, cocking her head. Sam had become utterly invisible as he watched the pair banter like old friends. Part of him hated it. Part of him was fascinated by how easily they chatted without overthinking everything.

Mac reached to the remaining original pile, lifted a few albums, and produced one. He slid it across to her.

Len's eyebrows went to her hair. "A second album?" she squealed, looking at him with her most excited smile yet. He nodded, and she broke out into an even more elaborate happy dance and reached for her wallet again. "I had no idea. I hope you know you're my new hero."

Mac flashed a wide grin and nodded. "Figured I'd have another disciple in you."

"I'm going to have a listen, okay?"

"Right on." Mac gestured to the hall of record booths and shoved Sam off the stool.

He had barely gotten to his feet when he was suddenly in her line of sight again.

She tilted her head. "Hey, not-employee. What to listen with me? It'll rock your world."

"Oh, uh, well, the booths are pretty small."

Her brows twitched, and Mac howled with laughter. Instantly, Sam was kicking his own awkward, naïve ass.

"Dude, take one for the team and check it out," Mac said, shoving his shoulder.

"Nah, don't stress yourself." Len flounced toward the booths. Just before she disappeared, she added, "But if you change your mind, do it in forty-five seconds, or I'm not letting you in."

They heard the soft click of the door, and Mac shoved him again. Pointing, he said, "I'm Lucy in the sky high right now, and I know you better move your ass."

Sam considered answering him. Instead, he ran after her so fast that he stumbled and had to vault a whining Myrtle.

"Eighteen seconds to spare," she greeted him when he opened the only illuminated booth in the hallway.

It really was the width of a confessional box in there. The bench and record player made things even more cramped. Speakers were mounted on the four corners of the ceiling.

Len dropped the vinyl on the turntable and stepped sideways to let him in. "Have a seat. We're listening to their first album because I know it."

Sam sat down on the bench while she stood by the record player. The needle touched. Right away, the room filled with a gritty, growling punk sound. The vocals were purposefully choppy and varied with a heavy blues influence.

Len lifted her brow. "It's a little dirty. In case you're easily offended."

Sam just crossed his arms and put his shoulders on the

wall.

So, are you in school? What other groups are you into? How do you know Monica and Jen? There were countless conversation starters he could've tried, but it was clear that the music, not chat, was her agenda. Len leaned on the wall with her eyes closed. He wanted to talk to her, but he respected her attention to the music too much to break it.

Their sound was different. Good for sure and interesting, but he was more entertained by watching her. She began by nodding to the beat. By the second track, the rhythm was in her shoulders and hips. She was essentially dancing for him, right in front of him. Her body was so close, all he'd have to do was cross his leg, and she'd feel it. Her eyes stayed closed, a content smile on her lips while she moved. Sam watched and didn't try to pretend like he wasn't.

She swiveled her hips halfway through the third song, and their knees touched. Sam sat up straighter when she startled. Her eyes fluttered open while her hand flew to her mouth.

"Sorry about that," she said, a shade breathless.

Her feathery gasp and the way he could still feel that brief connection shut off something in Sam's brain. Something that always held him back from just seizing a moment. Instead of mumbling that it was no problem, he grasped her wrist and flashed a half-smile.

"It's fine."

"No, now I'm embarrassed," she replied, sounding as composed as she had since walking into the store.

"Are you?"

"Humiliated, even."

He changed the topic. "Would you like to sit?"

She assessed the tiny bench. There were maybe six inches of free space. Even with her petite figure, there was no way they could both fit. Sam knew that logic and good manners would suggest he stand up, but her eyes sparkled with curiosity. Instead, he found himself sliding his thumb across the soft side of her wrist and saying, "I'm sure we can make it work."

"Someone's bold all of a sudden," she muttered.

He froze and cocked his jaw. "Too far?"

Her lips curled. "I'd love to sit, thanks."

She's going to squish beside me. She's definitely not going to sit on my lap. There is just no way I'm that lucky.

The track changed, and she—

She straddled him.

Sam's heart stopped, then exploded as her knees settled by his hips, her hands briefly on his shoulders while she situated. He kept his own hands balled into fists at his sides, terrified and elated all at once.

Her eyes crinkled. "Is this what you had in mind?"

"It wasn't what I'd expected, no." *More like hoped beyond my wildest dreams.* "But if you're comfortable, then by all means."

She adjusted again, rocking her hips, and even though there was daylight between their bodies, Sam's eyes fell shut while he tried to stifle a groan. Len giggled, and he opened one eye.

"I can't believe I'm sitting on you," she confessed, breathless again. "Do you think I'm a slut?"

His brows pulled together. "Not at all. Do you think I am?"

She held his shoulders and tilted her head back with a

laugh. When she sat forward again, her hands stayed. "It wasn't my first impression, no," she said, fingering his t-shirt.

The needle jumped and lifted on the old, heavily-used record player. Sam and Len looked up at the sudden silence.

"Dammit," they both muttered.

It was just too far for her to reach, so Sam's lap was vacated while she reset the needle. He barely had time to suck in a breath before the music resumed, and she was back.

"I'd just found a good spot," she grumbled as she shifted around.

Sam couldn't speak through his clenched jaw. He closed his eyes and tried to breathe evenly.

"God, you look tense."

"You're, um, squirming all over my lap," he said, eyes still closed.

"You said to be comfortable."

She repositioned again. This time, her hips rolled far too close to the undeniable ridge in his pants. The possibility that she would laugh at him for it made Sam grab her waist to keep distance between them.

Len froze. Sam's eyes opened. She settled on the middle of his thighs where he guided her. He didn't let go, and her eyelids drooped a little as her gaze flicked to his mouth.

I'm going to kiss her. I hope. Dammit, I wish I was a "pull her to me" kind of guy. Dammit, I'm going to mess this up. Dammit, she is so beautiful.

While he sat there, overthinking and staring into those emerald eyes, Len's shoulders dropped. Her hand floated back to his shirt.

"Do you like it?" she murmured.

"Do I like what?" he rasped.

"The music, of course. What else would I… be talking about?" Her voice grew softer as her fingers danced along his neck.

And, suddenly, Sam was absolutely a pull-her-to-him kind of guy.

I'm going to try, at least. For once in my life.

"I want to kiss you."

"Now?"

He wet his lips. "Right now."

Len blinked and nodded once. "Okay," she whispered.

His fingers played on the curve of her waist as he tightened his arms, inviting her forward. Acting on instinct and want, he glided one hand up to her jaw, then to the nape of her neck.

In that handful of seconds, Sam saw the thrill in her eyes, the way her tongue wet her lips, the blush in her cheeks.

He guided her mouth onto his with a surety that surprised him. What surprised him more was how he knew without a doubt what he wanted this kiss to be. He opened his mouth right away to pull on those petal-soft lips, taste them with a gentle swipe of his tongue that made her tremble and rest her other hand on his heart. She softened immediately, letting him suck her lower lip and lick the slickness just behind it.

The more of her he tasted, the more he wanted.

The tip of her tongue met his just inside her mouth. It took him a beat to realize that the growl he heard came from his own throat. Len whimpered and fidgeted, and his blood began to thunder like he'd never known.

Sam's touch made its way under her t-shirt to her warm, silky skin, but that snapped the moment. She broke the kiss.

Sam startled and removed his hand right away.

"Easy boy," Len gasped, gulping air. Her eyes were impossibly greener, her cheeks a deep rose over a brilliant smile.

"I'm sorry?" he wheezed, but it was a question. And Sam wasn't sure of the answer.

"Are you?"

"If… if you are?" He gazed at the face that was still leaning against his forehead. His next words came out rough and strange to his own ears. "But if you're not, then hell no, I'm not sorry."

She grinned. "Damn, who are you? You didn't even want to come in here, and now you kiss like that?"

"Like what?"

"Like fire. Like, let's get naked."

Sam's face warmed, but he asked, "You were hoping for something a little more boring?"

She eyed him.

The next thing Sam knew, she grabbed his shirt, her lips parting just before they met again. He leaned forward eagerly. Her arms hugged his neck, fingers tangling into his hair. She tugged, and he growled again as he used his tongue to open her wider. This time, Len planted his palms on her back and lifted the hem of her shirt. She sighed and rocked forward at his touch.

This time, Sam didn't care if she could feel how badly he wanted her.

A brief, wild fantasy of her whipping off his belt and them getting naked right there in the booth surged through him and fueled the urgency of his hands and mouth. Len moaned softly and ground against him again. She grabbed one of his wrists to bring his hand under her breast.

Oh, god, Beautiful. Gladly. Sam's thoughts were hazy and blissed as he tickled his fingertips over her bra.

He heard the clink of metal and felt her hands against his abs before he registered what was happening.

She pulled back and sucked on her bottom lip. It plumped out, flushed a deep red that had him mesmerized. "Should we?" she whispered. "Is this too, I don't know… wild?"

Holy shit.

Sam wasn't thinking of his family dinner or his father's comment just then. All he could think of was how hot this was.

"Maybe?" He dragged his thumbs over her breasts.

Her pupils dilated, but she smiled and echoed, "Maybe."

Then her hand slid into his jeans, and his head fell back against the wall.

"Are we doing this?" she murmured against his mouth.

"We're doing this."

4

ELEANOR

"Don't be a stranger."

"You know it," Eleanor called over her shoulder. Mac was dozing at the register. She'd made it to the door before the chime roused him.

Outside, she jumped into her car with an exhale. Her mother's voice echoed in her head from long ago: "A nice girl never just gives it away—never, ever, Eleanor Beatrice." She forced herself to look down at the damp smear across her jeans where she'd just wiped her hand.

She squeezed her eyes shut. *I didn't. I didn't really. No way did I actually...*

Pressing her thumb into the shiny, sticky spot on her palm, Eleanor sighed again. "Well, it's official. You're the girl your mother warned you about. Not even a month in Nashville, and here we are."

She groaned so loud that Mac probably heard it inside. A car parked in the space beside hers and shook her out of her thoughts. She had to get the hell out of there. Still groaning, she fired the engine of her VW Bug and headed back to Monica's.

Please don't let Dylan be there.

Monica's boyfriend was almost certainly working, but dammit, Eleanor blamed them for her sweaty fall from grace. He stayed over the night before, and the front room Eleanor occupied shared a wall with Monica's bedroom. An all-too-thin wall, it turned out. Hearing the two of them together had done something weird to Eleanor's hormones. It made her itch to be touched like she hadn't been in ages.

She turned onto the block and nodded at this oddly comforting thought as if it justified this crazy thing she'd done. "You're just hard-up," she said in the empty car. "He was cute. It's fine. It's done. Go to confession and move on."

Does confession work if you're Presbyterian? I'll ask Gran.

Monica was on the porch, painting her toenails a bright neon orange, when Eleanor pulled up to the house. "You look high," she greeted her.

"Might've been a contact buzz at the record store," Eleanor agreed.

She laughed. "Mac's Joint?"

Eleanor wasn't surprised that Monica knew the reference. Mac seemed like a character who'd be known by everyone. She nodded and plopped on the steps, still clutching the records.

"Was Myrtle in today, too?" Monica asked.

Something about her question made Eleanor's stomach clench. "How often are you over there?"

"Oh, we hang out at Mac's on the regular. It's a great place to waste time between class or on a rainy Saturday."

"Do you… or, I mean, you don't know… all his regulars, do you?" Her stranger had definitely seemed comfortable behind the counter.

Monica furrowed her brow. "I mean, his place is popular, especially when the semester starts. I don't know everyone. Why? Did you meet someone?"

Eleanor shrugged and studied the album art.

"Len," Monica chided.

She rolled her tongue and wrinkled her nose. "Nah. Well, maybe a little. There was a boy there. He just, I don't know. He—" she broke off, trying hard not to blush.

"A boy? You met a boy?" She swiped a strand of her straight black hair away from her mouth as her big brown eyes went wide.

"I didn't 'meet' anyone. He was just there," she defended, lying on the technicality that they hadn't, in fact, officially met.

"Go on." Monica grinned.

Eleanor blew her bangs off her face and said, "He, uh, he… he was really cute."

Just confessing it had her heart fluttering like it did when she threw out that silly pickup line from *Cosmo*.

Monica squealed and sat forward, almost dropping the nail polish. "What kind of really cute?"

"He looked like Blane from *Pretty in Pink*," Eleanor blurted. A nervous giggle escaped her, and she rolled her eyes. Eleanor hadn't had girl time in two years. Talking like this with her childhood best friend was silly—and so much fun.

Monica gasped. "Shut up! You did not meet Blane in real life."

She had introduced Eleanor to the movie on her first weekend in town. Her mission was to bring Eleanor back into "the real world" after all her time away by filling her in on pop culture.

"No, it wasn't him," Eleanor said

Monica rolled her eyes. "No duh. Keep talking."

"He was that type of adorable, minus Blane's rich boy vibe. Medium length, reddish-brown hair, dark blue eyes…a," she looked down, "killer smile," she whispered, then giggled again.

Monica jogged in her chair, her toes dancing up and down on the patio. "Look at you, Eleanor Field!" she squealed. "Please tell me you gave him our number."

Number? I barely remembered to take my records.

Eleanor deflated a little and shook her head. She flashed back too easily to the gorgeous sound he made when he climaxed in her grip, the way he reached for her waist right after. But Eleanor had jumped up, knees unsteady, and turned for the door. He called for her to stay, but she couldn't look at him anymore, couldn't think of anything but leaving. Before he could say another word, she'd hightailed it out of there.

"Len? Where'd you go? I asked if you gave him our number." Monica waved at her.

She crooked her lips in a sour smile. "Why would I do that? I already swore: no drama. No boys. Just hanging out and having fun. Besides, I'm leaving again soon."

Monica's face fell. "You're not really, are you? But what about the contest thingy with Sweetie's Bakery?"

Eleanor chewed on her lip. "I haven't decided if I'm going to go for it."

"What! With your talent? What do you mean you're not going to try? It's an internship that would let you live in New York City and learn from some of the top pastry chefs in the world. And then you'll get to come back here for good and become the raddest cake maker in town. I'm confused where the problem is."

Because I have to make three of the toughest pastries in the world, and I'm not that good, Monica. Because getting the internship would mean I had to commit to coming back to Sweetie's—coming back here—and working for at least two years. Because… because…

"I don't know if that's the right thing for me. And I was thinking of road-tripping for a few weeks. Or maybe all summer, just kind of see where I land next."

Shrewd eyes pinned her in place. "You just got back from saving the world for two years," Monica murmured. Eleanor nodded. "This is smacking strongly of running away if you ask me. From opportunity and from life."

"No," she said, too quickly for Monica to buy it for a second. Her gaze flared, and Eleanor tried again. "No, Mon, I just don't have much tying me down if I don't want, so why not enjoy it, you know?"

But Monica pressed on despite Eleanor's pleading eyes to change the subject. "I do know, but I also know the rest of the story—the story that's not your fault, for the billionth time."

Eleanor rolled her eyes. It was a practiced move to hide her flinch.

Monica growled. "Go for the Sweetie's internship. You know you'll love it. Why do you have to keep leaving?"

"Leaving what? It's not like I have a home or anything."

Eleanor knew she'd said the wrong thing. Monica's therapist vibe, which she'd been cultivating since they were in 8th grade, crumbled fast. Her mouth turned down in a wounded frown.

"This can be your home, Len. I already told you. Dylan and Brian can convert the room for you, and Jennifer doesn't mind at all."

She didn't answer.

"You meant the city, too," Monica said sadly. "Hon, how can you say that? Of course this is your home! Alex, your grandparents, me—we all thought you'd come back here."

Eleanor glanced up. "So, you're not going back to Atlanta after school?"

Monica didn't hesitate. "No, thank you, and you're not either."

"No way."

"Right. Nashville is home now. Why don't you think so?"

"It's where y'all live. It's where I spent a measly year floating along, trying to get my head on straight after——" she broke off with a sigh and threw up her hands.

Only then did she notice her dirty fingernails. "Do I have chocolate all over me?" she asked abruptly.

Monica eyed her and laughed. "Yep. Right here." She dragged her finger along Eleanor's neck, under her earlobe.

Eleanor groaned and collapsed onto the patio.

"Did Blane say anything about that?"

"Nope." For some reason, this solidified the queasy idea nagging her. That cute boy had written her off as nothing more than an easy good time. Whatever possessed her to be so crazy didn't matter. She was just a little afternoon delight.

An even more nauseating thought floated up. *Either he's already forgotten, or I'm going to be a hell of a story for his boys at the bar tonight. Oh, god, he wouldn't, like, carve this on the wall or something, right?*

You've been watching too many movies lately, Eleanor Field. Don't start drama, and there won't be none. She took a deep breath and thought about the guy again. Being a crazy story for all his friends seemed possible—except somehow it didn't.

With her eyes closed, Eleanor recalled his expression when she'd walked in. He'd seemed so stunned, and it had given her such an ego boost. There was something genuine in that navy gaze, something she wasn't used to seeing. He didn't seem to realize how cute he was.

Then, she thought of his kiss. He'd asked permission to kiss her. How hot was that? She recalled those too-perfect lips—really, they were indecently lovely for a man—and how hot and sweet and passionate he'd been with her.

Definitely, maybe he won't tell his boys.

Monica left her to her thoughts long enough that Eleanor was feeling drowsy by the time she stood and capped the polish. "The crew is going to Mulligan's tonight," she said. "You in?"

Eleanor shook her head. "Sorry, Alex has roped me into a blind date." She made a face. "Who wants a stuffy law student? Not that this is anything but a favor for my brother, but still."

Monica snorted. "Uh, plenty of ladies? Fine, but you're hanging out this weekend."

Eleanor smiled and promised as she followed her into the house.

They found Jennifer in the bathroom. The sink looked like a war zone of Cover Girl vs. Maybelline, with a curling iron and giant can of Aqua Net as incidental casualties. She was furiously combing her wavy brown hair, but it had gone past teased and into finger-in-the socket wild.

Monica and Eleanor traded a glance. "Jenny?" Monica crooned. "Len needs a shower, hon."

"Oh, I'm sorry," she gasped, blushing to meet their eyes in the mirror. "I just was trying to fix my hair. It's such a beast. What do you think?"

"I think you do know it's just Mulligan's, right?" Monica

pried the comb from her fingers.

Eleanor slipped around them and started peeling out of her clothes.

"Len! I'll leave, I swear. Just let me clean up." Jennifer turned away when she was down to her underwear.

Eleanor paused and wrinkled her brow. "No, it's fine. Just do your thing. Why are your ears blushing?"

"You're naked."

"Not yet," she said, then dropped her panties. "Now I am." She laughed and stepped into the shower, soaking in the abundant steam. "You lose your modesty quick when it's a row of communal showers with about ten minutes of hot water for the day."

"It helps if you've got a perfect bod," Jennifer grumbled.

Eleanor groaned, and Monica told her to shut up. Jennifer drank Tab soda and worried too much about her curves no matter how much the other girls insisted she was beautiful. Eleanor began to soap while the other two continued their conversation at the sink.

"I think my hair got too big," Jennifer said, and Monica hummed a gentle affirmation. "Ugh, now I have to shower again to beat it down and start over. I just wanted to look nice. Brian's coming tonight, and I haven't seen him in a few weeks."

Monica sighed. "Jennifer Marie, are we teasing our hair for Brian Greene?"

Silence.

"Honey, you know—"

"That he's a playboy? That he knows I'm in love with him? That I'm way too much of a geek for a guy like that? Yep, I sure do."

If she hadn't been soapy and naked, Eleanor would've hugged the girl for the defeat in her blunt words. As it was, she poked her head out with a frown.

"Then forget him."

"I know," Jennifer muttered. A tear spilled down her cheek. She set the hairspray down and sank onto the toilet. "I know. I just… am pathetic."

Monica hummed to life. She grabbed the flatiron and buzzed around. She began to yank the comb through her friend's hair and said, "You're pathetic when you decide you're pathetic. You have a crush on him."

"Unrequited love—dang, Mon, too rough!" Jennifer yowled.

"You don't love him," Monica insisted. "You want to do dirty things with him, which is totally fine, but it's not love. What you need is to get laid. Then you'll quit friggin pining for Brian."

Eleanor hid in the shower before either of them noticed her blush. She let them prattle on while she glanced down her still-achy body. *I need to get Blane off my mind.*

After the girls had drifted away, she dried off and slipped into the front room. Dylan had been sweet enough to install a pair of doors in the wide entryway for her the previous weekend. She shut the doors, climbed between the sheets of the pullout sofa, and slipped her hand between her legs, thinking about nothing but him.

5

SAM

Oh, hi Len! Wait, you know Monica? Wow, what a total coincidence!

Len, hey girl, you're looking rad tonight. What were the odds I'd see your fine ass here with my friends? Lucky me, I guess.

Heya, Len, you know the crew? That is so dope!

Sam rubbed his forehead. "You've never said dope in your life. You will sound like a dope if you go in there and try any of those corny lines."

He blew out a breath and stared through his windshield at the entrance to Mulligan's. The crew's usual haunt for Friday nights was the first and last place he wanted to be. He'd purposefully arrived late. Sitting in his car overthinking the whole evening hadn't been part of the plan.

"Man up and go in there. She's going to throw a drink in your face and call you a weasel. She's going to pretend like she doesn't even know you. She's going to… she's going to…"

Let me finish what we started. Jesus, wouldn't that be the dream?

He huffed a laugh. "Dream on, dude. Dream on."

Sam did all he could to keep a straight face as he forced himself to enter the bar. But when he spotted his friends at their usual booth, there was no blonde head among them. No emerald eyes fixed on him with horror, loathing, or unbridled lust.

There was no Len.

Of course, he couldn't ask. So, he did the only thing he

could do: he ordered a beer and took his seat. They greeted him with a cheers, including the date Brian had his arm slung around. Sam hadn't seen her before. By the message in his brother's eyes when they exchanged a look, he likely wouldn't see her much more after this.

Friday nights were for pub trivia and hanging out over chicken fingers and honey mustard dip. No agenda except for planning the weekend. They had decided to go out on the Greene's boat the next day for a little R&R. Sam promised to bring donuts when he met them at the house the next morning.

"Bring an extra chocolate and glazed, please, Sammy," Monica said.

Sam laughed. "Extra munchies after Saturday morning cartoons?"

"Hope so, but not mine. Len promised to join us tomorrow."

Sam took a long gulp of beer. "Who?"

"Oh, right, you two haven't met her yet," Dylan said, nodding between Brian and Sam. "Monica's friend from elementary school. She's rad."

Brian's date flashed a terse smile at this. "I think a day on the boat sounds fun," she said to him.

Brian winked. "We'll see how it goes."

Abruptly, Jennifer stood up from her seat. She motioned for Dylan and Monica to scoot down the booth and let her out. "Excuse me. I have a headache. Think I'll call it a night."

"Where you going, Jenny?" Sam asked, but she just shook her head and went for the door.

"What's her problem?" Brian's date wondered.

"Tired, I guess," Monica said in a way that ended the conversation.

Sam took another sip of beer. *Is that going to be me tomorrow? Enduring torturous moments while I choke on all the things I want to say?*

Almost certainly, he admitted to himself.

Whenever they met again, there was no way in hell that Sam could let on that he'd known about their connection in advance. No matter how things unfolded, he'd keep that technical lie forever. The fact would've bothered him if he weren't so busy being torn in half by white-hot memories and nauseating dread.

6

ELEANOR

"I had a great time. Sure I can't drive you home?"

Eleanor smiled and clutched her little purse. "I'll ride with my brother, thanks."

Jason, the lawyer, stepped closer, using his knuckle to tilt her chin up. "Let's do it again sometime, hmm?"

Eleanor turned her face just in time for his lips to glance off her cheek. Her vow of no boys, no drama, didn't even need repeating with a guy like this. This guy looked at her like she was a "pretty little thing," and he was used to having his pick of pretty little things.

She'd seen this guy before. Different body, same vibe.

Jason pulled back and touched her nose, then popped the collar of his Lacoste shirt and turned to his car.

Not his car. His 'Vette. He'd only mentioned the thing every twenty minutes or so over dinner, refusing to actually use the entire word Corvette even once. Eleanor shivered despite the warm summer air. It wasn't Jason's fault, but everything about him brought up far too many memories for her liking.

"Come on, sis. Let's hit it," Jason said to the young woman currently telling Alex goodnight.

Eleanor turned just in time to see her brother peck the girl's cheek before she hurried to the cherry red sports car. Eleanor followed Alex to his simple black Corolla. Their doors slammed simultaneously as they listened to the roar of the Corvette engine and "Rock Me, Amadeus" blaring into the night.

She looked at him. He looked at her.

"Well," she said.

"Well," he agreed and started the engine.

But then Alex flashed a grin that reminded her of childhood. In a good way. "Networking is over. Want to go have some fun?"

Eleanor laughed. "For sure. Oh, but let's stop by Monica's place first and get those new records you said you'd convert to tape for me."

"Monica's place? I thought you were living there."

"Whatever." She shrugged, again skirting the whole permanence issue.

"Fine, but if I'm driving, you're buying our beers."

At the house, Alex waited in the car while Eleanor jogged up the walk. She promised to only take two seconds. Inside, though, she found lights on in the den and the soundtrack to *St. Elmo's Fire* blaring.

Jennifer appeared in the hallway. Her arms stretched wide as she belted the titular song at the top of her lungs. She twirled in a circle that ended with a harsh jolt at the sight of Eleanor. "Oh, my goodness!" she gasped as her hand flew to her mouth.

"I'm sorry, I'm sorry! You sound great, though." Eleanor couldn't hide her smile.

"Ugh, stop," Jennifer groaned and darted away. A second later, the house was silent. She reappeared. Eleanor noticed that she was still dressed in her high-waist acid jeans and yellow silk blouse. But now, her hair was pulled into a low ponytail, and she'd washed off the electric blue eyeshadow she'd worn earlier.

"Just you here?" Eleanor asked, ducking into "her" room. Jennifer nodded as she leaned in the doorway. "Why'd you come home?"

She shrugged. "Just, you know, kind of got sick of the whole pining thing. Brian had a date tonight," she whispered with a swallow and brave smile. "I stayed through half of dinner and said I had a headache."

Eleanor hugged the albums and faced her. "My brother and I are going to shoot pool at a place in Green Hills. Want to come?"

Jennifer's hazelnut-colored eyes widened. "Really?" she asked, then bit her lip right away. "Oh, but no. You guys probably want to catch up and everything, and I don't really play pool. It's nice of you, though."

Eleanor pursed her lips and arched a brow. "Jen. Seriously? Come on. It's totally not a big deal."

She grabbed her hand and tugged Jennifer toward the door. Jennifer laughed but then dug her heels in.

"Well, if I'm going, maybe I should put my face on again. Oh, and my hair's a mess now. No, Len, just—"

"Ugh, It's not the runway at Milan, girl. You look awesome anyway."

"As if," Jennifer snorted, but she let herself be dragged outside to the car.

"Took you long enough," Alex greeted when Eleanor opened the passenger door.

She ignored him while she slid the seat up to let her friend climb in the back of the two-door. "This is Jennifer. Jen, Alex Field. He's thrilled to meet you."

Jennifer emitted a nervous gurgling sound. Alex reciprocated with a muttered apology for his rudeness. Eleanor swallowed a laugh, but then she realized the awkward silence that followed showed no signs of being broken. So, she decided to play DJ and dialed up WKDF. Alex and Jennifer began humming along to "Danger Zone" right away.

"But, seriously, do y'all even really like *Top Gun*?" Eleanor asked.

"It's a great movie about friendship and loyalty," Alex said with a nod.

Jennifer laughed in the back seat. "It's a love story about lowering your defenses and admitting when you need help." Alex hummed, and she added, "And it's Tom Cruise in a uniform."

Her brother chuckled. "Says you and the rest of American women."

"We sure do. Well, and also Val Kilmer in uniform. That part is important, too."

Eleanor ruffled Alex's close-cropped sandy hair once he'd parked. "See? Blond boys have fun, too—Iceman."

He snorted and ducked away to exit the car. "Have you done anything but watch movies and listen to music since you got back?"

"Very little," Eleanor said cheerfully.

But when she glanced at him, she realized he wasn't listening. Her brows lifted. Alex had his elbows on the roof, staring intently as Jennifer emerged from the back seat. She faced away from him while she smoothed her hair and straightened her blouse, then glanced at the bar's neon sign.

Eleanor cleared her throat and caught Jennifer's eye. "Take two: Jennifer, meet Alex."

Jennifer spun around, and he stood up straight. His gaze

turned into a squint and then a rapid blink as his eyes widened.

"Hi," he said at last.

"Hi," she whispered.

Hmm, Eleanor thought with a private smile. Alex had definitely not looked at his date like that earlier. He sensed her gaze, scowled briefly, and turned for the bar, motioning for the ladies to follow.

They staked a table while Jennifer insisted on buying a round of drinks. She perched on a stool and watched while they began a game of 8-ball that got serious fast—typical for the Field siblings.

"Eightball, side pocket," Eleanor muttered ten minutes later.

"Good luck."

"Dammit!" She collapsed onto the green felt while Alex cackled.

"But it went in," Jennifer said from her seat.

"Yeah, but she called side pocket, and it went in the corner. Since it did, she lost," Alex explained while Eleanor began racking up again.

"That stinks." Jennifer frowned.

Eleanor joined them at the table and finally took a sip of her beer. She'd been so intent on the game that she hadn't yet touched it. "It does stink, but it's cool because he's going down in the next round."

They didn't start another game right away, though. The three leaned on the little round table, drinking and talking. Alex and Jennifer kept their comments aimed at Eleanor until Jennifer suddenly glanced over and broke the ice. "So, you're a lawyer?"

Eleanor cheered inside her head. *Good job, Jen! Make that first move, girl!*

She excused herself to pee.

When she got back, she pointed to the pool table and snapped her fingers. Alex nodded and grabbed his cue, and she tossed him the chalk. He hesitated, then held the little blue square out to Jennifer.

"For luck?" he said with a sheepish smile.

Jennifer sat up straight, her cheeks tinged pink. She grabbed the chalk and rubbed it on the cue as if she were a surgeon removing a spleen.

"Blow on it," Alex muttered once she was done.

Eleanor's face split into a cheesy grin when she did. *Good lord, they're cute together. Who'd have thought?*

Alex walked up, his back to Jen, and whispered, "What'll it take for you to let me win this?"

"A lifetime debt," Eleanor whispered in reply as he bent to break.

Of course, she let him win.

"Good game!" Jennifer called when he sank the 8-ball. The siblings traded a glance. Alex mouthed, "thank you," before turning around, and her cheeks hurt with another grin.

This is the highlight of my day… Well, okay, it's the runner-up for highlights of my day.

She thought fondly of the afternoon while she watched her brother flirt like she'd never seen him do before. It reminded her of the way "Blane" had stared while they chatted.

Just thinking about him made a tingly warmth scatter over her skin. "Hey, Alex. Why don't you teach Jennifer how to shoot?" she blurted to get rid of the feeling.

"Oh, no, I'd mess it up," Jennifer said, breathless and sparkling with energy.

Alex drained his beer and set his glass down with a quiet thump. He jerked his head toward the pool table and flashed a smile. "Come on. It'll be fun."

"We, um, need to use the ladies' first." She grabbed Eleanor's arm and dragged her to the bathroom. As soon as the door closed, she gripped the sink and sucked in a deep breath. "Oh my gosh, oh my gosh. Len!"

"Yes?" she drawled.

"Your brother is..." Jennifer trailed off, blushing hard. "You didn't warn me!"

"I honestly didn't realize you'd think so."

"He's flirting with me—isn't he? Oh, I always act like such a fool. I never get this part right. Either I come on too strong or not interested enough. Do I sound like a geek out there? Oh, god, does my breath smell? I have Binaca in my purse—"

Eleanor laughed and put her hands on her shoulders. "He's waiting for you, and you're in here spazzing out. Is he flirting with you? That's a hell yes. Now, go let him teach you to hold his stick."

"Eleanor Field!"

"Stick," she said, hissing the S. "Now, go." She pushed her back out the door.

The next hour went exactly like Eleanor expected. Teaching Jennifer to shoot was a thinly veiled excuse for flirting and touching, and she couldn't be happier for them. When the second round was empty, though, they called it a night—but Eleanor totally let Jennifer ride up front. Alex walked the ladies to the door. Eleanor gave him a quick hug and slipped inside.

She'd barely stepped into the hall when the door opened again.

"What are you doing?" Eleanor hissed.

Jennifer blinked. "He asked if he could call. I said yes."

"Go kiss him!" She pointed to the door.

"No," Jennifer yelped. "We just met!"

Right, because nice girls don't do that kind of thing. And, unlike me, Jennifer is the nicest of nice girls.

But then Jennifer bit her lip. "Should I?"

Eleanor perked up and nodded.

"No, no, no. That'd be so—"

"Awesome, Jen. It would be awesome. Just go say something like, remember to make Len's tapes. See what happens. Go, before he leaves!"

Jennifer squeaked and ran back out. Eleanor held her breath and peeked out the open window in her room. Alex had barely shuffled halfway down the walk to the driveway. He spun around fast at the sound of the door and her feet running to him.

"Wait," she called softly.

"Yeah?" he asked in a rush.

"Um, Len said…" She slowed to a walk until they were toe-to-toe. "Her tapes. Sh-uh-she wanted you to… remember them."

He nodded. His hand drifted toward her, but then he paused. "Yeah, I will. Sure."

"Cool. Okay, so that's… cool." She lifted her face.

Alex studied her. Eleanor's viewpoint was close enough that it was easy to see them move, even though their expressions were shadowed in the moonlight. She heard her brother exhale a laugh just before he bent his head.

Her muffled cry of glee made them both jump back. "Piss off, Eleanor," Alex growled in her direction.

"Eleanor? Nobody here by that name," she called back, then snapped the window shut and lowered the blinds.

Eleanor had brushed her teeth and climbed into bed before Jennifer came back inside. She floated in and fell against the wall.

"Oh, Len," she sighed, the definition of dreamy. "You're the best."

She laughed. "Me? Don't you mean him?"

"No. You. You invited me out. You said he should teach me to shoot. You made me go back outside just now." She smiled. "He's pretty great, too. Thanks for being such a good friend," she added, standing up and turning for the door.

7

ELEANOR

Eleanor got to sleep around 2am. So, when Monica jumped on top of her at whatever-o'clock the next morning, the only time that mattered was too early. She groaned and shoved her friend away.

Monica rolled to her side and said, "Dylan and Brian are here. We're going out on the lake later. And by we, I mean you, too. For now, we're going to smoke weed and veg out over Saturday morning cartoons. Want to join?"

Eleanor opened one eye and laughed. "That's a fantastic plan, but I'm still a zombie and want to stay that way."

Her lip poked out. "Come on, you can zombie to *Muppet Babies*."

"I'll join you in an hour or so." She yawned and hid under the blanket.

Monica muttered threats of putting on an alarm but left her alone. Eleanor was asleep again in seconds. When she woke later to the beautiful summer day filtering through the window, she took her time dressing. Finally, her hair was in a fishtail braid, and she was dressed in denim cutoffs and a soft silk button-down with watercolor flowers on it. She knotted the shirttails just above her shorts and slipped to the bathroom.

She decided while she brushed her teeth that she wasn't going to smoke. She hadn't done it the whole time in Peru. Her first weekend in town, she'd lit up with Monica and felt nothing but dull and confused. Another thing best left in the past.

Jennifer was curled on her bed with a cup of coffee and a romance novel. She smiled when Eleanor peeked in her doorway, but before they could chat, a rustling of people in transition came from down the hall in the den.

Monica appeared with a yawn. "You're seriously late to the party."

Eleanor shrugged. "Sorry, it was a late night. What's going on?"

"We're waiting on donuts. Swear to Bob, I'm so hungry I could eat a dozen myself."

"And not gain a pound," Jennifer muttered.

Eleanor and Monica both pursed their lips at her.

"Get some coffee and come to the den," Monica instructed as Dylan squeezed past her and made for the bathroom with a mumbled, "morning."

Eleanor stepped across the hall into the kitchen, and her stomach hit the floor. Bloodshot navy eyes gazed at her over a glass of orange juice.

"Hey there."

"What?" she yelped.

Blane sipped, then smirked. "I think I said, hey there," he repeated in a sleepy murmur. "You must be Monica's friend."

Are you fucking with me? she almost hissed. Her stomach had gotten itself off the floor and was trying to crawl out of her throat. Meanwhile, he just stood there, high and cool as a cucumber, acting like they were total strangers.

Which, technically, we are.

"You look like you need some coffee." He grabbed a

mug from the cupboard like he knew exactly where they'd be and poured a cup. She took it, forgetting to hold the handle and burning her palm before finding the coherency to set it on the table. Blane watched, brows lifted slightly, but she couldn't do anything but gawk at him.

As the seconds ticked by, a strange tickle of doubt crept in. Eleanor was sure it was him… wasn't she? His hair seemed different. She thought she remembered it a little longer on the neck and temples. It was combed back and damp this morning, so maybe that was the difference. And she didn't remember that scruff on his jaw, but then again, it was a whole day ago—which could explain why he looked tanner, too, right?

But why was he acting like he didn't recognize her? Clearly, he was high, but seriously?

"Thanks," she said at last, reaching for the coffee—reaching for anything to hold on to in the face of her horror.

"What's your name, sweets?" he purred, flashing a flirty smile as he looked her over. Eleanor knew right away that a smile like that was practiced to perfection. It was not the sweet, endearing smile from yesterday. *Oh, god. Am I going crazy? Or am I that much of a hussy that I can't correctly remember a guy I—*

Dylan appeared from the door that led to the den and nodded. "This's Len."

"Len," he echoed like this was the first time he'd heard it. "Rad name. Nice to meet you, Len. I'm Brian."

Brian.

Brian.

Shit.

Click-click-click went Eleanor's mind around Jennifer's

Skye McDonald

drama yesterday. The term playboy had definitely been used to describe Dylan's roommate.

"You're Brian?" she asked, ignoring the flirt in his voice.

"The one and only," Brian affirmed. Dylan slid a glance at his roommate, who widened his eyes innocently. "What? I'm just saying I'm glad to meet her."

Something in that look made another thought click into place: He almost certainly told Dylan. The possibility had occurred to her yesterday during her chat with Monica, but now, she was sure. 'Dude, I swear I was just hanging out, and this chick came in. Next thing I knew, she was putting her hand down…'

Oh, my god. So much for no drama. I'm going to throw up.

Brian motioned toward the den. "Come on, let's go watch TV. *The Smurfs* is wrapping up, and we've got *Star Wars: Ewoks* next."

Eleanor trailed along to find Dylan and Monica snuggled deep into the overstuffed recliner. The blinds were drawn, and the room reeked. Brian gestured for her to sit on the sofa first. Then he settled in so that his side was pressed against hers.

Eleanor looked at their legs side-by-side and frowned. There was no hint of the tingly feeling she'd vibrated with yesterday. From the moment their knees had touched in that tiny booth, she'd felt electric all over. Now? Nothing.

He winked at her. Monica lifted her head and glared. "Stop flirting with her," she grumbled.

"Just being friendly." He smirked while they focused on the animated adventure playing out on the screen.

Are you friendly to Jennifer like this? Eleanor got a bitter taste in her mouth at that unspoken question, but she had to stop herself and admit the truth. *Jennifer didn't make out with him in a listening booth yesterday. Jennifer didn't put her hand down his pants. He's just being flirty. He wasn't flirty yesterday, but…*

This is too damn weird.

Brian sprawled out, his head on the back of the sofa, and somehow it put even less space between them. His arm was on the cushion behind her back, his eyes fixed on the TV. At the commercial, he glanced over and motioned to the bong on the coffee table. "Want a hit, sweets?"

She shook her head. "No, thanks. And can you not call me sweets?"

Monica snorted. "Go, girl."

Brian was unfazed. "Sorry, uh, Len. I think I'm just jonesing for those donuts. No harm meant."

"None taken." She had to appreciate his coolness.

The front door opened and shut, and the three of them grumbled a lazy cheer. Eleanor heard Jennifer shout hello. A male voice answered back. A second later, a figure filled the doorway.

Everything made so much more sense and got so much worse.

Her Blane stood with two green-and-white Krispy Kreme boxes in his arms. He gazed at her with a frozen horror that mimicked her own. Her Blane, whose hair was definitely a little longer, whose jaw was smooth, and who wasn't nearly as suntanned as his…

Twin brother.

Eleanor almost fell off the couch in nervous giggles.

"There you are," Brian growled approvingly, waving him into the room.

Her Blane flicked his eyes to his brother, then back to

Skye McDonald

her. The horror in his gaze became a flash of pain. It disappeared quickly, and he looked down and dropped the boxes on the table.

"This is Monica's friend Len." Brian hugged his arm around Eleanor's shoulder, then released her to attend to the gorgeous-smelling pastries.

"Hi," murmured her Blane—*Stop thinking of him like that, silly*—before backing toward the door again. His shoulder bumped the doorjamb.

The other three looked up at the sound, and he exhaled. "Uh, I—when do y'all want to hit the lake?"

Monica plucked a donut. "Eh, an hour or two. Sit down, chill with us."

"I… I'll make the beer run. Back in a bit." He almost fell over his own feet to escape.

Eleanor hid a smile. She surged with nonsensical affection at his awkwardness. "I'll come too."

Eight eyes fixed on her. Balling her hands into fists, she jumped up and shrugged. "I can help you carry it," she added lamely.

Her Blane—*Dammit! Stop that!*—shook his head, but Monica nodded. "Yeah, Len, go with Sam. Y'all get food and water, too. Plenty for the day. Oh, and ice would be good. Do you mind?"

Sam. His name is Sam. Hi, Sam, I'm Trouble. How's it going?

But she swallowed and shook her head. "Nope. I'll just grab some cash and get my shoes."

This required her to walk past where he stood by the door. Just being near him made her skin prickle. She glanced back at the two brothers, weirdly giddy with relief that at least she wasn't completely bonkers. All the rest of the mess could sort out later.

He walked out the front while she stepped into her jellies and hurried behind.

"Is that your car?" she blurted at the sight of the midnight blue sports car.

He nodded but didn't turn around.

"Nice," she whispered.

The white leather interior was soft and gorgeous. Eleanor tickled her fingers over it, but the sensation gave her less and less relief the longer he sat with his wrists on the steering wheel, head bent. She turned her knees toward him; she noticed when his gaze flicked to her legs, and his ears turned pink; she wondered if he could hear her heart beating.

They sat in silence for so long that Eleanor envisioned the rest of the group finishing their shows and coming outside to find them still sitting there. She had no idea what to say.

Her stomach broke the stalemate when it decided to announce the fact that the last meal she'd had was many, many hours ago. He stirred and glanced sideways. "Are you hungry?"

"I think that question just answered itself."

He drove to Mrs. Winner's. The regional chicken joint was widely considered the best place for fast-food breakfast south of the Mason-Dixon line. They decided to share a chicken biscuit and a cinnamon roll. Eleanor perched on a busted-up picnic bench behind the drive-through while he fetched their meal. As he strolled toward her, food bag in hand, her heart fluttered again. *This is terrible. What a disaster. And could you stop thinking about running your hands through that hair for two seconds, Eleanor Beatrice??*

Sam joined her on the bench without making eye contact. He tore the sandwich in half and gave her the bigger piece. They ate that in silence, then flipped the plastic lid on the cinnamon roll container and picked up forks. This required them to face each other and take turns.

While he stabbed a piece, he muttered, "Which is better? This or Krispy Kreme?"

"This," she answered, still avoiding his eyes. "But those donuts smelled amazing. Your, uh, brother had some serious munchies."

"I was halfway to the house when I remembered I'd promised to bring them."

Eleanor smiled at that, but he exhaled loudly.

"You didn't need to come with me," he said.

Food lodged in her throat. He saw her stunned expression but didn't recant. Swallowing hard, she choked, "I thought maybe we should talk or something."

His lovely lips sneered. "Why should we? You made a mistake, right? Dammit, I should've figured. How did I not see that coming?"

He sighed and dropped the fork, slurped his iced tea, and shoved his hand through his hair.

She ignored the sting his words gave her—and the itch to rake her own fingers across those soft auburn locks. She pursed her lips instead. "Yes, of course it was a mistake. If I'd had any idea that you knew my friends—what?"

He was eyeing her, a fortress of caution in his gaze. "You thought I was Brian," he grumbled.

"Of course I did. How could I have known there were two of you?"

"Of freaking course you did."

But Eleanor paused to replay his words in her head. "Wait. No. I thought *Brian* was *you*."

"What?"

"What?"

They frowned at each other. He stabbed another bite of the roll. She did the same as she mulled over his words.

Playboy. His brother probably has sex in those booths regularly. Eleanor understood suddenly and bit her tongue. She caught his gaze and softened her tone. "I met Brian this morning. And, when I did, I could not have been more confused."

Sam looked down fast, but he failed to mask the relief that washed his handsome features. "Oh," he mumbled.

They picked at the pastry with less and less enthusiasm. "Ugh, I'm full," she announced.

"You have to eat the center. That's the best part." He unwound the roll until all that was left was the core, coated in cinnamon and icing, and held it up.

"Do you want it?" he asked shyly.

Eleanor couldn't help herself. "Yeah, I do."

His cheeks flushed pink. "Then go for it."

She ate it off his fork, her gaze locked on his.

They sat on that table, playing with their straws and stealing little glances at each other in the silence of the summer morning. It was a beautiful day, hot but not sweltering, perfect for the lake. But boats and swimming were a million thoughts away while Eleanor let everything sink in.

"I'm sorry," she said at last. She got a confused look back. "I didn't know we knew the same people."

"No, but," he started, waving his hand.

She clapped a hand to her mouth. "You told them, didn't you? Dylan and Brian. Oh, god—did you know we'd see each other today?"

Navy eyes flashed. "No! I—no. I didn't tell anyone. I didn't tell anyone, I swear."

"It is humiliating." She looked down.

He inhaled deeply. "It was amazing," he insisted, soft and dark.

God, so amazing. Eleanor couldn't stop her silent agreement.

"But, yeah, it's," he exhaled a laugh, "a little awkward right now."

She jumped off the bench and dusted herself off. "This is silly. We can get through today, and then I'm gone again, so—"

"Gone?" he echoed before she could go on.

"Yeah, I'm just passing through." Something about saying this aloud made everything easier. "I'll be out of your way, I swear. Actually, know what? I can just go to my grandparents' house today. We'll tell Monica I forgot I'd promised to help them, and you won't even... even... um."

Her breezy words died a little when he stepped closer. They stopped completely when he put his hands on her shoulders, sending lightning and that weird sense of calm shooting through her just like yesterday.

He squeezed gently and said, "Nah. You should come spend the day with your friends—our friends—and quit worrying."

And that's what she did.

It was a perfect day. The kind Eleanor had seen in movies but hadn't lived herself. The kind where everyone was day drunk and laughing at everything because nothing mattered, not jobs or responsibilities or anyone's past. They waterskied, swam, coated themselves in Hawaiian Tropic, and basked in the sun while listening to the radio. They talked.

Sam and Eleanor talked a lot.

As the afternoon wore on, they found themselves side-by-side, deep in a conversation about music and life that no one else seemed interested in. They laughed about a shared love of Monty Python. Then, they began a game of musical trivia that could've lasted forever had the group not declared it time to go home, requiring Sam to stop to drive the boat back to the dock.

Riding back in his GTO with the other four squished into the back and singing at the top of their lungs, Eleanor traded a glance with her unexpected new friend. Wherever she ended up next, it would be a while before she stopped thinking of him.

8

SAM

The crew wrapped the day at the lake at the girls' house. They ate dinner and lazed on the porch in their usual places. Monica and Jennifer were in the chairs, Dylan and Brian sat on the rail, and Sam lounged on the stairs. Except, that night, he had company. Len sat facing him, their knees so close to touching that Sam had to drop his foot down two steps to give her space.

And to stop himself from thinking about yesterday.

The only problem was, yesterday had been a constant thought since, well, yesterday.

"Sam? Are you in?"

He startled from watching Len laugh and slap Brian's foot away from her face when Monica called his name. "What?"

"We're going next Saturday to see that new movie about a kid skipping school. It's supposed to be good. Are you in?"

"Yeah, I heard that was funny—somebody's day off, right? I'm in." He grinned and looked around. "Favorite movie these days, anyone?"

"*Top Gun*," Jennifer blurted, giggling and looking at Len.

"*Clue*," Monica shouted. "Love it!"

"You?" He asked the woman beside him.

"Eleanor's favorite movie is *Pretty in Pink*," Monica purred before she could answer.

Eleanor. Len is short for Eleanor. Sam's brain latched onto the answer to that puzzle with interest. Even more interesting was the blush that painted her face.

"Shut up, Monica," she hissed, suddenly very interested in the label on her beer bottle.

Monica giggled. "Oh, what's that blush for, silly? I just said you liked the movie. I didn't say you met—"

"One more word, and I'm out of here," Eleanor gritted through clenched teeth. She slid a glance at Sam that confused him even more.

Monica poked her tongue at Eleanor. "I thought you were gone anyway," she said sarcastically. "Leaving me desolate and lonely yet again without my BFF."

She flinched, then pursed her lips. "Stop that. You're totally fine without me."

"I absolutely am not," Monica retorted, voicing Sam's thoughts.

Eleanor turned dark red. "Stop it. I just like traveling, okay?"

Monica hummed and sat back in her chair with a huff.

"Where are you going?" Sam asked.

"I was going to go see the St. Louis Arch. And, I don't know, maybe Memphis."

"So you will be back for the movie," Jennifer reasoned cheerfully.

Eleanor shrugged. Her hair hid her face as she looked at the step.

"She won't if she finds another place to go first," Monica grumbled.

The group fell silent. Monica seemed to know that she'd pushed too hard, but her hurt was evident in her troubled gaze. Finally, she stood up and turned for the door. "I'm tired. Goodnight, y'all."

Dylan followed her inside. Jennifer muttered something about needing a shower and disappeared, too. That left Brian and Sam alone with Eleanor. The brothers silently conferred with their eyes. Then, Brian jumped down and crouched in front of their new friend. He tilted her chin up. The move seemed so natural on Brian, but Sam knew he'd probably poke his finger up her nose if he'd been the one to try it.

"Hey, sweets," he said, his voice nothing but kind. "It's your life. Live it like you want, right?"

Her lips curled with a mouthed thanks.

Brian winked. He touched her cheek and stood up. "I hope we meet again soon, though. See you later." Nodding at Sam, he jogged off to his car.

"I should go," Sam muttered.

"Yeah."

Neither of them moved. Sam looked over, and she flashed a faint smile.

"It'll be fine tomorrow," she whispered. "I'll be gone, and everything will go back to normal."

"You're right. What a shame," he said before he could consider it.

She blinked but didn't speak.

Sam knew he was veering close to pushing too far, but he continued. "Look, if you're into living off the land or whatever, that's cool. But… what?" His thoughts derailed at the smirk that twisted her lips.

"Why'd you say living off the land? Don't see me traveling first-class, hmm?"

"Uh, well, it's not that. It's just you seem kind of into a

THE NOT SO NICE GIRL

61

natural vibe. You had—"

He broke off at the mischievous glint in her eyes that said he'd walked into a corner. She hummed, so he finished. "You might've had a, uh, bit of dirt on you… yesterday."

Now that smirk was a smile, and Sam was all the worse for it. Eleanor shook her head at him. "Thanks so much for the heads up," she scolded.

"When was I supposed to tell you?"

"When I was babbling that *Cosmo* nonsense. 'Cute story, babe. By the way, you look like you've been playing in the mud. Go get a shower.'"

He cleared his throat and leaned a little closer. His voice had a rough edge he didn't recognize as he said, "I think it would've sounded more like, 'Cute story. By the way, you look like you could use a shower—want me to help with that?'"

You never would've said something like that in real life, doofus… But with her? Maybe I would. Holy shit, I just did.

The weird part was, Sam wasn't a bit nervous.

Her lips parted, and the ache he'd held in all day snapped one of its restraints. He didn't back up, just watched her scan his face.

"Well, it was chocolate ganache anyway." Her voice was soft. It made him hungry.

"Chocolate?" he echoed.

Eleanor wet her lips. "Mm-hmm. I work at Sweetie's Bakery. It's, um, I'm an assistant pastry chef."

Sam had questions about that, but instead, he grinned and shook his head. "Are you telling me I could've been licking chocolate off this skin? Can you at least tell me it was bitter or burnt or something?"

She blushed, but she also smiled. "I could, but that would be a lie. I'm good with chocolate. Chocolate is very diva-ish, but it's got the same attitude as I do, so we work well together. With buttercream, I'm nervous, but chocolate and I get each other."

He laughed. "I see."

Her cheeks got even redder as she looked down. "Um, anyway."

"Anyway." Sam let this current surge of boldness take him. He trailed a finger down her neck and watched her pupils dilate. She shivered, and nearly all the rest of his restraints dissolved.

He tucked her hair behind her ear. "I don't think you should leave for good, Eleanor."

"I don't think you should say that," she breathed. "I don't think you know me well enough."

"Exactly," he murmured.

They met halfway. Her lips trembled with a shaky breath, but her fingertips ran along his jaw and into his hair, pulling him in. Sam wanted nothing more than to pick up exactly where they'd left off yesterday. Words he'd thought on the picnic bench at Mrs. Winners' that morning sprang up again:

Dammit, Eleanor, you disappeared yesterday before I could return the favor, and it's not fair. I wanted my hands on you, in you, until you came all over me, and I'll do it right now if you say yes. That was the sexiest thing that's ever happened to me, and I hate that it didn't end with both of us satisfied.

But tonight, Sam knew what he had to do. So, when he'd kissed her long enough that her taste was all he knew, he pulled back gently and stood up. She blinked as a frown ghosted her features.

"I'll see you soon," he said, then turned and left, praying the whole way home that it was true.

9

ELEANOR

"What is that *smell?*"

Eleanor grinned, even while a bead of sweat rolled down her temple. She furiously swirled the saucepan, eyes riveted to the candy thermometer clipped to the far edge. A shriek hit her ears from the kitchen doorway.

"What the hell is this?" Monica screamed.

"Hang on," she muttered, squinting at the thermometer's little red line. The moment it hit its mark, she cut the heat and lifted the pan, adding cream, vanilla, salt, and—

"What's that?" Jennifer whispered from her seat at the table, far more awed than Monica's piercing yowls.

"Lavender." Eleanor folded in the ingredients and spread the caramel into a shallow pan. She stepped back and mopped her forehead. "Lavender caramels… I hope."

Monica clutched her head. She was still dressed in her pink scrubs from her assistant job at Baptist Hospital's psych ward. "I don't know where to look. When the hell did you get here, and what the hell are you doing in my kitchen?"

"Making caramels, duh." Jennifer laughed as she went to sniff the cooling confection. "She got in about four this afternoon. I'm in trouble with you around, Len. These look deadly delish."

Eleanor braced for Monica's tackle of a hug and laughed at the flurry of squeals and black hair that assaulted her. "I didn't think you'd come back."

"Well, I did."

It was Thursday, just shy of two weeks since that Saturday she spent with the crew. Eleanor had been on the road. She'd seen the St. Louis Arch, Beale Street, and had even driven along the Mississippi River a bit. But: "I just felt like I'd wandered enough. Thought maybe I should come back to Nashville. I'm, uh, going to go for the internship through Sweetie's."

It was a fair version of the truth. Her job at Sweetie's Bakery was open to her whenever she was in town. Eleanor had worked there the first and only year she'd attended Vanderbilt University. She'd had a knack for pastries since day one.

Dianne, Sweetie's owner, wanted Eleanor to take over the store when she retired. When Eleanor returned from Peru last month, Dianne had made her goals clear. She got Eleanor on the shortlist for a competitive six-month internship with her umbrella company. It started in the fall in New York City. The company would pay a stipend plus room and board. And it would allow Eleanor to train with some of the most talented pastry chefs in the country. Then she could return to Sweetie's, and Dianne would apprentice her to take over eventually.

Eleanor had hedged a firm answer ever since it came up. Making desserts and living in New York sounded totally awesome. It was the commitment she wasn't sure about. But it was a viable option for a new adventure and a good reason to come back to Nashville for the rest of the summer.

There was one catch. She had to prove her worth first by creating three of the toughest treats out there: macarons, a sourdough from scratch, and chocolate bonbons.

If I screw up, I'll just take off again. No big deal.

"I think you should make these caramels with weed in them," Monica declared when she peered at the pan.

Eleanor laughed and agreed to it immediately, so Monica fetched her black lacquer stash box. The girls settled in for an evening of confections and catch-up. Jennifer brought in a radio and filled three glasses with iced tea. Monica and Jennifer chattered at the table while Eleanor returned to the stove. They asked her about her last two weeks and then began making plans for summer fun for the three of them.

When the "magic" batch was in a pan and cooling, Eleanor kicked her feet up on the table and relaxed, nodding along to the music and listening to her friends gossip.

"…And that was 'Black Celebration' by Depeche Mode. We'll keep things rolling with some Dire Straits, mostly for Mac over at Stacked Records…"

She opened my eyes as the new song came on. "Wait. What are we listening to?"

Jennifer didn't hesitate. "WRVU. This is Sammy's show."

Eleanor lifted a brow as her heart started to thud. "Sam's show?"

"He DJs Tuesday and Thursday nights from nine to one," Jennifer clarified. "He's worked for the station since freshman year."

Monica nodded, then cut her eyes to Jen. "And speaking of the Greene brothers, you don't seem to be yearning for Brian the Flirt these days."

Jennifer's cheeks got pink. "I'm basically over him," she admitted, wiping condensation from her glass.

Eleanor squealed through a sip of tea. "Mmm! Speaking of! Did he ever call?"

"Who?" Monica asked. "Someone has you over your unrequited love of Brian Greene?"

Jennifer pinched her lips in a line. "Maybe, a little. But, uh, no, Len. Just that one night."

"That night?" Monica slapped a palm on the table. "Wait. Wait. Did you get laid?"

"No! Gah, Monica, I'm not that kind of girl!" Jennifer threw a desperate look to Eleanor for help.

Eleanor grinned. She had to admit how much she loved girl time, especially with these two.

"Jennifer met someone," she said. Monica's brows flew up, so Eleanor cleared her throat and smirked. "Jennifer met Alex."

Her best friend's eyes went from dark to obsidian. Her jaw dropped, then tightened into a face-splitting grin. Slowly, she turned to Jennifer. It was equally terrifying and hilarious.

"Alex Field?" whispered the girl Eleanor had known since third grade. "You're over Brian because of Alex Field?"

Their poor friend was crimson. "No, I, well," she blubbered. "It wasn't like that, but we—he—I—no, Monica."

"Yes, Monica," Eleanor whispered. "They were very interested in each other that Friday night."

Jennifer groaned, somehow getting redder.

"What!" Monica screeched.

Eleanor laughed and told it all. By the time she got to the "pool lesson," Jennifer had essentially hijacked the narrative, so she sat back and let her go on.

Her ears pricked up. Sam was speaking again, talking about The Cure and laughing just before "The Hanging

Garden" began to play. Chills dripped down her spine.

"Len?"

She jumped when Monica said her name. "Yeah?"

"Why hasn't he called her?"

She shrugged and scrunched her face. "He's hella busy with the bar this month, and… I don't know, honestly."

Jennifer smoothed her hair and met Eleanor's eyes. "It's fine," she said with a sad but genuine smile. "I don't want him to call if he doesn't want to. It was still fun—and exactly what I needed."

Eleanor grabbed a knife and cut the lavender caramels into little squares. She laid three on a napkin for them to sample. Her grade was B+, but her friends moaned and rushed to try another.

"I'm not eating the special ones until Saturday. Dylan will murder me," Monica declared as she fetched the plastic wrap.

"That's fine, but y'all go to bed. I've got the cleanup," Eleanor said.

They tried to protest, but she refused to hear it. Monica needed a shower from her shift, and Jennifer was toying with the corner of the novel by her elbow, so she shooed them away and snapped on the rubber gloves.

Now it's just me, Sam, and the dishes.

If she'd been given access to thousands of songs, Eleanor wouldn't have changed his lineup by a single track. He spun a lot of alternative stuff mixed with great classic and current rock, but it was those brief clips of him speaking that she enjoyed the most. Whenever he'd come on, Eleanor found herself smiling and whispering a commentary back. She acknowledged this was borderline creepy but didn't care in the least.

She took Jennifer's radio with her when she settled in on the fold-out sofa that night and decided to buy her own little Sony boombox the next day. A day of driving had left her weary, but there was no way she could go to sleep until after he signed off. She gazed at the ceiling and thought more about the offer from Sweetie's.

She really did love creating things. Every ingredient, every dough or batter or sauce had its own identity, its own precise texture, so beautifully unique. Chocolate was a specialty, but she liked the cold glide of butter on her fingers and the way she was starting to know measurements by their weight in her hands. She liked the idea of being a master at something so decadent and beautiful.

"Nashville's a good place to spend the summer," she reasoned to the dark room. "It'll make Monica and Alex happy, and I'll enjoy being around people. If I get the internship, we'll see how it goes. It's a good plan."

"It's time for me to say so long, but we've got a block coming. Joey's up next to see you through the night. I'll see you again soon, Nashville. This is Sam, signing off for another week."

"Goodnight, Sam," she whispered to the little radio, then laughed at herself for being so silly. She flopped onto her stomach and buried her face in the pillow to replay his voice until she fell asleep.

***

"Call the police."

Eleanor walked into the kitchen the following evening to find Monica with her hands on her hips.

"Call the police, Lenny! Someone stole six of my magic

caramels. Also, you look so cute it's definitely illegal. We're in the middle of a crime wave, all under one roof!" She put the back of her hand on her forehead.

Eleanor laughed. "I took a little box to Mac after work. A thank-you for that second Chili Peppers album he found me."

"Oh, lord," she snorted. "I bet he was in heaven."

"Totally."

She gestured to Eleanor's paisley peasant dress. "So, this cuteness is great, but you know we're just going to hang out here tonight, right?"

She shook her head. "No, um, I have a date."

Dark brows flew up. "Not that I think it's necessary, but I thought you said no boys?"

"I did, and I meant it. But Alex said the lawyer had tickets to a wine and cheese thing and was hoping to double date again. I can't tell Alex no, Mon."

But Monica already knew this. She nodded. "Bummer. I was pumped to surprise the guys with your return. Brian will certainly be thrilled," she teased. "Not that I in any way condone his slutty behavior. That boy's libido clearly speaks to an impulsive personality—or a need to compensate."

Eleanor giggled with her, but her face was hot. *If he's really identical to Sam, that's not an issue.* "I'm not interested in Brian, Dr. Huang," she vowed.

Out front, a horn beeped. Eleanor waved. "That's Alex. I'll see you later."

Jason hadn't crossed her mind once since they said goodbye that Friday night. He wasn't on her mind much while they sipped wine and nibbled cheeses in a swanky bar downtown, either. Mostly she thought about being at

Monica's house. She wished she could be in her shorts and a t-shirt on the patio, listening to the gang laugh and chat while she talked to Sam.

Alex politely declined Jason's invitation to go play mini-golf as the event ended. Eleanor could've hugged him for it, but instead, she hurried to follow him to the car. They didn't talk much on the drive home, though. She invited him inside, but he looked warily at the house and declined. With a pointed look, she wished him goodnight and hurried in.

No one was on the front porch. The house was quiet, too. But once she dropped her purse and headed down the hall, she could hear voices out back. Quickly, she slipped into the bathroom to wash her face and hands. She didn't bother to turn on the light in her hurry to join the fun.

She'd just buried her face in the hand towel when the door swung open and hit her squarely in the ass.

"Shit," they cried in harmony. Eleanor spun around, slapping on the lights in a panic.

The gorgeous navy-blue eyes that locked on hers made her pulse even more erratic.

"Hi," he said with a grin, then winced. "Shit—oh, fuck—oh, no, I'm sorry," he fumbled, more flustered with each profanity that fell from his mouth. Eleanor nearly melted from how cute he could be.

With a deep breath, Sam tried again. "I'm so sorry. I had no idea someone was in here—in the dark," he accused gently.

"No, it's totally fine. I was just washing my face. I had enough light from the hall."

He paused, leaned backward to peek out the door, then looked back at her.

Get out of here, her sensible side warned. Small spaces had a bad precedent between them, but Eleanor's feet weren't in a hurry. She leaned against the sink, knocking a can of Aqua Net to the ground when she did. The clatter made her jump.

"I've always been amazed at the sheer quantity of products that counter can hold and not buckle under the weight," he said lightly.

Eleanor grinned as she scooped the can up and found its place.

"Dare I ask for a tour of all this?"

"Oh, that's forbidden information," she replied, somewhere between relieved to banter with him again and dreading where it might lead.

Dreading? Oh please, Eleanor. You know that's not the right word.

"Come on. Just one. What does, hmm, this one do?" He reached around, too close for too short a time, and held the item aloft. The metal glinted in the low light.

"Okay, but only one. That's an eyelash curler. It's not mine, but you use it like this." She mimed the act of curling one's eyelashes, and his brows rose to his hairline.

"Why would you curl your lashes?"

"To make them pretty, duh." She dropped the device again and crossed her arms. "No more secrets."

He peered behind her. "What of this is yours?"

"None. I've got an abysmally tiny stash these days."

"Some tragedy befell your previous collection, I assume?" He leaned against the opposite wall, smirking until his shoulder bumped the towel rack. "Damn," he hissed, cringing. "That looked totally spazz, didn't it?"

She tried not to laugh. She held her lips in a line, but she could feel her nose wrinkling. A giggle slipped out. "Uh, it wasn't the smoothest, no."

The left side of his mouth curled sardonically—temptingly, Eleanor thought. He shrugged. "Typical me. But you probably noticed that already."

She hadn't, actually. Well, not exactly. Well, kind of, but it was precisely his lack of smooth that was so damn charming. Even high and sleepy, his brother had smooth down to a science. Sam was altogether something else.

Eleanor sucked in a deep breath when she realized her thoughts were getting too warm. She blinked, completely lost as to what they'd been talking about.

Sam tilted his head. "So, your beauty effects. Flood? Fire? What?"

"Trash. I dumped them when I left for the Peace Corps two years ago. Building irrigation systems for villages in Peru doesn't call for lipstick."

"That's where you were? Damn. Impressive."

She looked down with a shrug, and he cleared his throat. Eleanor could hear the smile in his voice when he said, "Monica mentioned at dinner that you'd come back."

"Yeah, for a couple months. Sorry about the surprise. I'll try not to wreak too much havoc on your friend circle."

He snorted. "God, thank you. That's exactly what I thought when I heard."

She snapped her eyes to him with a glare that was more of a smile. "No, I mean…"

"What?" he pushed when she didn't finish the thought.

"I mean… I really can be a nice girl. And, believe it or not, I'm not interested in… in… guys."

His brows hit his hairline.

Eleanor palmed her forehead. "Not like that. I mean, I'm not here trying to find any trouble."

"I'm not trouble."

"Well, I am."

They both startled at the snarl in her voice.

She drew a deep breath and tried again. "I know I was supposed to be your crazy one-and-done, and it's weird that we're in the same group, but I can be cool."

"Yeah?" he murmured.

"Yeah. So, um, I'm going outside now."

Except he caught her gaze when she walked past him to the door. And since he did, she heard herself saying, "It's fine. We can start over and be friends, right?"

He didn't answer, so she swallowed and fingered the cool metal doorknob. More words tumbled out as she stared at her hands. "See, what I meant to say was that I'm not some easy tart, I swear it. I-you-I'd never done anything like that before. I don't do things like that."

She finally made herself glance at him.

Sam nodded slowly. "I understand. And I wish you wouldn't worry. The only regret I have of that afternoon was that you left before I could return the favor."

Whoa. Wait. What??

She cut her eyes to him again. "What did you say?"

He smiled, scratching his ear with a little tug. "I think you heard."

"Don't say things like that. Just forget it, okay?"

"I won't. But I'll pretend to if you like."

"I do like," she insisted, spinning around with hands on hips. "I need a second chance. A redo on our meeting. To prove I'm a perfectly nice person who belongs in this amazing group of friends."

"I don't think you need that at all."

"I really do, though. Please?"

He nodded once. "Fine. Granted."

Fresh slate. I don't deserve it, but god knows I could use it.

Why, then, she shut the door and snapped the lock, she wasn't really sure.

She also couldn't be sure who moved first. All she knew was that one second, she was in control of this situation, and the next, she was against the wall with his tongue in her mouth, completely, blissfully, out of control.

"Oh, god," she moaned as his lips and teeth raked her jaw. "Oh, god," she sighed again when he sucked long and hard on her pulse.

"I'm sorry." His voice was muffled in her neck. "I'm so sorry, I—"

With a tug on his hair, she sealed their lips back together. Sam groaned. He threaded his fingers along the base of her scalp, rolling his body and making her cry out.

"Why is this happening? Why can't I stop?" she gasped when she tore away from his mouth.

Her head lolled while he worked on her neck again. She was so hot for him, for the way he held her, for those terribly perfect lips that she wanted everywhere.

Forget his lips. Just his smooth jaw under her fingertips was enough to make her wet.

Sam mumbled something against her skin. But then he kissed her again, one hand sliding down to cup her breast.

"What?" she panted as she squirmed.

"Science," he rumbled in a voice deep with lust.

Eleanor finally paused. "Excuse me?"

The tornado of their motion slowed, leaving them breathless and gazing at each other. She was still in his arms, but the touching had stopped. Slowly, his hands slid from their respective locations to meet around her shoulders.

"Science," he repeated.

The word never sounded so sinful.

He smiled. "That's why we can't stop, if you want a rational answer."

"Science?"

He nodded and licked his shiny lips. "Pheromones. En-dorphins. Adrenaline. I'm no biologist, but—"

She snorted. "Aren't you?"

His eyes glinted. "I'm a chemist."

"Oh."

"Yeah. But, yes. It's definitely biology that's to blame for the fact that I can't resist—"

That thought was finished with three burning kisses in rapid succession. She groaned, eyes fluttering open only when he pulled back.

Sam smirked. "Blame science for how aroused you are."

"Excuse me? Who says I'm aroused?" She pushed his chest, secretly pleased that it didn't budge him an inch.

"Your pupils have been dilated since you turned the light on. You've been flushed for that long, too. And your breath has been abnormally shallow."

She glared, but her lips were twitching. *This must be the sexiest nerd conversation ever.*

"I don't appreciate your insinuations, Sam Greene."

He didn't even blink. "Fine. Then me. My adrenaline spiked when I walked in: fight or flight."

Here he dipped his head to brush his lips across her

cheek as he continued. "That should've gone within seconds. It didn't. The whole time we've been standing here, my heart has been pounding, and my adrenaline has been high. It's hard to think straight. Science, see?"

Eleanor turned so they were nose-to-nose.

"She's a bitch," she whispered, thrilled at the way his eyes flared.

"I want you," he replied, too blunt and too tempting.

There was no point in saying she disagreed. But damn science, reason needed to have her say. "That's a huge mistake. We have to be friends. We can't fool around like this. We—I'm—"

A pounding on the door had her blood coursing cold. "Did you get lost, Sammy?" Monica called.

They leapt apart. He wiped his face and called out, "No, Mon. Just stopped for water in the kitchen first. Out in a sec."

"Okay, buddy," she sang.

They were silent for a long moment. Finally, Sam sighed and leaned against the wall beside her. "You want to be friends."

"I made a vow. No boys. No drama. No mess. Tennessee is a landing pad. It's time for me to get it right. To grow up and get my head on straight. I need to not come into this group and shake everything up. I'm not staying long, anyway. I'm sorry."

"No, it's fine. I... It's fine. Friends it is." He stood up, flashed a crooked smile, and held out his hand.

Eleanor shook it, rocked with regret from the moment their palms touched.

10

SAM

Friends. She wants to be friends. No woman has ever made me say things so illogical, so out-of-the-blue, so hot, as she does. From the first moment I tasted her, she's been on my tongue like no one ever. Science be dammed, it's true.

And now I'm not supposed to touch her again.

Sam stumbled back to the backyard party. Seconds later, he stared at his beer bottle while the group cheered loudly for Len's return. He couldn't bring himself to look up or make a sound. Monica's announcement that she was back had elated him earlier. Now, her soft hello just made him cringe.

That cringe got worse when Dylan brought her a chair and sat it beside him. Ten minutes ago, her tongue had licked his. Now, they were strangers at a party.

It was a bit much to handle.

They sat in silence while the others fell back to bantering.

"Chemist, huh?"

The question was so low and unexpected that it took him a beat to understand. He sipped his beer and nodded.

"Do you work in a lab?"

He nodded and added, "I'm going to grad school in Knoxville this fall to study at the Body Farm."

"The what?"

He noted with some surprise that nobody was paying

them any mind. Leaning an elbow on his knee, he turned toward her, forcing himself to look at her as a friend.

It was challenging.

After a quick breath to steel his nerves, Sam explained. He was going to study DNA and decomposition. His goal was to become a crime scene investigator or, less preferably, a DNA analyst.

She pursed her lips. "Pretend I'm not sure what that entails. Just for fun."

Sam laughed. "Chemists can do a lot of different things. It's kind of creepy, I know. But I'm most interested in forensic science—body chemistry. Basically, I want to be the person who solves a murder though, um, science."

Her cheeks flushed pink in the low light. He knew his had done the exact same. Sam cleared his throat. "So, what about you?"

When she spoke, her words were like a confession. "I'm trying to figure that out. The internship Sweetie's is offering—oh, right, you don't know anything about that. So, I think I mentioned I work at Sweetie's Bakery. Well, the owner…"

She told him about the New York opportunity and her boss's hopes that she'd take over the store.

"That sounds like a great plan," Sam said. "What are you still figuring out?"

Her tongue swiped her lips again. Every time she did that, it made him salivate.

"I'm just not sure about the commitment. Taking over the shop would be so permanent. It, um, would make this my... home."

"Is it not?"

"I don't really have a home," she whispered, again like a confession. A sad smile ghosted her features.

Sam opened his mouth to query, but Monica interrupted.

"What's all that? Are you stealing my BFF or what, Sam?" Her sassy question jolted them both.

"I was about to make her one of those goofy string bracelets," Sam agreed, turning his attention back to the group.

"Don't make me jealous." She made her fingers into claws.

"Speaking of jealous," Brian said with a grin, "Your car hasn't had enough proper attention lately. She was begging me when you pulled up to handle her right tonight. Want to take a drive?"

Sam rolled his eyes but fished for his keys like Brian knew he would. Monica and Dylan cheered, already on their feet.

"Wait, what's happening?" Eleanor asked.

"We're taking a drive," Brian explained, grabbing the keys when Sam threw them. He draped an arm around her shoulders and guided her to the driveway, "See, Len, I'm a really good driver, and my brother has a really great car. Want to ride up front with me?"

And so, Sam wound up jammed in the backseat of his own car. Brian had a Duran Duran cassette playing. It wasn't the worst, Sam reasoned, but he could have chosen better.

They cruised north of the city with the windows down until they were in the country. When they got to The Stretch—aka a long straight length of highway known as a popular drag racing spot in the 60s and 70s—Brian pulled to the curb and rolled his shoulders with a grin.

"Mind the clutch," Sam grumbled.

Eleanor looked out into the pitch-black night. "Is this where I'm being left for dead?"

"Buckle up," Jennifer said as she gripped Sam's fingers.

Brian eased the car back onto the road and let it idle for a second. Sam had to smile. He knew that a car would be his brother's first purchase once he got settled in a career, but for the time being, Sam was the one with the sweet ride.

With two quick revs of the engine, Brian flashed Eleanor a grin. "Sexy, right?"

"Excuse me?"

"The car, sweets," Brian laughed. "Well, and this sick move."

The car shot forward with a squeal of tires and a roar of engine and wind. Monica whooped. Eleanor grabbed the ceiling in the classic oh-shit move.

He cruised at top speed for a few minutes before gripping the wheel and expertly downshifting. They rode the momentum and drifted back down on the speedometer. Finally, a gentle tap on the brakes brought them back to idle.

"Oh, my god," Eleanor gasped. She turned to Brian with a brilliant smile.

Sam watched her beam at him, and that bitterness crawled right back up his throat. He clenched his teeth. *You can't do this to yourself. She's not yours. She doesn't want to be yours.*

It was sound advice. It did nothing to ease the feeling.

Abruptly that smile was on him, though. "Can you do that, too?" she asked.

Sam swallowed hard and nodded.

"He wishes he could handle this lady as good as I can.

I'm the man with the golden touch, Lenny." Brian was clearly joking. His comment still made Sam want to choke him.

Monica and Jennifer feigned vomiting.

But Eleanor's eyes didn't waver from Sam's gaze. "Oh, really?" she murmured faintly.

Sam's lips curled in a smirk. "She likes my touch better than yours any day," he said to his brother, ostensibly about the car.

Eleanor blinked rapidly and turned away.

Dylan jumped in. "I think I hear a challenge."

"Nah," Sam replied, sitting back in his seat. "Bry's having fun."

"Oh, by all means. Show us what you got, Sam." Brian laughed and popped the door so they could change places.

Sam eased into the white leather bucket seat, comforted to be back behind the wheel. He made a three-point turn to face them back toward town. Leaving the car idling, he yanked the cassette out and tossed it back to Brian. Then, he reached across Eleanor to the glove box and had "Thunder Road" blasting in seconds.

He stroked the wheel and clarified: "Brian's got skills with any car. I've seen him handle a Ford Pinto and get it roaring."

Brian harrumphed his appreciation.

Sam went on. "But this is my car. I rebuilt it from a junk heap in twelfth grade. Every damn paycheck I'd ever gotten, and a lot more afterward, went into her."

"She was orange," Brian supplied. "With green upholstery."

"She was defunct." Sam dropped his arm out the window of the 1972 GTO to pet the door. The midnight blue paint was invisible in the darkness. "So, yeah, Bry's the magic touch guy—with one exception."

And with that, he threw the car into drive. Sam smashed the gas pedal to the floor, and the engine roared. They hit 100 in seconds.

"Dweeb. I could've totally done that." Brian laughed and reached forward to smack Sam's head once he'd brought them safely back to a standstill.

Sam grinned into the rearview as the others applauded.

Eleanor peeked back at him when they were cruising. He lifted a brow and died inside when her nose wrinkled into a laugh. Things suddenly seemed a bit brighter.

Until Monica opened her infamous mouth.

"Sorry, but can I say how awesome it is to have you in Nashville?" she said to Eleanor, who nodded quickly. "And can we all agree that Len is a bitchin' new member of this pack?" No one argued.

But her next words dropped Sam's stomach to the floor-board. "When did Trish ever go riding? Never, that's when. Sorry, Sammy, but it's true, right?"

"Ugh, baby, we talked about not using the T-word any-more," Dylan groaned.

"Who?"

The question was quiet, but Sam didn't miss it.

"Sam's old lady," Brian supplied. "No, sorry. Sam's for-mer old lady."

"Fuck Trish, man," Dylan said, laughing at the "Nope" he got in unison from the brothers. "Exactly what I wanted to hear."

But Sam didn't like the way Eleanor looked out the win-dow. He didn't like the way her smile had vanished. He also didn't like thinking about Trish anymore. He hadn't thought of her much since the moment she walked out. Certainly not once since that Friday at the record store.

So, he said, as casually as he could, "Eleanor is definitely cooler."

The total lack of response didn't help anything.

At the house, they settled on the porch in their usual spots. Eleanor sat beside him, though, not across like last time. Sam was ready for it when she dropped her chin and spoke so only he could hear.

"I like your car."

Dammit, what man doesn't get hard at those four words? Sam swallowed a groan. "I'll take you for a drive if you want. We can go right now."

"We so can't."

"Do you want to?"

She didn't answer.

In a blink, Sam was on his feet. "I'm going to the 7-11 for a frozen Coke. Anyone want?"

They declined, but he knew no one would be interested in riding again so soon. The only problem was that Eleanor didn't move, either. He willed himself not to look at her while he grabbed his keys, asked again, then muttered he'd be back before retreating down the walk.

"Sam, wait!"

He looked up from opening the door at Monica's shout.

"Lenny wants to ride. Is that cool?"

"Huh? Oh, sure," he called back, limp with relief while she silently skipped down the walk and jumped in the car.

"Drive safe!" Monica shouted, waving.

"You are evil," he grumbled as he fired the engine.

She hummed.

While they cruised, Sam wrestled with himself. *Do I park us? Obviously, it's my only goal, fuck frozen Cokes, but what will she say? Is it too much?*

Yes, doofus. She just told you you're friends. Were you listening, or—

"She… uh… she really does like how you handle her, huh?"

With her barely audible question, Sam banked hard into a U-turn. He parked just inside Centennial Park in under five minutes.

The Parthenon was lit in the distance, but they stopped in a little lot by the road. Eleanor turned to stare at him.

He raised his brows. "She seems to," he said at last.

She pursed her lips, clearly debating with herself. Sam waited. He knew—hoped—patience was the right move.

It was. Eleanor opened her door, climbed out, and slid into the backseat. She crossed her arms and met his gaze in the rearview.

11

ELEANOR

You are a fool, Eleanor Field.

They gazed at each other for several long, tense moments that must've only been seconds in reality. Then he tumbled out, the seat fell forward, and they both reached for the locks before he was there, filling the space. Filling her with a tingly calm that she couldn't explain. Their sides pressed together as they turned to look at each other.

"You, uh, seem to know how to read her well. It's a little unfair."

"Unfair? How's that? What's wrong with knowing what she likes?" He smirked, confirming with his expression that they both knew how silly this car metaphor was.

His fingers on her neck made her forget about the shared joke. Eleanor struggled to keep her eyelids from fluttering or her words from becoming a breathy gasp. "Yeah, but she… likes it… too much."

"It's just science, Eleanor," he whispered.

And that was all the talk.

His mouth fit against hers, soft and sure. The familiarity and mystery raced like fire across her skin. She heard her own little groan, but she was too swept up to be embarrassed about how eager she was. But Sam heard it too, and in a breath, his arms tightened, drawing her closer. He licked across her lips, and Eleanor flicked her tongue out to catch his before it could withdraw.

And then she was in his lap, straddling him again, her fingers in his hair and his hands working up her bare thighs under her dress. It was instantly a thousand degrees in the car, with the windows only cracked and the intensity boiling between them, but Eleanor didn't care. She didn't care about anything but touching him, but feeling him touch her.

Sam dragged his wet mouth down her chin, cradling her head to angle her where he wanted as he sucked hard kisses up and down her pulse. Eleanor cried out. She called his name and felt his lips curve against her skin. She whispered it again, and he threw his head back, beaming.

"I like the sound of that," he panted. His hair was beginning to stick to his temples with perspiration.

They stared at each other. "Sam," Eleanor murmured again. "We can't do this."

"Eleanor," he returned, shifting underneath her. "We already are."

"This is the last time." She clutched his shirt as if it would anchor her to good sense.

He inhaled and sat forward. Both of his broad palms slid to her breasts, lifting them up and together before he bent his head and blew a cool stream of air across her cleavage. "Last time," he mused while she writhed at the tease of his mouth so close to her body. "Then let's make it count."

"Call me Elle if you don't like Len," she groaned when he sank his mouth into her flesh.

Sam paused and lifted his gaze. "Len is so bland for someone I think of as so… well…" He trailed off with a laugh.

"Finish that thought."

"Beautiful," he said simply. "So very, very beautiful. Elle

it is."

Eleanor had gotten compliments, of course. Certainly someone—maybe even him, the first one, the one who'd almost ruined her forever—had called her beautiful. But no one had ever said it like that. Sam made the word so much more than a compliment with the depth of honesty in his tone. He said it with conviction. Like she was so much more than what she was. Like she was really beautiful.

It stole her breath.

Well. Her breath might've also been stolen because he then began to flip open the tiny buttons at the top of her dress.

Navy eyes didn't waver from her gaze. "Is this okay, Elle?"

No. I've sworn off boys and reckless decisions. We're just friends, and… and… "Mm-hmm," she moaned, biting her lips together and nodding quickly. "Yes, it's okay."

He peeled the cotton away and yanked the satin of her bra down. Her difficulty breathing amplified when Sam's lips closed on the tip of her aching breast, his tongue lapping at the too-sensitive peak.

Eleanor heard "Oh, god," fall from her mouth as she arched backward, clutching his shoulders and spreading her knees wider.

His tongue circled, and her hips bucked involuntarily. Sam groaned. With a ragged breath, he paused just long enough to tug the fabric away from her left breast. Then, he dove back down, sucking gently. She wailed and writhed helplessly, certain that she'd never been this aroused. Certain, too, that sex with Sam would be utterly, life-changingly…

Beautiful.

She fumbled for his jeans, but this made him stop. "No, Elle," he growled. "You this time."

Like the first time he mentioned it, this idea did weird things to Eleanor's insides. A kind of sick thrill swept through her. Sam's hand curved around her inner thigh, slowly sneaking higher.

"No, please," she gasped. "Sam—don't."

He stilled instantly. "You don't want me to?"

"It's… it's not… you don't have to."

He chuckled softly and kissed her neck. "I want to," he murmured. "I want to see you come apart for me—if you want it, of course."

Oh, my god.

Sam kissed her neck again. "Well?"

She whimpered. That sick thrill kept swirling in her gut, but the achy curiosity at what his touch would be like was starting to win over her self-consciousness.

His whispers made her shiver. "I'm not going to do a damn thing you don't want, but I can feel your heat from here. I—fuck, I want to touch you."

Eleanor trembled all over and hid in his shoulder. "I want you to touch me."

The second the words were out, his fingers were there, inside her underwear and gliding along where she ached to have him. She whimpered again, twisting her hips and biting his neck. He soothed her and stroked again—then dipped two fingers into her.

"Oh, god," she mewled while his thumb petted her clit. "Oh, Sam, oh, fuck, I…"

He'd been right: she was going to lose it at any moment.

Her thighs tensed and jerked.

Sam's lips found her ear. "Come for me, beautiful," he breathed, skimming his tongue along her lobe, and she did.

When she went slack, she did it all the way. Her bones liquefied. She slumped against him, only to be caught in his steady embrace. He kissed her hair and held her close until she quit quivering and found the courage to sit up again. She couldn't look at him, though. Her eyes stayed low almost unconsciously.

He touched her chin. "What are you thinking?"

She shook her head and bit her lips.

"Elle. Eleanor. Look up."

It was physically difficult to do so, but finally, she peeked at him.

That's why she hadn't wanted to look. When she did, Eleanor tumbled hopelessly into total infatuation with Sam Greene.

She clapped both hands over her face to hide. "I can't believe you just did that."

He hummed. "I said if this was the last, I wanted it to be memorable. And I will never forget the sounds you make. The feel of you."

Eleanor knew what he meant. She'd learned those things well about him two weeks ago. *Now you're even*, she tried to reason, but most of her wailed for more. "Sam," she mumbled. "We—"

"I know."

"Because I—"

"*I know*, Eleanor."

It was hard for Eleanor to know if she was relieved or devastated that he was so agreeable.

Sam rubbed her arms and righted her bra. He sighed. "I know what you want, and I… I respect what you need."

Slowly, she lowered her hands and nodded. "Right. Um, good. Thank you."

On the drive home, Eleanor let the wind fluff her fuzzy hair with her face toward the window. With a sigh, she sat back in the soft leather seat. "You know what I regret most? There is nothing I can ever do to convince you I'm a nice girl."

He startled. "I think you're perfectly nice."

"No, I mean a nice girl. Like Jennifer. Respectable, like Monica. Not some hussy who's down for a good time in your car… or the bathroom… or the record shop. Oh, god, I've ruined this." She groaned.

Sam swung the car into the driveway and turned to her, an odd look on his face. "This is a conversation for later, if ever," he murmured, "but don't doubt my respect for you. Don't ever think I think of you as having ruined anything."

"I know," she blurted without stopping to consider her words. "I'll prove I'm nice—and that we can be friends. Will you help me get my internship?"

His eyes went wide. "What? How?"

"You're a chemist. Since you hang out at the house on Saturdays, maybe you could, like, give me your scientific opinion on my recipes?"

Sam drew his brows together, then arched them. "I mean, yeah. I could. If it would help you."

It would help me focus on something other than your lips when you're around. That would help a lot. She nodded, so he shrugged in agreement.

"Where in the hell did you go? Kentucky?" Monica

could wait no longer. Her shout broke their stare-off. They traded another glance and climbed out.

Eleanor pulled her hair back and walked to join the girls, who were the only two left on the porch. Brian's car was gone. She heard Dylan in the house through the screen door. "We cruised around awhile," Sam said from behind her. "Elle said she wanted to see downtown."

Monica pounced. "Elle?"

Eleanor felt him hesitate, so she jumped in. "Elle is fine. I was telling him about Peru. Elle is what they called me there. It's easier to say for Spanish speakers."

"Elle," Monica tried, making a face. "No. I can't."

She grinned. "And you shouldn't. You dubbed me Len a billion years ago. We're golden as long as you don't call me Nora."

Monica shuddered. Nora was Eleanor's mother's moniker for her. "Never, ever," she pledged, then pointed to Jennifer and Sam. "You call her Nora, I cut out your tongue."

"Goodnight, ladies," Sam said after he took his vow. "See y'all tomorrow."

Eleanor turned. "You're leaving?"

"Well, I'm not spending the night," he said lightly.

She bit her lip and turned away with a wave and a casual, "Thanks for the ride." She hoped he understood.

When the sound of his car faded, Monica eyed her friend. "You know, if it were anyone but Sam, I might be inclined to ask what you've really been doing tonight."

"Oh?"

"Mm-hmm. But my boy Sam's a bit too nice for me to need to worry about that vow of yours... right?"

Eleanor gazed at her, unblinking despite a thousand

knee-jerk reactions rioting inside her. "Sam seems very nice."

"He's a total doll," Jennifer agreed cheerfully. "And anyway, Mon, he just broke up with Trish. You're just being crazy—just like you were about Alex."

"Alex needs to feel you up ASAP," Monica snorted. "But that point was made already."

"Who is this Trish?" Eleanor asked, sitting in the empty chair.

The girls dished out the story, and it wasn't pretty. Monica and Jennifer clearly weren't fans of Sam's ex. They editorialized the long-term relationship, lauding how devoted he'd been and how flighty they found her to be. It made Eleanor angry. It made her jealous.

It made her sure that they shouldn't be doing any more of what they'd been doing.

She went to bed that night resolved: Sam Greene would be her buddy. If that meant they could never be alone together to avoid the temptation, so be it.

12

SAM

The first Saturday he showed up at the house, Sam wasn't sure if Elle would really want his help in the kitchen. He suspected she'd blurted that in a moment of panic, but she greeted him with a smile and an extra apron. So, he abandoned hours of mindless cartoons and got ready to put his chemistry skills to a whole new use.

Macarons were their first challenge. Elle explained that the trick was the humidity. She pointed to the two stand fans on the table and the window air conditioner unit. Sam recognized it from the den. This morning, it was perched in the kitchen window and on at full blast. She chewed on her lip as she assembled ingredients, but Sam quickly realized that he wasn't needed. Eleanor was a pro. She flew around, whipping egg whites and tossing him requests to do things like pass the sugar. Eventually, Sam found a spot by the counter. That let him be helpful and stay out of her way. Before the group was done with cartoons, she had two trays cooling on racks.

She and Sam gazed down at them. "At least they didn't crack. Try one. What do you think?"

The cookie dissolved in his mouth. Sam groaned. "Amazing."

Elle nibbled her own and crinkled her nose. "Too sweet. I'll have to try again, maybe get a different sugar. We'll do it again next weekend before I have to present them. Then we'll need to start the sourdough, too."

Sam grinned at her. *If it means I get two hours with you every weekend, we can do this from now till eternity.*

They learned about each other in the kitchen. While she worked, Elle told stories about Peru, how different it was, how fascinating. He didn't have the nerve to ask, but it seemed clear she had learned a lot about herself there, too. She peppered in random comments like, "It made me realize how strong I could be," and, "Being alone teaches you to look at yourself from the ceiling, you know?" He was dying to know more, so he got there half an hour early the next week, hoping he wasn't too obvious.

She was waiting for him on the front stoop, grin and apron both ready.

The macarons were a breeze for Elle's skill, but the sourdough was a different beast. Elle showed him a jar of goo that she called the "starter." She explained that she'd been "feeding" it since the afternoon she got back in town.

"The starter is what activates the dough, not yeast," she explained while Sam regarded the goo with pinched brows. "So if it's not right, I'm toast."

"But not sourdough toast." Sam cringed at his lame joke, but Elle burst into giggles and gave his arm a gentle push that had him ready to melt with relief.

The sourdough looked beautiful when she pulled it out of the oven, but even Sam could tell it was a little chewy. Elle gagged as if it were poison.

"It's not that bad," he said with a headshake.

"It's odious. Ugh, dammit, I've only got two weeks to get this right. The starter is crap. I worried it would be. The measurements were imprecise since all I had were measuring cups. If only I'd had a scale."

Sam's brows flew up. "I'll be back in twenty minutes." He jogged out of the kitchen, keys already in hand.

Twenty minutes later, he skidded back in to find Elle eyeing a measuring cup full of flour. "Here."

Her green eyes went wide as he laid a small scale on the counter. "You're my hero!"

Sam broke into a goofy grin. "Not at all. We have tons of them at the lab. I'll take it back with me this week."

"This is going to save my ass. So, um, can you measure out the flour while I…" And with that, she was buzzing around again.

Over those weeks in July, he learned the moods in her voice. He learned how she'd scratched below her ear, invariably end up with a streak of food there, and never once realize it. He learned that she stood on the outer edges of her feet when she worked. He learned that she had a thing about tactile sensations. She talked in depth about the way food felt and would make him touch sticky marshmallows or smooth batter while she smiled and wrinkled her nose. "Isn't it nice?" she'd ask each time, and of course he agreed.

What they never did, not once after that steamy night in the backseat of his car, was find themselves alone in the house together. At first, Sam thought it was a coincidence. After a couple weeks, it became clear that their ever-present company was by design.

It was maddening as hell. But it was also probably a damn good idea. There were still moments when her mischievous green eyes had him ready to fall to his knees and beg her to touch him.

The more they got comfortable with each other, the

more Sam had to make fists in his pockets to keep from putting his hands on her. Talk about tactile. The idea of touching her was almost an obsession. He fantasized about the simplest things, like pushing her bangs from her forehead or tickling her knee. He wanted to feel her.

He also fantasized about a lot more than that, though.

And none of it changed the way his heart ached for her.

* * *

On the last Friday of July, Sam found himself, as usual recently, in the girls' kitchen, watching Eleanor work. This time, it was a simple batch of cupcakes. They were talking about going out on the boat the next day to celebrate Monica and Jennifer's birthdays, which were a week apart. Elle was excited and hoping that the cupcakes would transport well.

She glanced at the oven clock and huffed so hard, her blonde bangs danced on her forehead. "I'm running late," she grumbled as she reached for the mixer. "Grab me the milk, please?"

"You're not coming to Mulligan's?"

Elle shook her head at his question.

"Another date?" He passed the carton and tried to keep his expression neutral.

She glared at the tablespoon as she poured several spoonsful into the bowl with confectioner's sugar. "Yup. We're going to line dance. Line dance, Sam." Emerald green eyes pinned him with a sardonic stare.

You have to be her buddy, dork. Don't get weird about it. "How… authentically Nashville. Maybe you can request a Cure song."

He grinned when she laughed. She quickly refocused on

the bowl, and his expression dissolved into a cringe. *What's the deal with this dude, the lawyer Monica keeps mentioning? Why do you always frown if you're going out regularly?*

Why doesn't he apply to your 'no boys' rule, but I do, dammit?

Sam swiped a finger into the frosting to get rid of the bitter taste in his mouth. Elle glanced over her shoulder from where she stood at the sink, hands already in yellow gloves.

"If you're stealing bites, steal one for me too, please?"

Sam didn't think about it one way or the other. He reached back into the bowl, walked up behind her, and brought his arm around. His finger hovered at her lips. It didn't seem like she thought about it, either, given the automatic way she opened her mouth.

But when her lips closed around him, they both thought about it.

Her tongue froze against the pad of his finger. His arm clenched, but neither of them moved. He felt her swallow.

Then, he felt her suck a little harder.

Pleasure rocketed through his system, stealing his vision for a beat. "How does it taste? Does it pass the test?" Sam's voice was ragged, and he couldn't do a damn thing about it.

She sucked again, her tongue lapping him once more before he was freed. "It's nice," she said, too softly.

They stood there for another breath. Then, balling his hand into a fist, Sam turned and fetched the plastic wrap. *I bet you anything that fucking lawyer doesn't make your voice bottom out like that, Elle. Or, if he does, tell me that. Maybe then, I can finally let this go.*

* * *

Monica decided they would go to dinner at Mulligan's, then over to the Zebra Lounge, aka the site of Trish's send-off party, to start the weekend. Everyone assembled on the porch in their usual positions.

When Alex arrived, Elle adjusted the collar of her white tuxedo shirt and pulled a black newsboy cap down on her head, then flashed Sam a look and mouthed, "Wish me luck."

"You don't look like a cowgirl," he whispered back.

"Shut up," she growled.

While Elle hopped off the stairs, Monica shouted toward the Corolla. "Hey, Alex! Did you know Jennifer's birthday was yesterday?"

Alex cocked his head while Jennifer hissed at her friend. "Oh, really?" he called back. He scratched his head and came around the car to walk halfway up the small front yard.

"Happy birthday, Jennifer," he said, clearly uncomfortable to be facing such a crowd.

Sam expected Jennifer to blush and mutter a thanks. Instead, she took a deep breath and stood up straight. Sam saw Alex's eyes follow her hands as they smoothed the gauzy white dress she wore, but then everyone's attention snapped to their normally sweet friend.

"Don't bother," she snipped. Jennifer lifted her chin, curled her lip, and flounced into the house.

The three guys gave a commiserative groan as Alex winced like she'd slapped him. Both girls' jaws dropped, but Monica recovered fast. She sneered. "You so deserved that, you fake yuppie."

The guys all winced again.

Alex threw his hands up. "Dammit, what do you want from me? I'm trying to—forget it. We've got to go. Len, come on."

Her eyes found Sam's once more before she hurried to the car.

Jennifer reappeared and sat studying her lap. She let out a huge sigh, and Sam silently joined her.

Best friend, the object of his desires—for everything she was, a night out wasn't as fun without Elle Field by his side.

13

ELEANOR

"Your friend never knows when to keep her mouth shut."

"You're learning that now? Jesus, Alex, you've known Monica for, like, fifteen years. And anyway, why in the hell haven't you called Jennifer?"

He sighed. "I've been swamped with work and the test. Besides." He shrugged.

"What? She's not cute enough? Because she's totally—"

"Adorable. Lovely. Sweet. No shit, Sherlock. She's totally awesome, and I'm… a… I don't know. Fake yuppie, like Monica said."

Eleanor scrunched her face and touched his arm. "Stop that. You're great, Al. Why wouldn't you think she thought so?"

His fingers flexed on the steering wheel. They'd just parked at the honky-tonk bar. Jason and Anna were waiting outside his 'Vette.

"Dad pulled his strings to get the info early. I passed the bar," he barely whispered.

Eleanor squealed, throwing her arms around her brother. His ire ebbed to a deep, relieved grin while he leaned into the embrace.

"It's confidential information for, like, two more months, so keep a lid on it, will you? You know how Dad likes to keep his connections quiet."

"Yeah, of course, but dude, that's so great!" She

squeezed him again. "Let's go celebrate!"

They paused and looked out the windshield. Alex turned back to her. His green eyes couldn't hide his truth fast enough.

Now it was Eleanor's turn to chuckle. "Let's go celebrate, Alex. You've passed the bar. You're going to be a lawyer. You can choose where you practice, what kind of work you do. It's all up to you."

He nodded. Then, Alex straightened his collar and opened the car's door. "You're right. I'll be right back."

Eleanor watched her brother cross the parking lot to meet Jason. They spoke for a moment and then nodded at each other. Then, Alex strode back to the car. Without a word, he fired the engine and zoomed away.

Eleanor screeched her delight. She threw her hands in the air. "There's my big bro!"

His grin was back, dimple carved deep in his cheek. "Shut up," he grumbled, failing totally to sell the sentiment. "I have to get her a gift," he added.

A swift glance at Eleanor made it clear who he meant. She hummed her agreement.

They stopped at the mall and went to the Hallmark store first, but Alex frowned at the stuffed animals and chintz. "I'm a fucking lawyer," he muttered when Eleanor offered a teddy bear. "I can do better than this."

So, they went to the jeweler. Eleanor dazzled over the cases of pretty stones and metals. "This is so... elegant," she whispered to him with a sheepish smile.

He bit his lip and nodded.

Eleanor roamed the store and pretended like she'd never had jewelry bought for her by a boy before. She imagined that she'd never had the surprise of a black velvet box. She liked the idea of it being true. How lovely it would be to feel that thrill from someone you longed for. How romantic to receive such a gift, not as a down payment, but because he cared. Not so he could get you in the backseat of his car, but because he wanted you to know he thought you were special.

Beautiful, even.

"What do you think?" Alex's question snapped her back to reality. They gazed at a gold chain with a modest teardrop ruby at the end.

"July's birthstone," the clerk explained.

Alex's choice was made.

They parked in front of the Zebra Lounge and took a collective breath. Eleanor exhaled with a laugh. "God, I'm excited for you right now."

His brows twitched. "I don't even know what I'm doing. Screw it, let's go."

She trailed him into the lounge. Strobe lights swirled to the beat of Wham!, but Eleanor spotted her friends easily. Dylan and Monica were on the dance floor. The twins and Jennifer were at a table in the corner, lounging on white couches. She touched her brother's arm and pointed.

Sam noticed them first, which didn't surprise her. They caught eyes, and she hurried around Alex to get a seat for what was going to be a great show. Her hip settled beside Sam's. She flashed him a hey-how-are-you smile like nothing was up, then looked at Jennifer.

Her friend's brown eyes grew wide at the purposeful way Alex strode to her. She jumped to her feet like she had on the porch, but this time her hands toyed nervously with her skirt.

"Jennifer," Alex said, all seriousness. "Happy birthday. I don't deserve a second chance, but you… You've been on my mind every damn day. Can you forgive me for being such a putz and not calling?"

Her lips fell open. "Uh… uh… uh-huh."

Alex reached out and put his hands on her shoulders. She swayed and fell against him as he pressed his mouth to hers.

Eleanor swooned.

14

SAM

Elle's hair tickled Sam's cheek. She buried her face in his shoulder and squeezed his arm over the PDA playing out in front of them. Jennifer's arms went around Alex's neck. He held her close and kissed her deeply until Brian laughed and let out a wolf whistle. They jumped and broke apart. Elle sat up, still holding his arm tight.

Brian applauded. "Bravo. Encore!"

Elle reached across to shove him, her hair under Sam's nose this time, flooding his senses with her strawberry-and-champagne scent. The newly-minted couple traded a look, gave their friends a wave, and walked to the exit. Eleanor's face was against his shoulder again. Her body vibrated with a squeal before she turned a giddy smile up to Sam.

Ow. How does her smile literally feel like a kick to the chest? Before Sam could reassemble his thoughts, his brother spoke up.

"Now that Jen's taken care of, I think it's time for some fun." Brian rolled his neck and rose, his gaze already across the room on a pair of women with umbrella drinks. He glanced down at Sam and Elle and smirked.

His eyes connected with Sam's, and the brothers held a silent conversation. It was a skill they'd had since childhood.

Brian: *You look comfy.*

Sam: *Piss off. She's my friend.*

Brian's response was to throw his head back and laugh. "Okay, sure, whatever. See you guys later."

He wasn't halfway across the room before the ladies were sitting up straight and smiling.

"Did I miss something?" Elle asked. She sat back, and instantly Sam longed for her warmth again.

"Nah," he grumbled.

"It seemed like I did."

"So. How was line dancing?" he said to change the subject.

Her eyes crinkled. "They wouldn't let me in. Said I wasn't properly attired."

"Shame," he murmured and let his gaze skim her again. "That's a real shame."

Her cheeks colored. She ducked her head, toying with those crisp white lapels. "Um, well," she stuttered, then looked up, fluttering her hands to the empty space where Alex had just stood. "Well, whatever. But can we talk about them?"

Sam grinned, half at the rare sight of Eleanor Field flustered and half at Jennifer and Alex. They replayed the evening and the weeks before, lauding Jennifer's boldness earlier and Alex's now. Eleanor reached for the margarita the server brought her. She stirred the little red straw and fixed her attention back on Sam. A dreamy sigh made her shoulders rise and fall.

He arched a curious brow. "What's that sigh for?"

"I don't know. It's just that I've never seen Alex like that. He's had girlfriends before, but the night they met—and now—I didn't know he could be so… romantic." She sipped as her eyes narrowed. "And Jennifer is so sweet, but she brings out something different in him. How incredible it must be to…"

She broke off with a wince and fixed her attention on her drink with a short shake of her head.

Sam knew where this was going. "To what? Say it, Elle."

"To meet someone who makes you act like you didn't know you could." She threw one hand in the air and sloshed her drink in the process. Sam handed her a napkin and let her clean up in silence. Finally, she fixed a guilty stare on him.

"It is pretty incredible, isn't it?" He kept his tone even. She was flustered, and it surprised him to realize that she hadn't looked at it like that before.

Eleanor Field had seen more of the world than Sam knew he may ever see, and she was obviously independent. But in that moment, she seemed so very young and innocent that Sam narrowed his eyes. Before he thought better of it, he asked, "How is the lawyer treating you?"

The wonder in her gaze shuttered. Eleanor recoiled. "Why do you ask?"

Sam scratched his head and wished he could press rewind. "Well, it's just that you said you weren't dating this summer, but it seems like you've got a regular thing going. So I guess I wondered—"

"Not that it's a bit of your business, but I am not dating him. And he doesn't make me act different if that's what you're asking."

"No, I didn't mean that," he said quickly.

She glared. "What did you mean, then?"

Good question. Too busy trying to be smooth to think it through, as usual. "I… I think I meant… have you ever been in a serious relationship?"

Storm clouds gathered on her face. Sam held his breath and braced for the fury that seemed imminent. But after a beat, Eleanor closed her eyes. When she opened them, her expression smoothed to a cold mask.

"Yep," she clipped out. "Maybe not as serious as you and your Trish, but yep, sure have."

Now it was Sam's turn to scowl. "You don't know anything about that."

"And you don't know anything about me."

They both frowned.

Her face fell. "I'm sor—" she began.

"You're wrong is what you are." Sam cut her off. He rose and drained his beer. "Actually, I'm kind of tired. I think I'll take off. See you tomorrow."

He found his friends and gave his goodnights. Seeing her sitting alone on that bench almost made him cave. But, he clenched his jaw and decided that, for Eleanor Field, being nice was running pretty damn short.

15

ELEANOR

"That was 'Get Up and Jump,' by a funky band out of California called The Red Hot Chili Peppers. I've been listening to this album all summer. Thanks for the recommendation, Elle. If you like it, call Mac. He'll hook you up. Next up, we've got Pink Floyd because *Dark Side of the Moon* is always in style."

"Eclipse" came through the speaker, and Eleanor sighed and smiled up at the ceiling. It had been a hell of a day at work. But now, her body was light and sated. "Alone time" was so easy with his sexy DJ purr in her ears.

Even if they hadn't spoken since that mess on Friday.

Impulsively, she jumped out of bed and tiptoed to the kitchen to grab the phone.

"WRVU."

Eleanor ignored the shiver that went through her and bubbled, "Am I the right caller? Oh, god, am I on air? I've always wanted to be on the radio! Please tell me I won!"

This is me apologizing, Sam. Please don't hate me anymore, she added silently.

There was a beat of silence, and then: "You're the ninth caller. Congratulations, you've won tickets for two to see Conway Twitty in concert."

She slid to the floor and covered her mouth to muffle her exaggerated squeal. He laughed.

"Hi Sam," she said in her regular voice, only quiet to

keep from being heard. *If someone comes in and interrupts this, I might lose my damn mind.*

"Elle, what a surprise. What are you doing up so late?"

Not much. Just lying in bed, touching myself while I think about you. Want to come watch when you get off your shift?

"I, uh, nothing."

He didn't speak, and she realized her answer made no sense. She tried again. "I was, uh, listening to your show. Just wanted to commend you on the lineup tonight. And say you're welcome, of course. It's always nice for my good taste to be acknowledged."

"You weren't supposed to hear that." His smile was audible.

"Then you shouldn't have said it," she teased.

"I didn't realize you'd be listening. Did the other girls laugh at me?"

Eleanor curled the phone cord around her finger. She knew she was about to tear down the wall between them more than she probably should. "Uh, no, they're asleep. And, I guess I… I listen to your show… a lot."

She cringed, hating the cowardice that made her edit her words at the last second. *I listen to your show every time you're on.*

Another beat of silence. Then, he cleared his throat. "Oh, yeah?"

Eleanor palmed her eyes and squeezed her thighs together. His DJ voice was a polished kind of murmur, languid and low and so fucking sexy it did dirty, dirty things to her body.

"Yeah," she said. It came out way too much like a sigh.

"Hold on."

The line went silent. Eleanor held her breath until it was live again.

"Okay," he said. "I've got three songs lined up before I've got to do my signoff. So, what made you call?"

"You know what made me call," she grumbled. "Although I don't suppose you have time to talk to me now, do you? I don't know, I just… wanted to."

"I like that you did. You want to talk?"

"Yeah."

"I could come over. The shift's up in ten. I'm on campus, so I'm close. If you wanted, I mean."

Her pulse was in her ears. "I'll see you soon," she whispered and leapt up to replace the receiver before he could say anything else.

Eleanor flew back to the bedroom. She didn't bother with lights as she peeled off her old sleep tee and stumbled into a pair of terrycloth shorts and a *Flashdance* style one-shoulder sweatshirt. Makeup wasn't part of her daily routine anyway, so she tied a high ponytail and dabbed on some strawberry Lip Smackers.

"Hope you enjoyed that block," Sam purred on the radio. "Let's pause for station identification—Ninety-one-point-one, WRVU, The Official Station of Vanderbilt University—And with that, my time's up. Joey Silver's coming on next to get you through the night. Tomorrow, during the day, be listening for a concert announcement. See you next week, Nashville, and thanks for listening. I think this is a good track to sign off with tonight."

It was "Call Me."

Eleanor grinned so hard her face hurt when the Blondie song began, but it had barely finished when she heard a car out front. The headlights died fast, and she hurried to the door.

It was just after 1am, and all the tree frogs and crickets were long to bed. The patio was warm under her bare feet while she watched Sam walk, hands in pockets, up the driveway. He stopped halfway to the porch and tilted his head, waiting for an invitation, so she waved him forward until he stood on the bottom step.

"Hey there," he murmured, more like his usual self.

Even in the light of a half-moon, his eyes held her captive. Even in the shadows, she studied the angle of his jaw and the soft wave of his hair. And, even if there had been no light at all, she knew him simply by the scent of Dial soap and him, and the inexplicable thrill she got whenever he was near.

She sat down. He joined her. They didn't speak at first, just looked out over the dark lawn. "How was the lab today?" she whispered at last.

"Good. Did you finish the sourdough?"

She nodded. "Monday. I got an eight-point-five out of ten, but it was enough for the contest. Today, I made croissants."

He high-fived her but drew his brows together. "You made what?"

"Croissants," she said, then smiled. "Cres-aunts," she drawled in the Tennessee version of the French word.

"Ah-ha. Confession: I've never eaten one. Is that shameful? It looks so boring."

Eleanor scoffed. "It's totally shameful, and if you eat a fresh one, it'll change your life. The flaky dough melts on your tongue."

"You don't say." His rumbled murmur didn't help the ache she already felt.

But she ignored the tingles and nodded. "Someday I want to go to Paris for a week. I'll live like a vagabond and exist on cheese, baguettes, pastries, coffee, and wine. I'll wear all black with a red scarf."

"You'll need sunglasses," he added seriously.

"Obviously."

"And probably some Ex-Lax with a diet like that."

She shoved his shoulder, and he laughed. "Sam! You're spoiling the fantasy."

"Sorry, sorry," he chuckled.

She shoved him again, ostensibly for good measure but mostly to feel his warm skin through his soft cotton polo.

Silence fell. Sam broke it by clearing his throat. "It's good to hear your voice again."

"It's good to hear yours. I'm sorry about last week. You, uh, you threw me with those questions."

"Wasn't my intention."

They fell into a stare-off, neither angry nor particularly happy. She knew what he was doing, and finally, she pursed her lips and lifted a brow. "You want me to talk first, don't you?"

He smirked. "You just did."

She pushed him again, then toyed with her sleeve. *You wanted him here. Talk to him.*

"I was wrong. You absolutely know things about me— but you don't know everything. You asked me about relationships like I was this innocent little airhead all bubbly over romance. It got to me."

Sam held up a hand. "I didn't mean it like that." He

paused. "Maybe it sounded that way—not an airhead, though, never. But I'm sorry."

She played with her sleeve again and said, "To answer your question, three boyfriends, I guess. Most recently, in Peru when I first got there. He was a rugged guy from Oregon, lots of fun, but he was finishing his tour and gone in three months. Before that, one during my year at Vandy. An art major and very, very kind to me. And one more."

She smiled at his intent expression. "You know your turn's coming, right? Anyway, the lawyer isn't a relationship. I've been double dating so Alex can network. I'd walk on coals for my brother, so I can certainly endure a few dates and some goodnight kisses."

His jaw clenched at the word kisses. She saw it but didn't comment.

"Now that Alex and Jennifer are a thing, I think the double dates are over. I could tell Jason was getting tired of me anyway. He could tell I'm not wife material."

Sam blinked rapidly. "Wife material? I need that defined."

Eleanor snorted. "Don't act like you don't know. Nice girl, passably intelligent, with enough interests to be moderately intriguing—not too much, though, can't threaten his own pursuits. Lives in the material world. Cool enough to be modern, but ready to shuck that for married life."

His dismay was almost comical. "What year is it? That sounds like the fifties."

"If you think it's changed, you're fucking fooling yourself."

He startled at the profanity, but Eleanor didn't blink as she sneered and said, "Oops, see what I did there? Language like that is definitely not wife material. And don't act like you don't know."

"I'd never thought about it." He rubbed his jaw.

"I don't want to be wife material, anyway."

"Mmm, too busy seeing the world."

She shot him a look. "That's part of it."

"What do you mean when you say you don't have a home?"

That made her look away. "What's not to understand? It's kind of like how I've got so many nicknames. Nora, ugh. Len. Elle. Different versions of Eleanor--of me. I guess I just don't have anything very permanent. As for a home, I grew up in Atlanta and... left. Alex, he, well. He arranged for me to come up here, but..."

Her story was falling apart, but she didn't know how to say the rest of it. She'd never spoken this part aloud. She didn't know if she even could. So instead, she flipped topics and put the spotlight on him.

"Tell me about Trish."

He looked at her, his shoulders and guard up all at once. "What should I tell?"

"All of it."

Sam took a deep breath, hesitated once, and then told it all.

"The Cure was playing on the stereo the last time I saw her. She never liked them. We had dinner at my place. Spaghetti. She was going to Spain in a few days, and I thought we were meeting to talk about our future. Turns out, we were—about the fact that we had no future together."

"She dumped you to go to Spain?"

"Mmm, not for the first time. We'd broken up a lot. The

most recent time was over Christmas, just last year. But I thought, hell. We've graduated. Time to get real. I thought she was nervous about going away. I, ah… was going to propose."

Sam might've flinched when Eleanor mentioned good-night kisses, but Eleanor knew she full-on blanched at his confession. He wore a self-deprecating smirk as he watched her reaction.

She tried to recover. "You loved her that much?"

"No. I thought it was the right thing to do." His words flowed out with a quiet confidence that made the story much easier to accept.

Not that you should have a hard time accepting that your friend loved someone else, goofball. Eleanor gave herself a mental slap and nodded for him to continue.

"Before I could ask, she dumped me. She kissed me goodbye. It tasted like parmesan, garlic, and Doublemint gum. It was a taste I wanted to forget as soon as it happened. I guess that's kind of a good summary of how the whole relationship left me feeling."

"If it was as unpleasant as gum and garlic, why did you stay together?" Eleanor realized she was perfectly torn between rapt attention and dread to hear all about the life Sam had been on track to lead.

"Oh, well, that's a little complicated," Sam said, but then he kept talking. He told her about five years, off and on. But, more than the story, he told it all, including how he felt at each stage of the relationship.

Eleanor was riveted. She was startled at how strongly she hated the way Trish had treated him. She'd never wanted vengeance before, not even for the people who had scarred her the most. But the story of selfish, unpredictable Trish made bile creep up her throat. Her fists clenched at how patient he was, and how completely she'd disregarded his kindness. His care. Him.

Sam looked over and narrowed his eyes. "You look close to murdering someone. What are you thinking?"

She exhaled slowly and tried to relax her jaw. "I don't like that story. She took you for granted. You could've been happier, you could've—"

His hand drifted to her fist sitting on her knee. He stroked her knuckles and eradicated her train of thought. "It was my fault as much as hers. I was naïve, too worried about making her happy because it's what I thought I was supposed to do—what a real man would do. Wife material? Husband material is as real as that. Be macho. Be strong. Make money to provide for her, and don't even think about admitting you don't know what the hell you're doing."

"That's fair," she murmured.

"Mm-hm. You're probably going to laugh at this, having traveled the world and all. I think I just figured our relationship was good enough. When you don't know better, you accept what is as what's normal."

He dropped his head as her throat closed up. His fingers began to slip away, but Eleanor gripped him so tight he looked back up, eyes wide at her haunted expression.

"I know exactly what you mean," she said fiercely. Two solitary tears slipped down her cheeks.

Looks like you're going to tell a little more. The thought made her purse her lips, but she knew she needed him to know.

"Elle?" Sam's expression had turned to confusion. He reached for her face with his free hand, but he lowered it again before making contact.

Eleanor wiped her own tears away and took a shaky breath. "Uh, yes. I know all about good enough. My first boyfriend, he—I was—there were… expectations." She tripped on her words. More tears leaked out while she watched his jaw set in understanding.

Sam hummed deep in his throat and reached again. This time he let his thumb coast over her wet cheek. "Expectations?"

"It's ancient history, thanks to Alex, but I absolutely understand accepting fucked-up as normal."

His eyes flicked over her face. At last, a faraway smile played on his lips. "Trish would have been total wife material… or a nightmare of infidelity. You wouldn't have gone to Peru."

He took a quick breath and continued. "We wouldn't be sitting here tonight. Thank *fuck* things don't work out as planned."

Her nose wrinkled to hide the shiver that went through her. Eleanor wanted to lick that word right out of his mouth, it sounded so good. Another piece of the wall she'd tried to build between them crumbled. She crooked her finger, beckoning him closer to whisper in his ear.

"You don't talk to nice girls like that, Sam," she said, allowing her fingertips to brush the soft stubble on his jaw.

His eyes fluttered closed at her touch. His nose touched her cheek, and Eleanor's breath hitched. She tried to steal one more sip of air, but too late. Their mouths met, and fire raced to her toes. They kissed gently, once… then again…

"Dammit, Brian Greene! I'm turning the hose on you!"

Monica's voice from inside the house made them jump

apart. Even slurred with sleep, she knew how to make herself known.

Eleanor noticed with vague relief that she'd neglected to flip on the porch light. "No, no, Mon. It's fine." She turned to the door while Sam bent his head between his legs and drew a deep breath. Her pulse throbbed in her ears. "We weren't—we were just talking."

She snorted. "Don't trust him, Lenny. He's the best friend in the world, but he's the worst with women."

"We were talking, Monica. And I'm leaving, okay?" Sam growled, head still bent. Eleanor realized then that she'd called him Brian.

"Yeah, o-kayy," she sneered. "Keep your hands off my best friend, or I'll tell her about that party where your two dates wound up fighting each other and getting arrested."

"Holy shit," Eleanor muttered, distracted but not shocked that a story like that would be attached to Brian Greene.

"Exactly," Monica affirmed.

"Thanks a lot, Monica," Sam grumbled in what Eleanor realized was a deliberately different voice, much closer to Brian's. She spied the smile creasing his cheek and bit her lips as she stood up.

"I'm coming inside," she promised her friend.

Monica grumbled before her footsteps shuffled back down the hallway. Sam stood, too. They faced each other in the silence.

"Huh," she muttered at last.

He laughed, and she loved it. She loved that his laugh gave them permission for this to be funny, not weird or anxious. She loved that she got to laugh, too, after so much seriousness.

"I have to wonder when this'll come back up," he chuckled.

"God only knows."

"True. Well, I… guess I should go."

I wish you didn't have to, though. With a final wave, she watched him stroll back to his car. As he drove away, the thought hit her hard: she didn't ever want Sam Greene to go.

16

SAM

How am I supposed to walk up these stairs and grin like the world's best buddy when a few hours ago I sat here and…

Sam dug the heels of his palms into his eyes and stomped up the front porch. He felt like he was living in *The Never-ending Story,* half in a fantasy realm of late-night kisses and unwavering stares, and half in this awesome, maddening reality of Saturday baking and the closest thing to a best friend he'd ever had outside of Brian.

But it was Saturday morning, and so he stuck his head in the house and called hello, only to be greeted by a knock-out scent of chocolate that made him dizzy.

"We're in here, Sammy," Monica called from the kitchen.

He expected the usual sight of Elle flying around. What greeted him instead was more like a vigil. The crew all sat around the table, gazing at a row of dark brown blobs on a sheet of parchment paper. Elle's brows were knitted, but she glanced up when he entered.

"I failed," she said simply.

"You did not," Monica insisted. "They smell great. I'm sure they taste great, too."

"Irrelevant. They're hideous. Look at those holes! That shape! The chocolate needs tempering again, and I have no idea how I can possibly create a shell with an ice cube tray." Elle groaned and buried her face in her hands.

Sam glanced at the sink and stove. Pots were on the burners, and, sure enough, an ice tray sat dripping chocolate on the counter.

"I thought you and chocolate understood each other," he said to lighten the mood.

Elle peeked up long enough to kick him in the chest with one of her cheeky glances, the kind that said she was impressed he'd remembered her comment from all those weeks ago. Sam chuckled under his breath. *I remember everything, Beautiful. Give me a break.*

"Chocolate, sure, but this has to become a shiny, perfectly built bonbon. Not even sort of the same. And between it being so damn finicky and not having the tools I need—"

Jennifer interrupted. "But you'll have them this week, right? You don't have to do this at home to qualify for the contest. Right?"

She shrugged a nod.

Sam reached around his brother and popped one of the blobs in his mouth. Its consistency was nowhere near a candy store bonbon. Still, the chocolate was rich and creamy and married well with the candied cherry center. He chewed and said, "I'm sure you'll kill it once you're at the bakery and can have the equipment you need."

The others snatched up the candies too and chorused their agreement.

Those blonde brows stayed stitched together. "But I've aced the other two right here. Why can't I get this one right, too? I need you."

"Len Field, you've always done things on your own," Monica jumped in. "Just because we're not there to cheer you on from the den doesn't mean we aren't all rooting for you. You can do this, girl."

Elle blinked, and Sam realized that her "I need you" hadn't been directed to the crew. His stomach flipped as she stole a glance his way, but he swallowed to keep his voice even. "When you're at work, just put on The Cure and pretend like we're—you're—right here. Easy."

She flicked the remaining chocolate so that it skittered across the table. Dylan caught it and tossed it into his mouth. Elle sighed and pushed a hand through her hair. "As if. Let's go do something. I don't want to smell chocolate anymore today."

* * *

"WRVU," Sam said into the phone. It was after midnight, so technically Wednesday. His shift had about 20 minutes to go.

"I took your advice. Kind of."

Elle's soft voice sent a pleasant jolt from his throat straight to his cock. Sam was grinning before her words even sunk in. "What do you mean? What advice?"

"In the battle of the bonbons."

"Battle of the Bonbons. A lesser-known skirmish in the War of 1812."

They both laughed. Sam shook his head. "Hang on, I have to drop a track."

He hit pause and leaned into the mic. "Here's 'Your Wildest Dreams' by The Moody Blues. Dream on, y'all." Then, he yanked off one headphone and grabbed the receiver again. "Okay, what about this epic battle?"

"Well, I figured, The Cure was too homogenous. I wanted these bonbons to really have some flair, you know? So instead, I stayed late here at Sweetie's and let you make the soundtrack for me. I've been working since your show started."

The idea of Elle listening to his show turned Sam on in ways he'd die to admit. He'd spent most of the summer half-pretending each show was a running conversation with her about music. Often after midnight, when he was drowsy, he'd lean back in his chair and imagine her there with him.

Usually straddling his lap like she did in that booth the first day.

He'd invented elaborate fantasies of her wearing his headphones and grinning her impish smile while her hands and lips did whatever they wanted to him.

When she called last Friday and confessed that she'd actually been listening, it was as if his silly daydreams were a half step closer to reality. The idea of her alone in her room while the radio played made it even hotter.

He'd never seen the bakery where she worked, but his mind had no problem filling in some blanks. Elle, wearing nothing but an apron, standing on the edges of her feet and grinning at his narrative, singing along with his lineup…

"Sam?"

Sam blinked and crashed back to reality. "Shit, oh, sorry, Elle. Dammit, hang on again." He fumbled all over himself to pull up three more songs, then returned to the receiver again with a strong headshake. *Get your head out of your ass, doofus.*

"Sorry, got tangled up there." *In my own pathetic daydreams.* "So, you've been at the bakery making the bonbons during my show?"

"Mm-hmm. I needed the, um, inspiration. And you did promise to help me. So, I guess technically this counts."

He chuckled. "Get real. This is the most helpful I've been for any of your projects."

"I should've had you spinning records all along then. Because… they came out, Sam. They're pretty."

The quiet pride in her voice made him grin for her. "You were the only one who had any doubts, you know."

She hummed. "Well, I definitely felt inspired, as usual, from your lineup. So, I wanted to say thank you before I headed back to the house."

Reality clicked in. "Wait. You're there all alone?"

"Yeah. I have keys. Going to go here in a minute."

His pulse kicked up. "Elle, it's not safe. Let me come get you."

"What? Don't be silly, Sam. I'm fine."

He blew out a hard breath. "Don't be a hero for a second. Just stay in the store till I get there, will you?"

She grumbled and hung up.

Sam didn't give a damn. He wrapped his shift, passed the mic to Joey as fast as he could, and jogged out of the station. An empty store in the dead of night was no place for one of his people to be navigating alone. He'd have run to his car for any of them. That it was Elle might've made him gun the engine a bit harder, but still.

He swung into the parking lot to see her little VW out front and flashed his headlights into the storefront. A second later, the door cracked, and Elle peeked out. She gestured for him to come in, so he locked his car and followed.

Light glowed from a door behind the counter. Despite his silly fantasy, Elle was wearing an apron—and clothes underneath. She was streaked in chocolate from her hair to her apron. Her eyes were tired, but she smiled brightly.

Skye McDonald

"Want to taste?"

Sam couldn't help it. He skimmed his finger from her bangs down the side of her face across a streak of chocolate. "Love to. Where should I start?"

Jesus, I actually said that.

Elle's cheeks flushed a perfect rose. "Sam, hush," she muttered.

And we're back to friends. Far fucking out.

He dropped his hand and shrugged. "Kidding."

But her breaths stayed shallow. "You were not."

"No, I was not."

"I... I..." she wet her lips and swallowed hard. "Friends," she wheezed. "We..."

Her hand floated out, almost like she didn't realize she was doing it. She skimmed her fingertips up his shirt. Sam stepped closer until she had to tilt her head to look at him. His heart thundered in his chest, but he kept his hands balled at his side. "We what? We're friends. But..."

That hand slid up to his cheek, one thumb swishing along his jaw.

"You've been here for two minutes, and all I can think is..." Elle's gaze, like her words, had gone hazy.

"I know, Elle. Should I kiss you or not?"

They looked around at the empty room. Sam could see it all. If he kissed her, it wouldn't be a kiss. It would be him, picking her up and carrying her to the closest surface. It would be her legs around his back and that apron—and the rest of her clothes—on the floor. If he kissed her now, the only thing that would stop him, the only thing that could stop him, would be her.

This isn't the place for what I have in mind for us.

Sam clasped her wrist gently and summoned all his will-power. He flashed a close-lipped smile. "I'm dying to see these bonbons. Show me."

Relief washed over her gorgeous face, but Sam saw the frustration there, too. There was no doubt her feelings were as muddled as his. It was a small solace.

The bonbons were professional quality. The flavor exploded in his mouth. The chocolate shell was smooth and snappy, just like it should be. When he finished moaning, she pursed her lips and flashed a sad smile.

"I know. I'm pleased. But, uh, this means… I've practically got the internship. I'll go to New York at the end of August."

Sam paused. "Wow, that's soon. I've been thinking about how I'll be in Knoxville for the upcoming school year. New York is a little bit of a different story."

She fluttered her hand. "Maybe I won't get it. Who knows? But if I do, probably time to move on anyway."

He shook his head and let that point rest. "Are you ready to go? I'll walk you to your car."

On the way out, she said, "You really didn't have to come here to walk me to my car."

"Hmm, I didn't. I came to walk you and follow you home."

"Nothing was going to happen to me!"

"Yeah? You can be sure of that? There was no chance you'd blow a flat in the middle of the night? There was absolute certainty no creep was hanging out in this parking lot?"

"I… I… thank you, Sam."

They faced each other. "I'd do it for any of my friends.

It's not a big deal."

"Well, and thank you for... everything. Helping me all summer. Being you."

"I'm not sure who else I could be," he chuckled. "Thank you for letting me bear witness to your amazing talent."

She rolled her eyes. "As if. So, um, goodnight."

"Goodnight, Beautiful. Drive safe and lock the door at Monica's behind you."

She pursed her lips in reply but did as he asked once they arrived at the house. Sam flashed his lights and headed home.

17

ELEANOR

"Woof!"

"Bowie's movie soundtrack: awesome or shit?"

Monica and Eleanor laughed at Mac's and Myrtle's simultaneous greeting when they hurried in from the rain Friday afternoon. It had been a soggy day. Eleanor had returned from work to find Monica vegging in front of the TV, bored out of her mind. Friday afternoons had become her usual time at Mac's Joint, so she threw some caramels in a baggie and dragged her friend along.

"Awesome," they chorused.

"Jury's still out," Mac grumbled.

He shelved a copy of the *Labyrinth* LP. Monica and Eleanor began singing the intro to the song, "Magic Dance." The phrase, *You remind me of the babe*, had been sung in the house at least once daily since they'd seen the movie two weeks ago.

Mac laughed at their antics. "Well, hell, let's put it on then."

Bowie came through the speakers while they browsed the aisles. Eleanor was poking through the INXS selection when Mac laughed again at the chime on the door.

"Where in the wide, wide world of sports have you been keeping yourself, man?" he called.

"Workin' my ass off building that new golf course, dude. Good to see you."

The girls whipped around to see Brian stroll in. His already broad smile deepened when they squealed hello. "Hey, ladies. I thought that was your car out front, Lenny."

The chime sounded again. "And the gang's all here," Mac announced.

Sam flashed Eleanor a hello smile that made her heart flutter. She glanced at Mon, seized momentarily with panic. *She's going to figure it out. I almost blacked out at the shop the other night. How can she not see right through me?*

Eleanor dreaded the thought. She dreaded the moment when her best friend finally realized how absolutely goofy she got when Sam was around. There was simply no way to predict what would come out of her mouth when it happened.

Monica sensed her gaze. Eleanor caught her breath, but she just flashed a quick smile and drifted down a row. Brian roamed around, and Mac chilled behind the register.

Hmm. Okay, maybe it's not as obvious as I thought? How can that possibly be true?

"Can't say I'm surprised to see you here," Sam greeted when he walked over. They traded another smile. "What are you shopping for today?"

She fingered the edges of the albums in the closest rack and shook her head. "Nothing. I'm just here to proposition Mac."

Sam startled. "Excuse me?"

She giggled. "I'm hoping to trade some pot caramels for a ticket to Echo & the Bunnymen."

He scratched his chin, brows still drawn. "Pot caramels?"

"Didn't you have any yet? I've been making them since I

got back from my road trip. Monica's request." She showed him the bag.

"I don't get high anymore. It makes me a total slug," he admitted, then twitched his brows. "But that is a genius idea. You could make a fortune. So, you're propositioning Mac for a trade. Think he'll go for it?"

"My caramels are awesome. He cannot resist the dark side of the Force." She winked, then frowned. "Wait, do girls wink? I shouldn't have winked, should I?"

"What would you have done instead?"

She lowered her lashes and glanced up at him. "Maybe that? But that doesn't make sense with the conversation, does it?"

Sam laughed, and she pursed her lips. Bantering with him gave her the best kind of flutters in her stomach. It had since the very first time they met.

"Wink again," he said.

She did.

He scanned her face, mock-serious. "Yeah, you can definitely get away with it. I advise you to wink at me on the regular, just to keep the practice."

Brian appeared behind him, slinging his arm around his twin's shoulder. After she realized there were two of them, Eleanor had never had a second's hesitation in knowing who was who, even though they were identical.

She eyed them. "Did you guys ever have one of those twin languages or anything?"

They traded a look. "Nope," Brian said. "But what we just did there? That's our code."

"What did you do?"

"We don't need to speak to communicate. We can talk

with our eyes," Sam explained.

"Really? What did you say?"

"We said, 'aw, that's cute she's asking.'" Brian grinned—and winked. Sam and Eleanor both laughed.

"Did you ever—" she started.

"No."

"Yes."

They traded another look and laughed again. She arched a brow and grumbled, "You didn't let me finish."

Brian explained again. "You were going to ask if we ever pretended to be each other. Am I right?"

"Wow. Yes, you are. Am I that predictable?"

"No, but it's a common question," Sam said gently.

"Oh, duh. I bet." There was a pause. Eleanor waved her hand in a circle. "It might be a common question, but that answer needs explaining, please."

Brian said, "No and yes. When we get mistaken for each other by people who can't tell us apart, we usually just go with it. It's kind of a joke."

"We never swapped places or bullshit like that," Sam clarified. "Pretended to be each other for a date or an exam or anything."

"Or to avoid getting busted with a girl in the middle of the night?" Eleanor added innocently.

Brian burst out laughing while Eleanor winked at Sam's widening eyes. He flashed a look that made her shiver. But before either brother could reply, the door chimed, and Myrtle woofed.

"Afternoon," Mac called from the counter.

"Yeah, you got any copies of *True Blue* on cassette?"

Oh, god.

Sam's brows drew together, and Brian stopped laughing. Both were in response to the way Eleanor suddenly went pale. Her stomach hit the floor.

Mac called, "Aisle three. I think we got a couple."

And then Jason the Lawyer was striding their way.

"Excuse me," he said. He stepped around the guys and stopped short when he saw her. "Eleanor! How are you, sweetheart?"

She didn't miss the look Sam and Bry traded while she crooked her lips and said hello. He glanced at them, then skimmed his gaze over her pink tank-top and jeans. The way he did it made her feel naked, especially compared to the suit he wore. His leer turned into a playful glare and a wagging brow.

"Alex said y'all were busy tonight, but you don't look busy." The smell of alcohol was strong on his breath, and his tie was askew. "I just won a big case today. Maybe you and me could celebrate tonight? Think you'd want to come over?"

The way he said it, all familiar and patronizing like she'd come over dozens of times before—or even once—made her cringe. She started to make an excuse, but then paused and remembered: Alex had told her he'd spoken to Jason about the end of their double dating routine. Her brother hadn't given a lot of details, but she knew he'd given Jason the message.

This is all for show in front of my friends. He's claiming me.

Jason's lips curled as he gave her another leering look. "I've been hunting Madonna's album all over town. What are you shopping for today? How 'bout I buy it for you? A little present for my girl here?"

Presents.

Ancient memories rocked her senses and froze her where she stood. Flowers and jewelry, shoes and trinkets, all in exchange—as a down payment—for…

For suede driving gloves inching higher under ball gowns. For back-seats and expectations from nice girls. For me.

"No, thank you." Eleanor hated how thick her tongue was suddenly, how weak she sounded. She mentally raced for stable ground. *Think of all the moments you've been strong. Think about Peru. Think about Sweetie's. Think about waterskiing.*

Think about the first time you were in this store.

She knew that was silly. Getting frisky in a listening booth wasn't the kind of thing that was supposed to give someone power, but for her, it did. She'd taken what she wanted that afternoon. It might be weird, but it was a moment of strength.

Eleanor looked over at Sam. He watched them with a guarded expression. The same look was mirrored but different on his brother. But when she looked into those navy eyes, it unlocked her tongue.

Turning back to Jason, she stood up straighter. "I said no, thank you."

"Aw, baby." He stepped closer to her, again glancing at Brian and Sam. His wrists rested on her shoulders. "Don't do me like that. Why're you acting like you don't know me? Don't tell me I need to be jealous."

His eyes were hazy, but the lightly scolding look in them was laced with threat. "Don't tell me you've been sneaking behind my back with these dorks, hmm?"

She heard the collective intake of breath behind her, but Eleanor stepped away from his arms with a scowl. "I don't have to tell you anything because you don't have a claim to me. I am not your girl, your baby, or your anything, and I never was. Goodbye, Jason."

Just like the movie says. You have no power over me. Take that, Bobby-uh, Jason. Whatever.

Old memories and this horrible moment made clammy goosebumps sheet across her skin. Eleanor spun to look at the racks of albums, but Jason grabbed her arm and whirled her back around. Myrtle barked and came bounding up with Monica right behind.

"Don't touch me," she seethed, wresting out of his grip. "Get your cassette and get lost, okay? Just leave me alone."

His face was red as he growled, "Your brother said you were a nice girl, but you're just a little slut, aren't you?"

"Enough."

The word was barely breathed, but in the next moment, Jason disappeared from her view, replaced by Sam's back. She gazed at the list of cities that Springsteen had played in '84, printed on his t-shirt, as her blood boiled.

"Stop talking. Walk away." Sam's voice was quiet. Menacing.

"Sam, I've got it," she said, stepping beside him.

"I was talking to the girl, asshole, not you," Jason said.

Monica and Eleanor traded a look. Monica moved forward, but Eleanor sliced her hand across her throat to hold her back. *Go away, Jason. Just leave us alone. You don't give a shit about me. Just make this stop.*

"I'm not the asshole here. You're embarrassing yourself. Walk away," Sam repeated.

Jason sneered. "Or what? You're gonna punch me? Try it. I'm an attorney. I'll sue you so hard you'll be my servant

136   Skye McDonald

for life."

"Yeah, but you'd have to prove it." Mac shuffled down the aisle, hands stuffed in the pockets of his baggy jeans. He shrugged. "And the security cameras in this section are on the fritz today. Funny how that happens, huh?"

He grinned mirthlessly and lifted two cassettes from the row, adding them to his pocket. "Funny too, but we're out of your album. Maybe you just get the hell out and leave our girl Len alone in that case. Your business isn't wanted here."

Jason scowled at him, then at Eleanor. This made Sam cross his arms and nudge her back with his shoulder, just a little. Alarm bells wailed in her head. Sam was never controlling, and she had no idea what he was about to do.

But when Eleanor shuffled half a step back, Jason squared his shoulders and stepped toe-to-toe with Sam. "What do you want to do?" he growled.

"Aw, Jesus, Sam, just do it," Brian muttered, but Sam held his ground, gazing impassively.

It was too much for Eleanor. Too much drama over absolutely nothing. She huffed and threw up her hands. "How many people need to tell you to leave before you get the hell out?"

She shoved Jason's arm. He whirled on her, the back of his palm raised high. Eleanor cowered. Before the blow could fall, Sam grabbed his wrist. He pulled his arm behind his back and slammed Jason to the ground. Jason cursed and belched, which only added to the utter disgrace he was suddenly in. Eleanor clapped a hand on her mouth to swallow an hysterical giggle at this absurd sight.

Sam brought his sneaker to rest on Jason's chest, leaving a muddy footprint on his expensive dress shirt. Brian shouted his approval and knelt down. He wrapped his arm around Jason's neck and lifted his head.

"Look at her," he growled, and the dirtbag's bleary eyes settled on her.

"Guys, this is nuts," she muttered.

"No, it's awesome," Monica corrected, kicking at his shoe. "What an asshole!"

"Look at her," Brian repeated. "Now, apologize."

"Fuck all of you," Jason seethed. "I'm not apologizing to that—ughh, fuck!"

He broke off in a groan when Sam's foot connected with his side. Brian grinned like a demon and tightened his grip.

"Try that one more time," he said softly.

Eleanor wasn't sure she'd ever seen someone as mad as Jason looked. And Eleanor had made a man *furious*. She held her breath. His apology meant nothing. She just wanted him to vanish, wanted to erase the last ten minutes from everyone's memory.

Jason gnashed his teeth, but he gritted out, "Apologies, Eleanor."

She took a tight breath. She couldn't look into his eyes anymore, couldn't bear any more fury. "Just leave me the hell alone," she muttered softly.

The twins sprang back and let him crawl to his feet. Once upright, Jason jerked his coat straight and put a death glare on all of them. "This place is a dump," he snapped at Mac, who just laughed. "Fuck all of you," he said again before storming out.

The moment the door chimed, Eleanor exhaled—but Brian and Sam jumped into motion.

"Shit," Brian hissed as he raced his brother to the door. They skidded out at a full run, shouting into the rain, "Don't touch it!"

Eleanor couldn't find the energy to wonder what was going on. She sagged to the ground and let Myrtle nuzzle her. Monica knelt down and hugged her tight.

Heat flooded her face. "Sorry, Mac."

He laughed. "Kid, don't you know we don't pay no attention to kangaroos? Don't sell to them, either."

Eleanor knitted her brows together at the strange euphemism, but the sentiment wasn't lost.

Curving her lips, she got to her feet. "Well, thanks. Here."

She tossed him the caramels and looked down at Monica. Concert tickets suddenly didn't matter. "Let's go," she whispered, and Monica was up in a blink.

The door chimed again, and the guys appeared, shaking rain off their hair. "He didn't key your car, did he, man?" Mac asked, and the girls traded a startled look. The thought clearly hadn't occurred to either of them.

"Nah, but the asshole was thinking of it. He had his keys in his hand," Brian reported, then flashed her a smile. "How you doing over there, Len?"

She shrugged. "Glad he's gone. Good riddance."

He chuckled. "Yeah, but that was fun. I haven't been ready to fight since high school. Shit, I'm ready to play some Whitesnake or Poison now."

"We're out." Monica slid her arm through Eleanor's. "See you later, Rocky Balboa."

Sam and Eleanor traded a look as Monica guided her to the door.

Back at the house, Eleanor tumbled onto Monica's bed and hugged a pillow while Monica fetched the ice cream.

"Want to build a fort?" she asked when she returned with the carton and two spoons.

Eleanor grinned. Even as seniors in high school, building a fort and huddling in their sleeping bags was their place to tell secrets and hide from the world. She opened her mouth to say no, that they didn't have to be that silly anymore.

"Hell yeah," was what came out.

They tied her bedspread to a chair and her footboard and sat under it, then traded a laugh. "Oh, god, I'm so happy you're here," Monica blurted. She threw herself on Eleanor, and they tumbled down on the blanket and pillows to lie on their backs.

Eleanor sighed, then looked at her. "That was a nightmare. He was a little too familiar, right?"

She rolled her eyes. "Gag me with a spoon. Too fucking familiar, thanks. That was your lawyer?"

Eleanor waved that thought away. "He was drunk. He's been… fine until now. You know I've been doing this for Alex anyway—oh, god, what if this comes up at work?"

She shook her head. "You think that dick will tell Alex what he said to you? Or that the twins took him down for it? Not hardly."

Eleanor nodded at that but then groaned. "That was like a scene from a bad movie."

Monica grinned. "Dude, did you see how Sam laid him flat? That was awesome. And Brian making him apologize—damn, they were kind of sexy." She giggled.

Eleanor smiled, her cheeks warm. She suddenly knew that this was the moment she was ready to tell Monica how she ached for Sam. This was where it'd be right for her to ask if she thought anyone would care if they explored being more than friends. This was when it would be safe to giggle and ask how the hell she didn't think he looked like Blane, to admit she was ready to smash her silly vow for a date with him. To admit that she was tired of outrunning her past.

This was the moment that the window in her heart was open.

But Monica missed it. She didn't catch the look in her friend's eyes before she was gazing up at the quilt and telling Eleanor how well she'd handled him, too. And after that, the window closed again, and Sam was just her secret.

18

SAM

"Up next is 'The Queen is Dead,' the eponymous first track off the new album by The Smiths. Enjoy." Sam punched play and sat back in his chair with a glance at the clock. Fifteen minutes till his segment was up. That meant time for one more track, then a signoff song.

Sam liked the last song of his show to be meaningful, but no inspiration had struck that night. The Smiths ended, so he leaned into the mic again, closed his eyes, and said the one thing on his mind.

"It's getting late, Nashville. I hope you've enjoyed tonight's lineup. Hope it's gotten you where you needed to be. I'm on my way out in a minute. But right now, I'm sitting here debating saying this aloud. I've been debating for the past four hours. Now, I figure it's so late I've got nothing to lose. If you're listening—you know who you are—give me a call. I want to ask you something completely absurd. Ring me if you're game. In the meantime, here's Elvis Costello."

The phone rang before he could pull off his headphones.

"Morrissey's voice is possibly sexier than Bowie's. Your thoughts?"

He grinned and punched his fist into the air at the sound of her playful murmur. But the song was short, and he knew he had to get back to business. "I think this requires some discussion. And right now, I have to close out the show."

"Ah. Too bad then," she said before the line went dead.

"Alright, Nashville, I'll catch you next Tuesday. Joey Silver will be on in a few to take you through the night. What should we close with? Well, in the immortal words of Monty Python: and now for something completely different."

Grinning, Sam yanked a disc from deep in the drawers and let it drop. "I Think We're Alone Now," the old 60s pop song, filled the studio as he dropped the headphones and gathered his stuff. He arrived at the girls' house fifteen minutes later, still muttering the lyrics.

"Speaking of," he whispered under his breath. He killed the engine and fixed his eyes on her blonde hair in the moonlight. She was seated on the front porch, arms around her knees. Sam tumbled out and jogged to her.

"Well?" she greeted.

It took him a second to remember. "Oh, right. Bowie is a god. Morrissey is a prince."

"That wasn't the question. The question was about the sex level of their voices."

He sat beside her. "I stand by my declaration. And your thoughts?"

She pondered it. "Bowie's got that plaintive wail thing nailed, but Morrissey's voice is, mmm," she shivered for effect. "This may be an unanswerable question."

They lapsed into silence. Sam's head filled with a vision of making love with a mixed tape in the background. The idea warmed his skin in the still summer air. He tugged at his t-shirt and cleared his throat.

She seemed to interpret that as a prompt to speak. "Oh. Well, so… you asked me to call."

Sam knitted his brows. "When?"

Elle blinked rapidly. "Oh, I—oh, shit, I thought," she

fumbled but stopped when he laughed.

Sam expected a shove or at least a smile, but she still frowned. "Don't laugh at me. I thought you meant me when you said someone should call."

Her cheek was hot when he reached for her. "Of course I meant you," he murmured, and her shoulders lowered. "Guess I'm lucky you were listening again."

"I always listen. Every time you're on."

Sam's heart went into free fall at the words he'd hoped to hear the first night they'd sat together after his shift. His arm clenched to control the urge to pull her close. He gritted his teeth. "Really?"

She nodded, eyes lowered.

"Elle, I—" Sam reined in his libido and swallowed hard. He flashed a smile and reached into his back pocket. "I've got something for you."

She accepted the concert tickets. Her brows inched up her forehead. Mac had confirmed that she hadn't bought them once the girls left last Friday, so Sam bought two. He had been working up the nerve to show her ever since.

When she didn't speak, he said, "Having a friend with such good taste as to appreciate an Echo & the Bunnymen show is an opportunity I couldn't pass up. It's cool if we go together, right?"

Elle ran her finger over the face of the tickets, then nodded once and flickered a smile at him. She put the tickets on the porch and sucked on her lip. Worry creased her brows.

Sam reached for her cheek again. "What's on your mind?"

"This isn't working, Sam," she blurted, pulling away.

Sam froze.

Elle jumped up and paced around barefoot in the grass. "The bonbons were my best score yet. I got the details of the internship yesterday. It's six months in New York City, and then I have to agree to a year's employment with one of their subsidiaries. One of them. That means I might not even need to come back to Sweetie's if I don't want to. I could wind up in Chicago, or stay in NYC, or… or a dozen other options."

"Still looking for your home," he murmured.

She pivoted toward him and nodded. "Exactly. Still avoiding Atlanta, still not ready to settle down."

Sam sighed and rubbed his eyes.

Eleanor spoke again. "Except this summer is changing me. I, ha, I like it here. I like me here. I'm starting to trust myself more. That probably doesn't make sense, but—"

"It does."

She kept her gaze on the grass as she continued to pace. "I want to say I'm not coming back because coming back means this is home." Her strides paused. "And if I'm honest, I'm not sure I'm ready to admit that to myself, much less Monica, or Alex, or the world. What if I do, and it all blows up? What if I'm not made to have a home?"

Her head dropped with a sigh.

Sam took a deep breath before he spoke. He knew he had to be a voice of reason despite all his selfish desires. "I mean, I could assure you that's nonsense, but I don't think that's what you want to hear. So maybe just don't say it. Don't promise this is home. Just go to New York and see how you feel."

Ow. Even in the shadows, her gaze could twist his heart.

"I know how I feel," she murmured, then wet her lips.

"Sam, I… I'm going to have to leave because I… can't stand being your friend."

She heaved a shaky breath and looked down again. Sam's lungs burned. Nauseating dread began to creep from his stomach to his throat.

"I tried. I love the guys. I love Jen, and I love that my brother's in this group now, too. But I can't with you, Sam. I'm sorry."

She lifted her face to reveal tear-tracked cheeks and huffed a dry laugh. "I tried so fucking hard to be nice," she said to the sky.

She wiped her face, lowered her gaze to him, and lifted both palms up in surrender. "I can't stop thinking about you. I don't know what else to do. All I want is for you to touch me."

Through her whole confession, Sam took about two sips of air as he walked that knife's edge of ambiguity. But with those words, his world crashed down. His jaw dropped as he sucked for air, almost blind with the sudden and absolute knowledge that Eleanor Field was going to change his life.

And then he leapt to his feet and took her in his arms.

She fell against him, trembling hard. So was he. He buried his face in her silky hair and tried to just breathe. Her sweet scent filled his brain, so familiar. In that moment, so utterly his.

"Eleanor," he muttered while her delicate fingers clenched at his t-shirt. "Beautiful Elle."

She shuddered harder, and Sam shifted his stance.

"Please don't let go yet." Her words were muffled in his chest.

Sam laughed and squeezed her tighter. "I'm not," he pledged. *Ever,* he added silently, unsure if it was what she needed to hear yet.

"What are we going to do?" She lifted her face, her shadowed features etched with genuine concern.

Sam met her gaze as confidently as he'd ever been about anything. "We're going to hold each other, and we're going to stop pretending like we don't want to. And when we're ready, we'll tell the rest of them, and they'll be cool. But you're not going to worry that this isn't okay, and you're not going to leave here and not come back because you have this idea that we were a one-and-done. And the rest of it will work out."

She sucked her lip. It made him hungry. "But what if—"

He squeezed her again, and she stilled. "Eleanor," he scolded gently. "Trust."

"Trust you?"

"Trust *you*," he corrected, touching his forehead to hers. "You know as well as I do that we should be together. Trust that it's right."

Her face lifted, but she whispered, "Please don't kiss me."

"Why not?"

Her eyes were still closed as she murmured, "Because if you do, I won't be able to stop. And the walls in this house are thin, even if we're really quiet."

Sam grunted. His brain flooded with an even more potent vision than a few minutes ago. His arms constricted even tighter, and she looked at him. He dodged her lips and bent to her ear.

"You and I aren't going to be quiet, and we're sure as

hell not going to be nice. You and me, Elle, we're going to be… wild."

He licked her lobe, and she moaned and melted into him a little more. Flexing his hips into hers, he laughed. "You like that idea?"

"Uh-huh, but don't tell," she whispered. "I told Monica about my vow to be good this summer."

"You're the fucking best, Beautiful."

She flexed back, blinding him with the sweet pressure of her body against his. He bit her neck to muffle his own moan.

"Sam, stop," she panted. "I—god, I can't handle another interruption."

With a groan of frustration, he tore himself away but kept hold of her waist. Her hands rested on his arms. They were both breathless with tense energy.

"Science," they whispered at the same time.

Their mutual laughter eased the tension just a bit. Eleanor shuffled, looked down, then back up with a shy smile. Something about it made him remember what had really been on his mind forever ago at the station.

"Um, so, change of topics, but the concert wasn't why I asked you to call."

"Oh?"

"I wanted to ask if you'd come with me on Saturday to my parents' silver anniversary party. It's at their country club and sure to be lame and corny."

"Sell it a little more, please," she laughed.

Sam relaxed even more and let himself appreciate holding onto her for this conversation. *I will hold you for every conversation I can, Beautiful. I will hold you until my fucking arms fall*

off.

"Hey, I want to be honest. I was hoping maybe you'd come with me to keep it interesting. If you don't, I get to spend the afternoon avoiding my cousin Janet, who's convinced we're enough DNA strands apart to make something happen." Her eyes widened, so he added, "Brian scared her off by hinting at a threesome with her mom two Christmases ago. I wasn't that brave."

A giggle burst from her lips, and she leaned into his shoulder to muffle her mirth. "Oh, god, I totally believe that."

Her hands slid around his shoulders in a hug. Sam pulled her closer but then tensed and frowned. He stepped back just enough to meet her gaze again.

"I didn't realize that this would become our first official date. It's a horrible excuse for a first date. But tomorrow Bry and I are going to dinner with the parents. Maybe we shouldn't—"

Elle shook her head with another smile. "Can we drink boozy punch and foxtrot? Will you promise to introduce me with a different backstory to each of your relatives?"

Sam stared. *This is the perfect woman.* "Of course."

"Then it'll be an awesome first date."

"So, you're in?"

"Definitely."

He grinned and hugged her, then twisted his lips. "I should go home."

She wrinkled her nose. "Yeah, you probably should before Monica comes out with the hose."

He dropped his head until their breaths mingled. "This is me, not kissing you goodnight, Eleanor. This is the last time I leave you unkissed, okay?"

Her lips parted over a short gasp. "Uh-huh," she breathed.

Sam smiled and stepped back. "See you Saturday," he promised, walking backward to his car just to keep his eyes on her as long as possible.

19

ELEANOR

Oh, god, what have I done?

Eleanor could practically feel roots growing from her feet. Her pulse pounded while she stared at the ceiling, unable to sleep.

"This is the last time I leave you unkissed."

Sam's words rang in her head. The promises behind such a vow unfolded in her mind. There would be kisses, plural, until they became as natural as laughing with him. There would be his absurdly perfect lips against hers. There would be her heart pounding, unable to control the urge to lick him just to hear him groan and feel him answer back.

How the hell would she ever, ever get enough of that to leave again?

"This is the last time I leave you unkissed."

Eleanor sighed. She scrunched her face tight but couldn't stop the giddy smile that spread from ear to ear. "Oh, god, Sam," she whispered to the darkness. "I've done it now."

* * *

"You look high."

"You like to say that," Eleanor answered when she found Monica in the backyard the next afternoon after work.

"You do, though. All dreamy."

"Guess I'm just tired," she muttered. "Might go to bed early tonight."

Jennifer flipped to her back and pushed her sunglasses

on. "Have a sit. It's girls' night anyway."

"No boys?" Eleanor plopped on the grass.

Monica nodded. "The twins are busy, so I told Dylan I was with my ladies. And everyone knows it's been forty hours and thirty-seven minutes since Alex left for that workshop in Knoxville."

Jennifer pushed her with a laugh, then fingered the necklace she now sported 24/7. "Yeah, but he'll be back in twenty hours and, uh," she made a show of looking at her bare wrist like there was a watch there, "eight minutes."

They all giggled.

Monica looked over at Eleanor again. "So, Jennifer will obviously be majorly 'busy' tomorrow afternoon. Are you free?" Eleanor hesitated, and she went on: "The twins' parents are having an anniversary party. Brian's recruited Dylan and me to keep it fun."

She bit her tongue to keep a neutral expression. "Oh? So, what, I'd be his date?"

Monica shook her head. "You know how I feel about Brian Greene." She cut a look at Jennifer but mercifully didn't mention that night on the stoop. "And anyway, he's bringing a girl named Angela. She's cool enough. I just thought we could go as a group. I guess if anything, Sammy'll be stag. You two talk all the time, so you probably won't hate it, right?"

Eleanor felt Jennifer's eyes on her through her sunglasses, but she just nodded. The conversation drifted off as the girls lazed in the sun.

They were sprawled in the den watching *The Breakfast Club* and arguing Emilio vs. Judd when the phone rang. Eleanor jumped up before either of them could move. "Hello?"

"I heard about tomorrow."

She faced the wall and hummed in commiseration. "A group thing, apparently."

Sam sighed. "This doesn't count as a date. I'll take you out after, okay? Houston's," he said, naming the swanky downtown spot. "And a movie if you want."

"What if I don't?"

Eleanor's stomach dipped. There was no way that her tone implied anything innocent in that question. Even through the phone, the tension grew palpable. She ached between her legs at his heavy silence. The rumble in his words made her swallow a moan when he finally said, "Then we'll do exactly what you want."

"I gotta go. See you tomorrow." She hung up and prepared for Monica to ask if she'd gotten into the caramels when she walked back into the den.

But Eleanor didn't care. She could feel more roots growing as she walked through the house that she could now navigate in the dark. She knew the promise of tomorrow, of exactly what she wanted, was even more of an anchor to this place. And she knew she'd likely never see herself as good enough to deserve all this comfort and kindness. To deserve the thrill he gave her that curled her toes and stilled her nerves all at once.

She still didn't care.

Eleanor was floating. And she would keep floating for the next sixteen hours and forty-two minutes, according to the stove's clock.

* * *

Dylan parked at the country club the following afternoon. The three of them exited the car, and he proffered both elbows. "Well, ladies. Shall we?"

They spotted Sam, Brian, and Angela on the stairs, greeting guests. Brian was decked in a loose-fitted teal suit with a collarless black shirt underneath. Angela, his date, waved at Monica. Her bangles clinked as she teetered on bright blue heels in her silver sequined dress. They looked like they belonged at a disco, not a stuffy old country club. Eleanor had to admit they were the picture of hip.

Sam sported dark jeans and a blue dress shirt with a tan linen blazer. Eleanor glanced down at her Grecian dress and lace-up sandals. She smoothed her braid that began at her temple and snaked down her back. *It's not a date... but, damn, he looks good. Blane times ten.*

Even better was the glint in his eyes when they locked on her. Eleanor's heart fluttered like it always did, but this time everything was different. She slipped her arm off Dylan's and made straight for Sam. No one paid them any mind. By that point in the summer, the two of them gravitated to each other habitually.

"I didn't know sequins were an option," she whispered with a nod toward Angela as they followed the group inside.

"This is 1986. Sequins are always an option, aren't they?"

"Mm-hmm. So, why'd you leave yours at home, Boy George?"

Her pulse hummed in her veins. Eleanor knew her tone held the same kind of energy she'd first walked into Mac's with—flirty and playful. Her cheekiness was usually more fraternal with the group around. With them, it was a silly comment that made everyone laugh. This was different.

This was for him.

He stepped closer and whispered, "This jacket is reversible. I'm waiting for the right moment to break out the sparkles. I'm thinking it'll be when things start to get crazy once my Uncle Barry has drunk enough of the punch."

Her hand flew to her mouth to cover a laugh. "I assume you're expecting us to launch into a *Saturday Night Fever*-style dance at that moment?"

"Obviously." Sam chuckled and shook his head. "No, really, I almost wore a suit. But I looked like a waiter, or at best, a Beatle circa 1964."

Elle skimmed her hand over his sleeve. "I'm sure you looked great. But this seems more you."

They stepped to the side once they entered the ballroom. Sam swept his eyes over her twice. "Well, good. Because this dress you're wearing is very you, too."

She smirked, but she could feel her heartbeat from her throat to her fingertips. "Is that code for you like it?"

Sam glanced around, then shrugged like he didn't give a damn and slid an arm around her waist. He pulled her close to whisper in her ear. "It's code for you're absolutely beautiful."

His lips grazed her ear before he stepped back and looked into her bright eyes. "Now, let's get some punch and tell some lies about who you are and how we met."

Eleanor felt so high that she wanted to giggle. She watched Sam ladle the pale pink beverage into two crystal cups and tried to relax the perma-grin that threatened to break loose on her face at any moment.

"Now wait, wait, don't tell me. It's Brian, right?" came

a voice from behind them.

They turned to see a man in a cheap plaid polyester suit with a lariat in place of a tie. He was chewing on the stump of an old cigar.

Sam glanced at her and cleared his throat. "That's right, Uncle Barry. How are you, sir?"

Barry pumped his hand and babbled about crops. Meanwhile, Eleanor slid to Sam's side, so close that he instinctively put his arm around her waist.

That shut Barry up. "Who's this little beauty?"

"Oh, this is Eleanor."

"Ellie?"

"Sure. She's… French. She's studying languages at Vanderbilt. We met at a Godard film festival. Elle-uh, Ellie, this is Uncle Barry from Bucksnort. It's a small town between here and Memphis," Sam added at her startled blink.

Given his hazy expression, Eleanor assumed Barry caught the gist of about half of what Sam said. She smiled and murmured, "Bonjour. Parlez-vous Francais?"

Barry guffawed. "Well, I tell you what. I never known a French girl before. Say something else, sweetheart."

She began rambling off any French word that popped in her head. Some of the words might've been Italian. She spoke quickly so that it sounded like conversation. Sam cleared his throat when she rolled the word croissants off her tongue like she had that night on the porch.

Barry was enthralled. "Look at that," he laughed. "What do you know?"

Eleanor turned her face up to Sam and smiled sweetly. "Voulez-vous coucher avec moi?" she purred.

Sam choked on his punch.

"It's, uh, good to see you, Uncle Barry," he said, leading her away.

"You too, Brian," he called.

"What did you say to him?" he muttered while they walked the room's perimeter.

She laughed. "I have no idea. Just anything I could think of."

He hummed. "Well then, what did you say to me?"

She cut her eyes up. "I don't know, Sam. What *did* I say to you?"

Sam flashed a grin and mimicked her tone. "I don't know, Elle. But it sounded pretty good."

She bit her lip and broke the eye contact. Grabbing his hand, she led them toward the finger foods. "So, French student was a good start. Who will I be next?"

She was an artist from New York. She was a fellow Chem student he'd met in the lab. She was a fan who'd called the radio station. She fronted his favorite local band and had finally agreed to go out with him.

She was perfectly happy.

"I'm afraid if we meet too many more people, we'll get caught," Sam said after the fifth story. "We can join the group if you want. Or I guess we could… dance?"

They looked at the older couples foxtrotting to the jazz band.

"You did promise me a turn. I know you've got the sequins on standby, but I think it'd be more fun if we turned this into *Footloose* instead."

He laughed. "I never knew I could have this much fun at a country club. Hell yes, we can."

They took three steps toward the dance floor before two

older couples descended on them. The younger man they had in tow blatantly ogled Eleanor.

The auburn-haired woman was breathless as she exclaimed, "Sam! There you are. I've been trying to catch up with you for an hour—who is this?"

Sam stood up straighter and put his hand on Eleanor's elbow. His voice adopted an adorably formal tone as he said, "Mom, Dad, this is Eleanor Field. Eleanor, meet my parents, Claire and Paul Greene. These are their friends, Mr. and Mrs. Robinson, and their son, Jeff."

"So very pleased to meet you. Congratulations on your anniversary!" Eleanor shook their hands with a warm smile.

His mother glowed. "You said you weren't bringing a date," she said to Sam as she eyed Eleanor again.

"Oh, uh... Elle is friends with Monica. Brian mentioned she was coming yesterday."

Jeff pounced. "So, she's not your date?"

They all looked at him, but he grinned at Eleanor. "Would you like to dance?"

She eyed him up and down, and then stepped sideways so that her shoulder touched Sam's. "No, thank you."

Jeff deflated, and his mother made it worse by scolding him. Sam looked down, but Eleanor caught his smirk.

Mrs. Greene hummed with delight. "So, Eleanor, are you from Nashville? Where did you go to school?"

She shook her head. "No, ma'am, I grew up just outside of Atlanta."

"You don't say! I'm a Georgia peach myself. I was a Druid Hills debutante in my day. Although, I'm sure that sounds perfectly old-fashioned now, hmm?" She laughed.

Eleanor tossed her hair. Her stomach fluttered, but she

kept a pleasant smile. "No, ma'am, not at all. I'm from Buckhead. I was a debutante, too. So was Monica."

Mrs. Greene's eyes almost fell out of her head. So did Sam's. Mr. Greene's brows hit his hairline. Clearly, the family recognized her name-drop of the wealthiest suburb in Atlanta.

Mrs. Greene tried to recover herself. "Buckhead! You don't say! Who are your parents, sweetheart?"

Eleanor wondered how to skirt the pothole she had suddenly created in the conversation. *Why the hell didn't you just tell another lie? You could've at least acted like you knew nothing of cotillions and society parties. Why did you feel like you needed to be so honest with his parents?*

… Because they're his parents. And he means something to you. This is why we don't let roots grow, Eleanor.

But she knew that it was too late. She couldn't backtrack or swerve into a made-up story now. "My mother is a housewife. My father is, uh, Greg Field."

"The quarterback?" Mr. Greene blurted.

Eleanor affirmed.

Mrs. Greene eyed her up and down with a new level of curiosity. "My, my. And now you're studying at Vanderbilt, I assume?" Eleanor was about to disagree, but she continued. "We'll have to have you over some time. You and I can talk cotillions, hmm?"

Her cheeks got hot. "I'm afraid I was a terrible debutante, Mrs. Greene."

"Darling, so was I." Mrs. Greene laughed and snaked her arm through her husband's. "You all have fun. Jeff, I'd love a punch."

"Yes, ma'am," he mumbled as the party strolled away.

Sam put his fingers on her elbow and guided them out to the terrace. Once they were alone, he faced her and threaded his hands in his hair. "Holy shit, Eleanor. Those were my parents."

She nodded, blinking up at him in confusion. "They seemed lovely. Why?"

"You just—we were telling stories to uncles and people I barely know! Not my parents!"

Her confusion cleared. Eleanor pursed her lips. "I embarrassed you?"

He exhaled. "No, don't worry about it."

"There you go, Sam. Being too nice again."

"What do you want me to do, spank you?"

They blinked at each other. Her ears got hot. A dark red flush crept up Sam's neck.

Eleanor took a quick breath. "Maybe you could just believe me, hmm? Have a bit of confidence that someone you call a friend wouldn't tell bald-faced lies to your parents? Come on. Is the idea of me and Monica in ball gowns really that implausible?"

"Yes," he insisted. But then, he paused. "But you were serious, weren't you?"

She nodded.

"Holy shit."

She stepped a little closer. "Are you still embarrassed?"

"I'm never embarrassed around you. And that is definitely saying something."

The air between them electrified. Sam's lips parted as he stepped closer, but suddenly, they were surrounded by their friends.

"What have y'all been doing?" Monica demanded.

"Keeping things interesting," Sam replied. He turned to his brother. "We should toast soon."

The twins made their way to the microphone by the band and did their filial duties while the group took their seats. After they spoke, there was hardly a dry eye in the room. The group clapped as the brothers dropped into their chairs.

Brian checked his watch. "Well, look at that. It is exactly three minutes before get me the hell out of here." He slung his arm around Angela and looked around. "I say we go to our respective places and... get comfortable... then find some proper fun, hmm? Real booze, too. Everyone in?"

Brian's tone implied that getting comfortable would be a partner activity. Eleanor's thighs ached. She didn't dare glance at Sam, but she prayed he'd take his cue and offer to drive her home. Then they could get out of there and...

But before he could open his mouth, a waiter clapped loudly. "Is there an Eleanor Field here? Miss Field, anyone?"

Every one of them jolted. Eleanor's hand flew to her face as she got to her feet. *Me? What did I do?* She forced her legs to carry her down a hallway and accept the telephone the waiter handed her. The cold plastic touched her ear as Jennifer's frantic voice sank into her brain.

Alex called... your dad... Emory hospital... I didn't know how to tell you but...

She returned to the table a ghost.

When she'd sunk into her chair without a word, Monica jumped up and shooed Sam to vacate his seat. Drawing the chair closer to her friend, she touched her shoulder. "Lenny?" she whispered.

Eleanor startled. "That was Jen. It's Dad. He had a

heart attack."

Her gaze circled the table at the collective intake of breath. She swallowed hard and continued as coherently as possible, but shadows were building in her heart. Shadows of worry.

Shadows of dread.

"Uh, Alex called the house looking for me. His roommate had called him when Mother rang this morning. Jennifer called three different country clubs trying to find me, bless her heart."

Monica squeezed her hand. "What's the status, love?"

"I don't know. He's in ICU. Al's on his way straight from Knoxville. I—oh, god, I have to go." She rose, then dropped down again and looked at Monica. "I have to go… home."

Monica sat up straight. "Len," she began, then sighed. "Yeah, you do. Shit, I've got shifts the next three days. Screw it, I'll call and—"

Eleanor spoke over her. "No, I just need to go get my car. You're not coming."

"You're not going alone." "Alex will be there."

The girls eyed each other as they spoke at the same time. Monica pursed her lips. Elle mirrored her.

"You're not going alone," Monica repeated. "You're as pale as a sheet. You're not driving four hours in the dark by yourself, not for this."

"I'll take you."

They both turned when Sam spoke up. Eleanor sensed that the whole table had suddenly fixed their attention on him.

He looked around, then squared his shoulders and nodded. "My car can make that drive no problem. I'll take you to Atlanta."

20

SAM

Elle wet her lips. It was the first time in his memory that Sam didn't ache to lick them for her. Her ghostly expression left no room for such thoughts. The offer to drive her this afternoon had suddenly gone from loaded with anticipation to the offer of a friend.

Elle shook her head at him. Her lips parted to decline.

But Monica beat her to speaking. "Sam, you are the absolute most."

"No. I don't want you to go," she whispered.

The pure fear in her green eyes made his blood cold. It was clear that this was about more than the imposition. A thrill of trepidation shot through him, but Sam shook his head.

"You don't have much choice."

"I absolutely do. I can go alone. I can take a bus. I can…"

Tears slid down her cheeks, and she hid her face. The guys and Monica traded a look that said one thing: she could absolutely not make this drive alone. The decision was made. Sam jumped up, keys already in hand.

Eleanor didn't argue again. She just let Monica hustle her out to Sam's car with Brian and Dylan flanking them to avoid any more of a scene. Sam swung up to the front, shouted a reminder to his brother to tell their parents what happened, and watched Monica buckle her into the passenger seat.

Monica ran around the front of the car to the driver's side, her dark hair bouncing on her shoulders, and motioned for Sam to step out. She lowered her voice to a hissing whisper. "Listen to me. Take good care of her, Sam. Atlanta isn't a good place for Lenny. And whatever you do, watch out for her mother."

Her eyes clouded with fury. She blinked and swallowed. "Alex will know what to do, though. Don't worry."

She gave him a squeeze and a nod, then pushed him back toward the car.

Sam looked down for a second at Monica Huang, barely five feet tall and without a doubt one of the most formidable human beings in the world. Her ferocious loyalty and razor-sharp insight would make her the perfect psychologist. Certainly, they made her the perfect friend, too.

They were hurtling down the interstate before Elle lifted her head. "Monica warned you, didn't she?"

"Mm-hmm. I didn't ask questions."

"I don't want you to come, Sam. Atlanta is where I hate myself the most."

He whipped his head to her. "What does that mean? How can you hate yourself?"

She sighed. "Monica said once she thought I was doing the humanitarian aid as penance. She's right, but not in the way she thought she was. I'm guilty, Sam. I'm guilty of… not feeling guilty."

"Elle," he said over a tight throat. "Are you sure about going?"

She nodded. "It's my dad. I love him to death. He never did anything to make me hate myself."

Watch out for her mother… Holy shit, what are we getting into?

They didn't talk much on the ride, just listened to the radio until the Nashville stations lost their bandwidth and turned into static. Elle looked at the tuner when the reception started fading. Sam sensed her hesitation. It made him grin.

He nodded toward the glove compartment. "You can play DJ. I've got plenty of stuff."

"You trust me that much?" she teased.

"I do, actually."

She selected his favorite mixed tape. Why he was surprised, Sam didn't know. By now, it seemed logical that she'd pick the mix he loved the most. As they began to sing along together, the mood in the car lightened considerably. There was none of their usual banter, but the storm clouds seemed to be pushed to the backseat at least.

Her father was at Emory University Hospital. Sam had to stop and get directions just outside of town, but it was easy enough for him to find. Elle was out of the car almost before he could shift into park. He hurried after her to the cardiac floor, where she rushed to the reception desk.

"Len!"

They both whirled at Alex's shout from down the hallway. Eleanor flew to him, and he caught her in a hug.

His brows rose to see Sam standing a few feet away. "Sam?"

Alex had been hanging with the crew since that night at Zebra a couple weeks ago. Sam thought he seemed cool, a little quiet, but that would be expected when someone walked into a group like theirs. But they had barely spoken more than a few words so far. Sam was a bit surprised at the surety with which he identified him. Most people took a while to discern him and his brother on sight.

Are you really surprised? You're the guy who's always sitting with his sister. You think he didn't notice that?

Sam shook his hand while Elle explained getting the news at the party and Sam's offer to drive. Alex's eyes, the same shade as hers, narrowed thoughtfully.

"Thank you," he murmured, saying a lot with the weight of those two words. He turned to Elle. "Dad's been moved out of ICU, but they're keeping him a couple days for observation."

"How is he?"

"He's all right. The doctor said it was a pretty serious event, but they don't think he'll need surgery. There's been a lot of talk of lifestyle changes. Dad's been joking that he'll have to go back into training camp, but I think a lot of it is dietary. You know he can't resist sweets."

Her lips curved. "So, he's awake?"

Alex nodded. "He knew you were on your way. He said he'd stay up until you got here."

"Let's go, then." They turned for the hallway.

"I'll be over here in the, uh, waiting room," Sam said.

Eleanor's head snapped back around. "No, come with me."

He saw Alex's look of surprise, but he shook his head and waved her on with her brother. She bit her lip but turned away and followed him down the hall.

Before he sat down, Sam went to the pay phone and placed a reverse-charge call to Monica. Everyone was at the house, waiting for news. He reported what he knew, then settled into the hard plastic chair and stared into space. For as out of place as he felt, there was nowhere else he could imagine being.

"Sam."

Her fingertips on his cheek jolted him out of a doze. Sam jerked to attention, focusing on the face he knew so well.

She smiled. "Come."

"Come where?" He rubbed his eyes and yawned.

Elle took his hand and gave him a gentle tug. "Dad wants to meet you."

Sam shook himself awake and followed her down the hall. At the door, she turned and straightened his collar. Then, she tugged his sleeves straight and smoothed his hair. While he tried to resist the urge to melt into her, she opened the door and took him inside.

"Daddy? This is Sam."

Her father was exactly what Sam expected of a retired quarterback. Greg Field filled that hospital bed with his size and air of authority. He was a broad-chested man with graying hair and the same eyes as his children.

Sam gulped hard to swallow his nerves, but Mr. Field grinned broadly and motioned him over to shake his hand.

"So, you're Sam. I appreciate you driving my baby down to me, son."

"It was no trouble, Mr. Field."

He boomed a laugh. "Aw, call me Greg and quit lying. Four hours at a moment's notice is trouble indeed."

Sam smiled. "I was happy to do it," he amended.

His brow shot up. "Were you?" he muttered slyly.

"Daddy," Eleanor chided.

Sam had no idea what to say because, *Yessir, I'd have*

crawled here if your daughter asked me to didn't seem like a comfortable fact to drop.

Besides, he was pretty sure everyone in the room already knew it was true.

They didn't stay more than half an hour longer. Visiting hours were nearly over, and everyone was tired. Alex nodded at the clock and said they should go.

Their father nodded brusquely. "Go on home and get some sleep. Damn, I wish I could join you. This place smells of sick people."

Alex stiffened. "I think we'll probably just get a hotel, but we'll be back in the—"

"Hotel?" his father interrupted. "Your mother is waiting for you. You haven't been home in years. Why would you need a hotel?"

The siblings traded a loaded glance, then hugged their father goodnight. On the way to the parking lot, they conferred quietly. Sam gave them space, even though his ears strained for any clues to this cryptic mystery.

When they were in the car, Eleanor sighed. "I guess we're on our way to Buckhead."

Sam followed her directions to an enormous colonial house on a street where every driveway displayed a Mercedes, BMW, or both. When Alex parked behind them, they filed in a line to the porch. With a single knock, Alex opened the front door.

Two small dogs yipped a noisy greeting. A pair of teacup Poodles skittered into the foyer. Eleanor and Alex knelt to pet them, so Sam was the first one to see their mother appear. She was dressed in a long silk robe with heeled slippers on her feet.

"My babies," she cried drowsily, and they rose to accept her cheek kisses. "It's been too long. Look at you, so grown!"

Sam couldn't understand why Alex and Elle were so tense, or why Monica had warned him about this lady. She seemed fine. Maybe a little glam, but wasn't that to be expected in a place like this? Mostly she seemed thrilled to see her children.

The family murmured about the events of the day. Alex updated his mother on Mr. Field while Sam stood back, invisible until she noticed him at last.

Her penciled brows arched. "Where are my manners?" she asked in a Georgia drawl. "I don't believe we've met."

"I'm Sam Greene, Mrs. Field."

She gave him her hand over the top, with her knuckles out and her manicured nails toward the floor. Sam clasped her fingers, unsure if he was supposed to kiss them.

"Ah-ha. And you're friends with…"

Alex spoke up. He met Sam's gaze confidently and said, "Both of us. He drove Len down from Nashville."

"How kind of you," she murmured. With another cursory glance at him, she turned away. Sam got the message: he was dismissed as a person of interest.

"We'll have to put him up in the study. The guest room doesn't have linens on, but you can get him a pillow and blanket from the hall, can't you, Nora? Well, darlings, get on up to bed. Your poor mother is about to fall out from this horrible day." She gave them a brave smile and touched their faces before sweeping away down the hall, the dogs at her heels.

There were two showers upstairs. Eleanor took one. Alex let Sam shower first. Then, he led him to the study at the end of the hall. A plush sectional couch sat against one wall.

"Sorry about this, man," Alex sighed.

"Honestly, that thing looks as comfortable as a bed."

Alex chuckled and handed him a pillow and blankets. His smile faded. "Listen, Sam. I want Len out of here tomorrow. I'll probably stay until Monday, but she needs to go."

Sam agreed, and Alex nodded and left.

Sam had just closed his eyes when he heard the soft click of the door. He smiled into the darkness. He knew it was her before her hand was in his hair.

"Sam," she whispered. "Are you awake?"

"Kind of."

Her touch trailed down his arm until she caught his hand. "Come," she said for the second time that night.

This time, Sam didn't ask. He just rose and let her lead him where she would.

Straight to her bedroom.

There was a little bedside lamp to illuminate the room. When his eyes adjusted, he looked at her. Eleanor was dressed in one of her father's old jerseys and nothing else, as far as he could see. The curves of her breasts were outlined, clearly without a bra. Sam had to look away fast since he was now only dressed in his boxers and a t-shirt.

She breathed a laugh and tugged the fabric away from her body. "Um, I… well. Are you going to make me say it?"

He crooked his lips. "I'm afraid I'm not sure what you're trying to say, so yeah."

Her voice dropped to a whisper. "I don't want to sleep alone, Sam. This is the worst. Our date was ruined. Our day was ruined, and now I'm exhausted and nervous and…"

She looked down and shook her head.

Sam clasped her hand and led her to the bed. They lay down together. Eleanor flipped out the lamp, and they burrowed under the covers, staring at each other in the darkness.

Before she fell asleep, though, he kissed her.

She gasped, but her mouth softened in answer. Her body arched until he pulled her into his arms. They kissed, slow and sweet, knowing it wasn't more tonight.

At last, he pulled away and nosed her cheek. "I promised, Elle. The other night was the last time I left you unkissed."

She nodded and snuggled against his shoulder. "I know, Sam."

They held each other all night.

21

ELEANOR

Eleanor woke up *hungry*. Not hungry for food, although the last meal she'd had was pimento cheese finger sandwiches at the country club. No, she woke up hungry for Sam.

It was a delirious feeling, fueled by all the anticipation she'd been carrying since Thursday night. Fueled, too, by a sick wish to be wild and reckless right there in her childhood bed.

Her mother's reaction to Sam had been exactly what Eleanor expected: complete disinterest. He didn't ooze money or authority, so why should she consider him further?

"Nice girls catch nice boys, Eleanor Beatrice." Well, Mom, I'm not nice, and I guess I'm not going to become nice anytime soon. But as for Sam… Oh, he's nice, alright.

She opened her eyes and studied him in the early light. He lay on his back, her head on his shoulder. His far arm was tucked under the pillow. The outline of his bicep curved against the linen. His other arm held her close to his side.

Eleanor lifted her head, her pulse thrumming faster. His face was smooth with sleep but with the shadow of a day's scruff lining his jaw. His lips were closed but relaxed. *Why do these lips fit against mine like they're custom-made to do it?* She pushed a lock of his auburn hair off his forehead, and her mouth started to water.

Eleanor knew if she climbed on top of him, if she woke him with a bite on his neck and her hand on his cock, that he wouldn't deny her. She knew it as sure as she knew she wouldn't do it. Making that move right now would be so wrong. To come so far, to want him so bad, only to reduce their passion to a symbolic rebellion against all her old demons. Against the sick, warped rules her mother had taught her—rules that had gotten Eleanor in trouble.

The kind of trouble you try and fight as long as you can. The kind that overtakes you with whispers of, "just relax" and, "I'll take care of you." The kind of trouble that you can get out of but never really leaves you. The kind of trouble that shakes everything about who you are.

The kind of trouble that made her leave home.

No, if she took them there now, she would validate the whisper in the dark places of her heart that wondered if she deserved the peace she felt with him. If she deserved the connection they shared.

If she deserved him.

And she wanted to. Oh, god, did she ever. "Trust you," he'd said, and when he held onto her, she did.

As if he read her mind—a common occurrence, actually—Sam stirred. He rolled to his side and pulled her closer to his chest. His eyes opened slowly with a yawn, those sleepy navy blues crinkling into a look of unfiltered delight.

"Hi."

Eleanor's hunger rolled back, and she was glad she'd kept it in check.

"Hi," she managed to say, breathless at how happy she suddenly was, how content this moment had become. They were huddled under the sheet, his leg over both of hers. Two people completely tangled together. Eleanor was very sure that she would never, ever get tired of it.

Home. The word whispered softly in the back of her

brain, so faint she didn't dare consider it.

After several long, warm minutes in their cocoon, Sam stirred but didn't release her. "Um," he said, then bit his lips. "Damn, I have morning breath," he mumbled, not moving his mouth.

She laughed and kissed him. "Don't really care… But, ugh, now I'm thinking about it."

She bit her own lips together, and they laughed. His forehead pressed to hers, and she melted into him.

Sam turned his head a little to say, "Um, do you know what's going on this morning?"

"Nothing as far as I know. I want to visit Dad again in the afternoon. Alex wants me to leave today, I know. He's probably right."

Sam nodded. "Well, since I'm in Atlanta and nothing's going on this morning, I thought I might pay my grandmother a quick visit. Unless you need me to stay around here."

He hesitated. "Unless you'd come, too. I'd like it if you did."

Her brows rose. "Well… sure."

Alex was already downstairs at the breakfast nook when Eleanor jogged down, Sam a discreet five minutes behind. They ate with him, no Mrs. Field in sight. Alex was going to the hospital to catch up with their dad a bit more. They agreed to meet him back at the house for lunch in a few hours.

They drove 30 minutes north to a suburb called Kennesaw. Sam turned into a modest subdivision and parked at a quaint, single-story home on the end of a cul-de-sac. He killed the engine and flashed her an enigmatic smile before heading to the front door.

"What's that smile for?" Eleanor asked, but the door was already opening.

A tiny woman dressed in a pink cotton house dress appeared. Her blue eyes widened in shock at the sight of Sam.

"Sammy? What in the world are you doing here?" she gasped, a question of disbelief but no doubt about which twin it was.

Sam folded her carefully into a big hug. "Hi, Nana. I was in town and thought I'd come see you."

"Well, what a lovely surprise on this Sunday morning! I was just watching the TV preacher. Come on in and sit awhile." She beamed, then looked over his shoulder at Eleanor. "Oh, and you brought a girlfriend."

Sam didn't correct her. He just cleared his throat. "This is Eleanor, Nana."

She took Eleanor's hand in both of hers, her skin soft and papery but her grip sure. "Eleanor, so nice to meet you. Oh, my, you are a beauty, dear."

She blushed hard. "It's a pleasure, Mrs.—"

She squeezed her and laughed, then waved them inside. "Nana is fine, or you can call me Marianne if you must. Come, come. You must be hungry."

They weren't, but she fed them raisin bread and coffee anyway. The TV volume got muted, but the sermon continued onscreen while Sam told her family news out of Nashville. Eleanor stayed silent and sipped politely.

"I don't suppose Brian's found himself a girlfriend, too?"

"Not yet." Sam laughed, again not correcting her.

Elle bit her lip. *But am I his girlfriend? Is that what we meant Thursday?... Maybe it was. Holy shit.*

Before she could get too lost in thought, Nana's gaze settled on her. "Now, Eleanor, tell me about you."

Sam turned toward her, his elbow on the table, an expectant arch in his brows and a playful glint in his eyes.

Eleanor nibbled the toast. "Well, I'm friends with Sam and Brian's group of friends from Vanderbilt."

"You're a student?"

"No, ma'am. I work at a cake shop. I, uh, was abroad for a couple of years doing volunteer work. I'm from here. Atlanta, I mean."

"I see." Her eyes narrowed in a sharply assessing gaze that seemed to say, "*What aren't you telling me?*"

Eleanor startled at the silent question. It was potent, as if she'd said it aloud. She recalled Brian and Sam talking about how they could communicate with their eyes. *Must run in the family.*

She sipped her coffee, unsure what to say next.

"Elle is going to live in New York in the fall," Sam volunteered. "She's going to study to be a pastry chef."

Nana hummed but didn't say much to that. Sam excused himself to the restroom, and Eleanor had the irrational desire to ask him not to leave. *Don't be silly. This is the sweetest lady.*

But as soon as the door clicked down the hall, Nana put that shrewd gaze on her again. "You're a bit remarkable, aren't you?" It was an honest question, admiring and not a bit sarcastic.

"Not at all, ma'am," Eleanor said quickly.

This made Nana laugh. "Volunteer work abroad for two years. Now, moving to New York alone to study. If that's not remarkable, then how would you define the word?"

Eleanor wrinkled her nose. No answer came to mind.

Nana's coffee spoon clinked against the china when she stirred thoughtfully. Her next words were so soft that Eleanor almost didn't hear.

"You don't need to be ashamed, Eleanor. We all have hard choices we've had to make. They aren't all that define us, you know."

Eleanor flash-froze to her chair. "What?"

Nana stopped stirring and looked up with raised brows and a small smile. "You deserve to be happy. And Sam makes you happy."

Eleanor didn't speak, didn't move, but she knew that somehow she conveyed her agreement.

Nana smiled wider. "Good. Because he's certainly enamored of you. He's also listening to us. Aren't you, Samuel Joseph Greene?"

He appeared wearing a guilty grin. "Nope. Don't even know what the question is for."

She laughed and reached across the table to pinch his cheek when he sat down. Their humor eased the moment, but Eleanor still reeled from Nana's words.

And she knew she would for a long, long time to come. Like, forever.

They stayed about an hour more. Nana refilled the coffee and then put Sam to work. He repaired a broken knob on her dresser, programmed the microwave clock, and checked her car's oil. The women shadowed him around while he worked.

When he was bent over the car's hood, Eleanor admired the way his shoulders stretched in the blue dress shirt he'd been wearing since the day before.

Nana looked at her and smiled. "He's a good one, isn't he?"

"He's the best," she admitted, ducking her head when he winked at her over his shoulder.

They were sent away with a sandwich bag full of Oreos for the road and plenty of hugs. Eleanor fell into the GTO's soft leather seat with a deep sigh as he backed out of the drive.

"Is, um, your Nana psychic?" she asked at last.

"I'm a scientist, Elle. So, as a scientist, I'll tell you that's ludicrous. But as her grandson? I'll tell you… she's extremely insightful."

She grunted and stared out the window, replaying it all in her head. Sam didn't say more, didn't ask what she meant, and she appreciated the privacy.

He's certainly enamored of you.

She snuck a glance at his profile. With another sigh, she lifted his hand from the gear shift and laced their fingers together, then set them on her thigh. He didn't take his gaze from the road. He just squeezed her hand and grinned.

"Let's take off," she blurted. "Dad's going to be okay. Let's get ho-um-back to Nashville. I'll call Alex from the road."

His brows rose. "Really? I will if you want. You don't want to go to the hospital again?"

They were at the interstate on-ramp. Sam pulled to the shoulder, waiting to decide if they headed north or south.

Eleanor opened her mouth to affirm but glanced at the floorboard and winced. "Shit. I left my purse. It's got my money, ID, keys, birth control—yeah, no, I can't leave it, not even for a day or two. Damn."

Sam turned right. The engine revved as they went south. "Run inside, grab it, and say bye. We'll swing by the hospital and be home before it gets dark."

They couldn't know that *dark* was coming much sooner than that.

22

SAM

Visiting Nana had put Sam in an excellent mood. He was more than willing to get out of Atlanta ASAP. He'd already decided that they were going straight to his apartment.

But then they rolled up to the Field's house. Half a dozen cars were parked in the drive and along the curb. A man in a suit and a woman in a wide-brimmed white hat strolled up the walk. Sam and Eleanor sat and gaped, then traded a glance and slowly exited the car.

The living room buzzed with conversation. Scents of casseroles and cake wafted from the dining room. Sam shadowed Elle, who was clearly trying to make herself invisible. They made it to the first stair when a woman bawled out, "Is that little Nora?"

Mrs. Field appeared in a Sunday dress and high heels. Beside her was a carefully coiffed woman whose red sequined dress matched her hair.

"It is indeed. Can you believe it? Home at last," Mrs. Field crooned. "Nora, come let Mrs. Watson give you a hug."

Alex appeared. His shoulders were at his ears. Elle was suddenly flanked by a bevy of women, all variations of her mother.

"I walked into this ten minutes ago," he hissed at Sam. "Mother said they asked to come by, but I say that's bullshit."

Sam grunted, unsure how to commiserate better.

Elle was trying to speak. "We were on our way to check up on Daddy…"

Her mother waggled her fingers. "Nonsense! Greg is resting fine, and anyway, Alex was just there. Stay and visit. Have some tea. The Tisdales are here, including Becky! You were debutantes together. Surely you'd like to chat a bit?"

The flock was moving. Alex grabbed Sam's elbow, his jaw locked. "Within the hour, Len's out of here. She's doing well, but too much of this is bad news. Out within the hour, yeah?"

"Not a problem for me."

Alex was about to say more, but he was suddenly caught in a headlock from behind by a man who was at least fifty years old. His eyes widened, but the man guffawed, releasing him and ruffling his hair.

Jesus Christ, I'm in the Twilight Zone.

Up until then, Sam had felt comfortably invisible thanks to their mother. He found it funny how little interest she had in him. The men, though, weren't so easy to escape. Their testosterone-fueled excuse for chitchat made the minutes crawl by. Sam was introduced as "Alex's buddy." He was therefore subjected to patronizing jokes and queries to test his masculinity. He could've told them he spear-hunted in Africa, and they'd have had a crack about him being a wuss for not using a shotgun. Sam couldn't care less what any of them thought. All he could think about was Eleanor.

But then another man entered the fray. Pushing the rest of them aside, he slung his arm around Alex's shoulder. "Field, where the hell you been? When are you coming home to work for me, dammit? I need a new junior attorney—I'll make you partner in five years. In the meantime, my Dana's here with us. She's looking more like her mother every day. Come say hi." He winked. With a good amount of hooting from the rest of the men, he dragged Alex away.

Sam used the diversion to hurry after Elle.

It was hard to find her. The women had been on the move. He roamed through the den, the dining room, and then into the living room. Finally, he spied her, still surrounded by ladies and now some girls their age, too. But before Sam could cross the room, the front door opened.

Another couple appeared from the foyer. Behind them strolled a younger man wearing a seersucker suit. He looked every inch the Southern gentleman, from his oiled-back hair to his white leather shoes. Although he wore a pleasant expression, something about him made Sam's blood run cold.

A ripple ran through the girls, but Elle stepped back once, then again, before her mother grabbed her arm and shouted in a teasing lilt.

"Debbie, you didn't tell me your son was coming! Bobby Jones, what are you doing in my house, looking more handsome than the devil himself? And what good timing—Nora's come home!"

Mrs. Field dragged her daughter forward to face "The devil himself."

23

ELEANOR

Eleanor registered the ripple of appreciative giggles that ran through the girls around her. But her heart had suddenly gone from racing to barely beating. Her fingertips were cold, but her mother's vise grip on her arm burned her skin.

Bobby's eyes walked all over Eleanor as he murmured, "I can see that, Mrs. Field. Wow, Nor. You've grown up."

No reply came to mind. Eleanor's brain had gone silent. All she could do was bite her tongue to keep from vomiting while her heart continued that slow thud in her chest.

"You two go catch up a little, why don't you?" Mrs. Field shoved her into his arms.

She tried to slip away, but he deftly took her elbow. Eleanor could hear the girls giggling as he guided her toward the hall. Her mother's voice again lifted over the din:

"Let's hope they take their time. They did use to be so close. He was her first real beau, you know. Escorted her during her season. I was sure they'd make a match…"

She wanted to turn, to call for Sam or Alex or anyone, but she couldn't. It was like he'd cast a spell over her. Again. The same spell that made her get into the backseat of his car the first time—and then helped her shut off her brain every time it happened after.

The same spell that had rendered her barely verbal when she first arrived in Nashville.

But I've come so far. I'm not that person anymore.

Eleanor blinked as that feeble thought finally formed. She was standing at the end of the upstairs hallway, her back against the door to the study. Bobby loomed over her, one hand planted on the wall by her head. He grinned, and she could smell breath mints and cologne. The combination brought on an assault of memories.

"Let's go chat a little, honey."

Eleanor shook her head.

Bobby flashed a cajoling smile that made him even more sinister-looking, in her opinion. "Aw, Nor, it's been years. I just want to catch up, hear how you're doing. Tell me everything, sweetheart."

"I'm not going in there."

I don't want to park with you, Bobby. I'm not ready for that… Aw, Nor, it's no big deal. I want to show you how much I care about you… Nice girls catch nice boys, Eleanor Beatrice. And Bobby Jones is quite the catch. If he wants to park a little, there's nothing wrong with that.

There was everything wrong with that.

Eleanor crossed her arms. She wasn't 17 anymore, and nice wasn't part of her makeup. So be it. She'd never be a Buckhead momma, hosting parties and coaching her own daughter to keep a boy interested by consenting to whatever he wanted. If that was nice, then Eleanor Field wanted nothing to do with nice.

"I'm not going in there," she repeated. "And I'm not your sweetheart."

"Elle? Want to get out of here?"

Bobby whirled at Sam's voice. Meanwhile, Eleanor was torn between sweet relief and dread. *Sam, get out of here. You can't be part of this.*

But he stood quietly, arms crossed just like in the record store, waiting for her. Bobby glanced at him, then turned back to pin her to the door again. "We're already getting interrupted," he murmured, loud enough to be sure Sam heard. "And I've missed you so much."

Eleanor snorted, but in a flurry of motion, Sam grabbed his shoulders and shoved him into the wall.

"Get the fuck away from her," Sam said in a weird, cold voice that sounded nothing like him.

Bobby jerked from his grip and spun on Sam, but Eleanor planted herself in the middle of the two men. "No way. This isn't happening with all these people here. Get the hell out of here, Bobby."

"You stupid loser," he spat at Sam, ignoring her. "Nora's my girl. She always was."

The color drained from Eleanor's face. She trembled all over and swallowed hard, but fury, not fear, coursed through her. She glared at him. "How dare you say that? I am not yours. You—you threw me out. You…you…"

You told me to take care of it. You said I was careless and stupid. You made me walk two miles down the highway to a gas station. All because I'd been "nice." All because you'd "cared about me so much."

She bit her lip and shook her head. "I wish I'd never met you. I wish that every day."

"Aw, babe, that was all a misunderstanding." He reached to stroke her face.

She slapped his hand away. Her voice broke as she said, "It was not. I hate you. Don't you get that?"

I hate you for what you made me do. For the decision I had to make. I was 17, for god's sake. And I had to…

But he just smiled like she was a child having a tantrum.

"You always were so feisty. I've missed that."

She trembled from head to toe again. A weird noise started in her chest and bubbled up her throat before she lunged forward, her fingers around his neck. Her nails dug into his skin in a deliciously vile way. So long she'd fantasized about hurting him. He was a behemoth in her memory, and as his skin flushed bright red under her grip, he suddenly didn't seem so invincible. She'd been dragged through hell, and he'd never even mussed a hair on his head. The thought made her dig in deeper.

Bobby's head cracked on the door with the force of her shove. His patronizing smirk transformed into a menacing snarl as he grabbed her wrists, and just like that, the monster was back. Eleanor cried out at his grip and wrestled to free herself. Suddenly, Sam's arm hooked her waist and pulled her back.

Just as her shoulders touched his chest, they both stumbled backward. Sam caught his footing, and Eleanor blinked to see Alex push his way between them. He pinned Bobby to the door with one arm across his throat.

"Hold onto her," she heard him say to Sam.

But Eleanor flailed wildly. She could see her nail impressions on Bobby's neck, and all she could think was, *the job isn't done.*

"No, let me go, let me go, I'm going to kill him. I'm going to fucking kill him," she seethed. Her voice was a hissing rasp.

"Get the fuck off me, Field," Bobby said.

"Hold on. Let her cool down," Alex snapped back.

The fury slowly ebbed the longer Sam held onto her. She stilled in his arms even though she continued to shake.

"Okay?" Sam murmured in her ear, and she nodded. "Let's get out of here."

She blinked up as reality set in. *We can still escape. Bobby hasn't ruined this, too.* "Yes. Okay. Let's go," she said.

Everyone stood down. Bobby straightened his coat and ran a palm across the part in his hair. Eleanor gloated to see a single lock had fallen out of place. To her, it was a victory.

"Damn, Nora, that's no way to treat your old beau," he drawled.

She should've walked away. Instead, the loathing inside of her—for him, for herself, for the past—reared its head. The not-so-nice girl in her couldn't help but fire back.

"You know, Bobby, I'd say go fuck yourself, but your dick is so small, I'm not sure how successful you'd be at it."

Sam chuckled softly and hugged her, but Bobby's lips curled in a wolfish sneer. Before he spoke, Eleanor knew that the devil was about to win another round with her.

"It was enough to get you in trouble, wasn't it, sweetheart?"

24

SAM

Those words slammed into Sam's head like a sledgehammer. But he didn't have time to let it sink in because Eleanor jumped out of his arms with a roar. This time, Bobby raised his arms to block her. Sam stared, stunned, as Alex hauled her off, urged her toward Sam, and then swung on the prick himself.

Bobby didn't see Alex's hook coming. He'd lowered his hands, wearing that same sneer for another millisecond before Alex's fist connected with his temple.

"Get her out, Sam."

It took him a second to understand Alex's command. Everything had lurched into slow motion. Those words still rang in his head as he watched laid-back Alex collar the bastard with impressive authority.

Alex bared his teeth. "I beat the shit out of you once, and damn if this time isn't going to be better."

His fist connected with Jones's nose this time. Bright red blood spurted down his face. "Fuck," he groaned and slid to the floor.

Alex stepped on his white leather shoe. "Go downstairs now, why don't you. Tell this fancy party how much of an asshole you are, talking to my sister like that. See if I give a fuck what they think of me. Or you can get up and see if you can fight back this time. I wish you'd try. That'd make this even more fun for me."

Sam really wanted in on this fight. His blood was rushing, every muscle in his body primed to jump in, but he had Eleanor in his arms. They had to leave. Gripping her hand, he ducked them into her bedroom and thrust her purse into her hand. They sprinted down the stairs and straight for the door.

"What on earth is all the commotion?" Her mother's confused shout stopped them on the front porch. She hurried outside and shut the door behind her. "Nora? Where's Bobby? What did you do?"

Sam's blood pounded in his temples, but he didn't move beyond sliding his gaze to Elle. Her face was ashen as she stared her mother down. "I told him no, Momma. Like I should've the first time he ever… Why did you tell me to indulge him? Why did I have to keep him happy back then? Why couldn't I just be me?" Her lips quivered.

Mrs. Field put her hands on her hips. "Baby girl, you always did get so dramatic about boys. They always come to their senses. Didn't I tell you? Nothing wrong with being courted, with a little give-and-take."

Elle shook her head so hard her hair danced. "That's not how it works. I get to choose, and any man—not boy, Momma, they're not children—any man who's worth it will be happy with me for me. Not because I indulge his expectations in exchange for trinkets. Not because I'm a nice girl who'll make a good wife. Because I'm me. And if that's not enough, then he can piss up a tree."

"Eleanor Beatrice, such language!"

Elle continued as if her mother hadn't spoken. "And maybe no guy will ever want me. Maybe I'm not wife material. But never again, Momma. Never, ever again will I give myself like that. No matter what I get to 'take' in exchange. Even if that means I live alone for the rest of my life."

Through all his adrenaline and panic, Sam still had to clamp down on his tongue to keep from shouting, "Christ, Elle, I'm right here. I will want you every fucking day I draw breath. How do you not see that yet?" A weird gurgle rumbled in his throat, but neither Elle nor her mother glanced over.

Mrs. Field pursed her lips. "My baby girl. Don't talk like that."

Elle breathed a dry laugh. Her cheeks began to go from pale to flushed with frustration. "You just don't get it. I know I'm your failure, Mother. But I can't be here anymore. I'm leaving, so just go back to your party and soak in the attention. Tell them whatever you want. You won't have to make excuses for me anymore after this."

"Nora, calm down and—" Mrs. Field reached for her daughter, but Elle flung her away.

"I said no. Just like I said to Bobby. Not anymore. Not again. No more of your games. Goodbye, Mother."

And with that, Elle spun on her heel and marched to Sam's car. Sam stole one more glance at her mother's pinched expression and read more disappointment than anything else on her face. She looked over at Sam.

"Well, that was unpleasant, hmm?"

Sam didn't speak.

For a brief moment, regret flashed in her eyes. But then she lifted her chin and put on a saccharine smile. "We can hope for the best for our children. But in the end, they make their own choices. Do drive safe, Sam. My daughter is precious to me, no matter what."

"I will."

With a single nod, she turned back to the house. Sam hurried to join Elle.

"Take me to my dad, please."

Inside the car, her voice was hollow and dead, but Sam obliged. He waited for her in the waiting room until she emerged, red-eyed and sniffling.

"He wants to see you," she said.

She dropped into a seat and stared straight ahead, so Sam hurried away. "Mr. Field?"

"It's Greg, dammit," he boomed. "I know y'all are on your way back to Nashville. Heard my little girl had a tough morning."

Sam grimaced and nodded.

The older man hummed. "Well, that's life sometimes. I hate that she couldn't be back for a day without it, but her mother has her ways." He sighed and shook his head. "I don't even know what all this is about. Did you know that? Eleanor won't tell me, and if she doesn't want me to know... Ah, hell, I'm talking in circles. I wanted to shake your hand, son. Tell you thanks again for bringing her to me."

Sam took his hand and gave it a firm shake. "It was good to meet you, sir."

He lifted a sly brow. "Got anything you want to ask me?"

Sam's own brows knitted. "Um, no, sir?"

He laughed. "Not yet, maybe. Well, that's okay. Just know when you do, my answer'll be yes."

Sam's jaw dropped. *Holy shit, he meant did I want to ask...*

Mr. Field laughed again. "Don't look so stunned, boy. I see it. And I'll see you again. Take care of my baby girl."

"Yes, sir."

Sam didn't exhale until after he'd closed the door. He found Eleanor in the waiting room. She fell in step beside him out to the car.

"I'm getting in the backseat, okay?" she whispered.

"Whatever you need."

She crawled into the backseat and lay on her back. Every time he glanced in the rearview, she was staring at the ceiling, not blinking, her hands folded over her abdomen. She didn't move or speak the entire drive. When he turned into the driveway of his parents' property, though, she sat up.

"Where are we?" she asked, her voice groggy.

"My home." Sam coasted past the house to the end of the lane. On the edge of their property sat the garage, above which was his apartment. It in no way felt like living at home, and it afforded him a much nicer space than the musty, lived-in rentals available to a student's income. Sam had lived there all four years of school. Although the commute was a pain, he'd never regretted it.

Elle peered up at the white building with a frown. "No. I don't want to be here."

Sam flinched but shook his head. "Look. We've been on the road for hours. I'm going to piss my pants if we keep going. Let's just freshen up, eat something, and figure out what's next."

But she shook her head and lay back down. "I'm not going inside. Take your time."

He exhaled loudly. He didn't want to leave her, but nature was more than calling. "Fine. I'll be back in two minutes, okay?" She didn't reply, so he got out.

When he returned, she was in the front seat, nibbling on

an Oreo. Sam realized she'd not met his gaze since they left her parents' house.

"Take me to Monica's. And that's the last thing I'll ask of you."

"You'll ask whatever you need." He turned the car around and headed back out.

"Don't even think of obliging me like that."

Her voice was so bitter that Sam could taste it in his own mouth.

At the girls' house, she looked up again. "Don't park. Don't even stop the car. Just let me out."

"Elle," he tried.

"No, Sam. I don't—I can't do this right now. Just— leave. Please. I need… time."

She was steel, and he couldn't bend it. He was afraid if he tried, she might break. So, he did as she asked. Elle didn't speak. She just got out, slammed the door, and didn't look back.

"I'll see you soon," he called after her and then drove away.

25

ELEANOR

Her insides were sludge. A quivery mess of all the ugliest emotions. Eleanor stood in the driveway until she couldn't hear Sam's car anymore. The house was quiet, the front door shut. Instead of going in, she fished her keys from her purse and ran to her own little car. Realizing only when she reached for the steering wheel that she was still holding that baggie of Oreos, she dropped them on her lap and got the hell out of there.

Cruising around was okay, but Eleanor couldn't focus on the road. Even on a lazy Southern Sunday, two horns honked at her within fifteen minutes of driving. She knew she needed to stop. So, she went to the only place she could think of being.

"You know, I'm about ready to put you on the payroll. You're here so doggone much."

"Woof!"

Tears spilled down her cheek the moment she walked into Mac's Joint.

"Awesome," she croaked as she knelt to greet Myrtle. Hugging the dog made more tears flow as Myrtle leaned her silky head onto Eleanor's shoulder.

"What's with you, kiddo?" Mac slid off his stool and shuffled toward her, but Eleanor shook her head. Myrtle licked her face, and she laughed through the tears.

"No, really, Len. What's wrong?"

She sniffled and rose slowly. "I'm messed up, Mac. Seriously."

He nodded, asked nothing more, and scratched his beard. "Want a hit?"

Another laugh coughed out. "No. Thanks, though. I want some tunes. Is that cool?"

His kind eyes crinkled with a smile. "That was my second idea. Take whatever you want. Be my guest."

"I may be here a while," she warned. "Kick me out when you want."

"Without hesitation," he said cheerfully.

She took *Pornography*, her favorite Cure album, and *All Things Must Pass* by George Harrison into a listening booth. Not the booth from that first afternoon with Sam. Pulling her feet up on the bench, she curled into the tiniest ball she could. The music washed over her while she ate the rest of the Oreos.

Both albums played through. Eleanor had just set the needle to listen to *Pornography* again when Mac knocked softly and stuck his head in.

He held out a different album. "I think you need this one, kiddo."

Eleanor took it and gazed at the cover. It was green, with a funny illustration of a boy with a pointed yellow head. The whole thing was made to look like a needlepoint tapestry. "Nilsson: *The Point!*" was printed at the top.

She looked up at Mac. "Harry Nilsson? As in *Midnight Cowboy*?"

He nodded. "Very good, young one. This is the soundtrack to the animated movie he wrote and scored. It's some deep shit. Let your mind go and enjoy."

Eleanor was in love from the first track on. She listened to Nilsson tell the story of Oblio, a little misfit boy. The musician's narration interspersed the beautifully harmonious story-songs that took her on his journey, complete with a canine companion, to the "pointless forest" and back. Along the way, little Oblio learned that "you don't have to have a point to have a point."

She took that lesson and tucked it deep in her heart.

That album played through twice. Once it had, Eleanor realized she felt enormously better.

I have to go see Sam. Right after I play the song "Life Line" one more time.

When it ended, she sleeved the disc and stepped out. She hugged it tight as she walked down the hallway. "Mac, I need this album. Tell me it's not a limited edition."

"It's yours," he said.

But Eleanor skidded to a stop as soon as she rounded the corner.

Sam leaned on the counter with his eyes trained steadily on her.

26

SAM

Sam got home and stood in the middle of his living room, lost for what else to do with himself. Too much was unsaid and unknown. He fell onto his couch and stared into space, trying to reason out what to do. Go back to the house? Let Monica care for her? He had no clue.

His phone rang over an hour into this torment. "Where are you?" Monica demanded without a hello.

"You called me, Monica. Where else would I be but home?"

"Right. I meant to say where is she?"

"What?"

"Len's car is gone. What happened, Sam?"

His stomach hit the floor. *No, please no, Elle, don't run off.*

He took a deep breath and told her things hadn't gone well. He skirted the details, but she clearly suspected the worst. He concluded with what had happened when they arrived back in town, stopping at the point when he drove away.

"Goddammit. Well, she's definitely not here. All her stuff is, though, so maybe… maybe she didn't go far." She sighed hard. "Okay, listen, we're on Len watch. You hear anything, you call me, got it?"

"Ditto," he said grimly.

It was another long hour before the phone rang again. Sam fell off the couch from a fitful doze and raced to answer it.

"Sam, buddy, what it be?"

He blinked and looked at the receiver. "Mac?"

"The one and only. Listen, I think you ought to get over here. Our friend Len's holed up in a booth and has been for a couple hours now."

He was out the door in two strides.

When he screeched up to the front of the record store and saw her VW there, warm relief coursed through him even as he sprinted to the door. Myrtle woofed, but Sam barely gave her a pat in his rush.

"Ease up, buddy," Mac said as Sam crashed down the aisle to the counter. "There's no fire."

"Len—is she—what the heck?"

Sam's feet tangled to a halt when his eyes came into focus. Mac was seated on his stool behind the register with a child in his lap. The little girl smiled up at him and waved a fist, gasping a baby's laugh. Mac grinned and smoothed her light brown curls.

"In the booth," he said, and Sam had to remember they were talking about Eleanor. "She's been here for ages. I've got her listening to Nilsson. Good for the soul, and she looked like she needed it."

"She did," he said slowly, still mesmerized by the girl's wide blue gaze. "Thanks for calling."

"Who else would I call? She's your girl. Has been since she walked in here, I'd say."

Sam tore his attention away from the baby and onto Mac. "She's," he started, then sighed. "She's her own person. I think I'm just lucky to know her."

The baby waved her hand and squealed, and Mac blew

a raspberry on her neck. She laughed, a sound of pure delight that lifted some of the darkness of the nasty day.

Sam twisted his mouth and gestured to Mac's companion. "Sorry, but who is this?"

"This is Emily," he said, tickling her.

"Of course it is?" It was more of a question.

"Of course it is," he agreed and stood her up on the glass counter. "This's my daughter. Em, say hi to Sam."

Sam's jaw hit the floor. Hesitantly, he reached out and let her grasp his finger. Her feet stomped merrily as she laughed again.

"Someday," Mac declared, "she's going to run this world."

"No doubt," Sam murmured. "Sorry, I… I had no idea you had a kid."

Another laugh, and Mac and Emily sat back down. "I realize it doesn't fit with my badass persona around here. But the wife works the night shift at the hospital, and I should've closed over an hour ago."

Sam marveled at Mac. They'd known each other for years, but Sam realized suddenly that he really knew nothing about him at all. It made him laugh.

Mac grinned and asked when he thought Springsteen would release another album, yet again bringing them back to their running conversation. So, Sam leaned on the counter and went with it. He didn't want to beat down the listening booth door and drag Elle out. He could wait, so long as he knew she was safe.

Not fifteen minutes later, Elle appeared. Her praise for the album Mac had picked stopped mid-sentence when she saw him. Sam froze, too. The ugly day rushed back at the sight of her. Eleanor lifted her chin and shuffled forward. Sam chuckled at her double-take when she caught sight of Emily.

Mac insisted she take the record at no charge. Then, he got to his feet. "Okay, sportsfans, you don't gotta go home, but you can't stay here anymore tonight. My little one needs her beauty sleep."

They traded a glance, nodded, and both thanked Mac profusely. Elle hesitated, then walked to the counter and held her finger out for the baby. Emily gripped her, doing her happy kicks again.

"Oh, god," Elle sighed, closing her eyes for a long moment. When she opened them again, she beamed at Mac. "You're the greatest."

"Aw, I know." He laughed and shooed them out.

The air was dense when they stepped through the door. The night sky hung so low it practically touched their shoulders. Lightning cracked, and a breeze swirled around their legs.

Elle looked at the sky, then at Sam.

He rolled his shoulders and knew he needed to be the one to do the thinking at that moment. "Get in my car or follow me home. And be quick—it's about to monsoon."

She got in his car, and they took off again. Sam left the windows down and hightailed it back to his apartment. He was ready to not drive again for a week after all this.

They almost made it in time. They were on the stairs to his apartment when the skies opened up. Elle shrieked at the cold rain that poured down so hard it bounced off the pavement below. Sam grabbed her hand and hurried her inside.

They tumbled through the door and turned to each other. The clothes they'd been wearing since the anniversary party a million years before dripped audibly on the floor.

But Sam didn't give a damn about the stream running from his hair down his back. All he cared about was the woman in front of him. "Elle," he rasped.

"I'm sorry, Sam," she whispered. "I'm so sorry."

"For what?"

She barked a sound almost like a laugh. "Try the last twenty-four hours. For dragging you through this, then running away. For... for bringing you into my mess at all. I don't deserve..."

"Stop."

"No," she insisted, pointing at him. "You heard him, didn't you."

It wasn't a question. Sam could tell by the growing momentum in her tone that she needed to get this out. He flipped on the lamp and crossed his arms.

"He wasn't exaggerating. I was pregnant, Sam. He—he was—Mom...." She covered her mouth.

"Say it all," he murmured. "Just say it, Eleanor."

Her hand dropped. "Alex was perfect. So smart, so talented. And me? I was a debutante who cared more about volleyball and rock and roll. Bobby was my escort for my coming out season. It's exactly like something out of olden times. He bought me gifts, took me to parties, courted me. Like I said, there were expectations. The first time scared me to death. After that, I just held my breath and got into the backseat so it would be over fast. But I was crap at remembering birth control once Mother put me on—"

"Your mother knew?"

Nod. "She told me to... oblige him. She told me that a

nice girl never just gives it away—never, ever. But she said that a lady knows how to keep her man. And when a man invests in her, it's all right for him to expect things in return."

Nausea threatened to knock Sam off his feet, but he let her keep going.

Elle looked at the ceiling. "Easter weekend of my senior year. I told him I was late. Bobby was furious. He called me careless and stupid, told me to take care of it, and cursed me for the expense it'd be to him when he had just bought a new stereo. The expense. Because there was no question what choice I was to make. No discussion of options. There was only how irresponsible I'd been to let this happen. He wouldn't drive me home. I walked along the highway to the gas station two miles from his place and used the payphone to call home.

"Alex answered. He…he…" Her dams broke, and she bent in half, weeping. "He took care of me. He took me to Monica's house. I didn't see Bobby after that, but the next day when Al came to take me to the clinic, he had a black eye."

She hiccupped. "He did everything for me. He and Monica…"

She broke into sobs for long minutes. Finally, she stood up straight and wiped her face as her color started to slowly fade back to normal. When she spoke again, her voice was controlled.

"Um, so. When we went to the clinic, Alex told me the decision was mine of what to do. He said that, either way, he'd make sure I was safe. But I knew what I had to do. And afterward, he arranged for me to come to Nashville and live with our grandparents as soon as I graduated. He didn't want me with Mom. I was so naïve. I didn't even realize how fucked-up her advice had been.

"Anyway, that Easter weekend was when I kind of lost my way. Maybe I never had one. That's probably more true, actually. And since then," she shrugged. "I've been finding it."

Her eyes locked onto his, her mouth set in a line. "I don't regret my decision, even though I'll carry it forever. It wasn't the right way to bring a child into the world, and at seventeen years old, I absolutely couldn't have given it the life it deserved. Mother said… she said I should've waited. That Bobby would've calmed down and done right by me."

"Jesus," Sam breathed.

"But money isn't enough to equal a good life for a child, you know?"

He nodded.

"What I said, guilty of not being guilty?" She wet her lips. "I've been atoning for the fact that I never doubted the decision. Judge me if you want."

"Judge you?" he echoed. "Judge you? Eleanor, you— you don't—" Sam broke off in a splutter, gripping his wet hair just to have something to hold on to.

She trembled. Tears made her emerald eyes glitter. "Your Nana said I didn't have to be ashamed. When she said that, it was like… absolution."

"She also said you deserve to be happy. I heard that part."

She blinked and nodded once.

Sam stepped closer to her and rested his hands on her shoulders. "She said I make you happy."

Her trembling stopped. She lifted her face. "So much."

And with that, Sam brought his mouth down on hers.

Eleanor swayed into him. Her knees buckled as she threw her arms around his neck. Sam wrapped his around her waist and let his tongue swipe against her lips until they parted.

But she groaned and pushed away. "No, no, this isn't right. I can't—this isn't how it should be, all broken, and… I've ruined us." Her head touched his shoulder, still shaking no. "It's too ugly now. You'll never think of me the same. I can't bear it."

Sam laughed. Not a simple chuckle; he threw his head back and laughed, refusing her attempt to disentangle from his arms. "Jesus Christ, Eleanor. What do I have to do to make you see how much you mean to me? Do you not get that none of this 'ruins' you? Life is full of dark days. You make me happy, Beautiful. Accept it."

She whined and punched his chest. "No, Sam. I don't deserve this—we can't—"

He hooked her chin to bring her gaze up. As soon as those eyes were on him, he burned with need. "We do deserve it, Elle. And I'm not obliging any arguments on that point."

Her pupils dilated. Slowly, her fingers lifted to his scruffy cheek. "You're soaked," she muttered.

"So are you."

A smile ghosted her mouth. "Yeah, I am."

Her words raced through him like fire.

She began unbuttoning his shirt. "You deserve a nice girl, Sam Greene."

He touched his nose to hers, his lips almost against her mouth. "You seem pretty nice to me."

"It's a sham," she whispered back as she rested her palms on his bare chest. "I'm the worst kind of trouble."

He grinned. "You're the kind of trouble I've been waiting to find my whole life, Elle Field."

She smiled a little deeper. "If we're doing this, don't you dare let up, okay? I think I'll break if we have to stop again."

Sam grunted an agreement.

She sucked in a breath. "So, are we doing this?"

"We're doing this."

27

ELEANOR

His tongue licked across her lips and into her mouth. Eleanor's knees buckled again, but he held her tight. Instead of collapsing, Eleanor slammed her shoulders against the door. Sam lifted her easily, and her legs knew to wrap around his back. He groaned and thrust his hips until she squealed and raked his scalp with her nails.

They were hot skin and wet clothes, as steamy as the summer itself.

Penance. Redemption. Absolution. Eleanor wasn't religious, but she understood those concepts with enormous depth. If Nana's words were absolution, then the passion radiating from Sam was most definitely her redemption.

He kissed her hard and deep, his mouth punishing and perfect. She bent her head, doubtless that he would hold her safely, and ran her teeth along his neck.

"Yes, please. Harder," he groaned.

Eleanor bit down until he moaned again. That hunger was back, an animal inside of her that had her claws out and left her blinded by want. She tugged his hair and pushed his mouth to her shoulder. He bit, and she squealed and bucked against his hold.

Sam lifted her off the wall and carried her across the living room. He eased her into a cushioned bowl chair and stood over her, his gaze dark and hooded while he unbuttoned the rest of his shirt and shrugged out of it. Eleanor pulled her dress off and fell back to her elbows. She arched her back and beckoned him down.

His mouth met her breast above her satin bra. His warm body pinned her to the chair's mint green cushion, and she gasped at the rough pressure of his mouth and the scratch of his unshaven cheek.

Eleanor didn't remember propping her knees up, only that he fell between them, flexing through his jeans against her soaked underwear. The sounds of their heavy breaths filled the room and nearly drowned out the pouring rain on the roof.

"Sam." His name cut in the silence with so much need that it took her a breath to realize it was she who'd spoken.

"Elle."

Oh, god, the way he growled for her was so—

The telephone's shrill ring froze them in place. His back tensed under her hands as she caught her breath.

Riing, riing. They both groaned.

Eleanor pulled him closer. "Let it ring. They'll call back."

But Sam shook his head. "They're worried about you."

He stood up—and pulled her along, too, all the way to the kitchen wall where the phone was mounted. He pinned her against the wall with a wicked grin and answered the phone with his lips against hers.

"Hello? Oh, hey, yeah." Sam cleared his throat, then ran his tongue over her lips.

Eleanor shivered all over as his words dimly floated into her brain:

"I've got her, Mom. She was at Mac's, just hanging out. We got to my place just before the rain started. Uh-huh, no, she seems fine, actually. Do you want to talk to her? Sure, hang on." He rumbled an evil laugh and thrust the receiver to her ear.

"H-hello?" she stuttered, captivated by the mischief in his eyes.

Monica's chatter couldn't compete for Eleanor's attention when Sam knelt down. She gaped while he untied her sandals and slipped them off, then sat up higher and began to kiss her thighs as he ran his thumb along her hip crease.

"Oh," she gasped.

"What?" Monica asked.

"Oh, uh, no. It wasn't—Atlanta wasn't… I'll tell you everything later."

"Are you okay, Len? I've been worried sick."

Sam pressed his nose against the apex of her thighs, and she shuddered.

"I'm good," she gasped, covering her eyes as he rumbled a laugh. "Oh, god—I-I mean, I'm pretty good, but god, am I exhausted."

"This storm is supposed to be bad. We're in a tornado watch. Maybe you should stay put at Sam's for a while."

"Uh-huh, I'll stay—well, hang on. I should ask first. Sam?" she called loudly as if he wasn't inches from her body. He sat back on his heels as she continued in that false pitch. "Monica says the storms are supposed to be bad tonight. Do you mind if I crash here?"

"Nah, that's cool," he shouted back.

"He says it's cool," she reported, then bit her cheek as his mouth sank onto her inner thigh.

"I'm ready to nominate him for sainthood," Monica said.

"I wouldn't be too sure about that, Monica." *If you knew where his fingers were right now, I'm not sure the Vatican would agree.*

"Y'all stay safe. I'll see you tomorrow after work, okay, love?"

"Yep. Later, Mon." It almost came out as a whimper when Sam stroked lightly over her underwear.

The receiver hit its cradle with a bang. "Damn you!" she groaned with a laugh.

"You said not to let up."

They tumbled to the kitchen floor, ignoring the cold linoleum in their frenzy. There was nothing *nice* about their passion. They were wild and rough and perfectly sweet. But nice had nothing to do with it.

The rhythmic sound of skin pressing and lifting against linoleum filled the room. Eleanor's back arched against the floor as they rocked their hips together. She pushed his jeans down his thighs. His cock pressed into her with no barrier but their thin cotton underwear, and the sensation made her skin burn all over.

"Sam, Sam," she gasped at last, unable to take any more halfway business.

He took one look at her and understood. In a blink, he hauled her to her feet and held her close as he walked her to the bedroom, kissing her lips the entire way. Her bra fell to the floor. Sam eased her to the bed and rolled her panties down her legs. She gazed intently as he stepped out of his boxers and crawled over her.

"The most beautiful woman I've ever seen."

He kissed down her neck to her aching nipples. His lapping tongue made her gasp and twist for more, and he gave it, sucking hard and pinching at the same time before swapping sides. Eleanor reached for his cock and guided him to press against where she needed him most.

"Oh, god, Elle," he groaned suddenly when she rubbed him against her pussy.

"Come here," she whispered.

He paused. "Hang on. I have condoms."

She smiled. "I don't forget my pills anymore, I swear. Nine am, every day."

Sam grinned and kissed her again. He pressed against her, teasing and testing. Eleanor felt him tense all over as he dragged out the moment.

We're here. We're finally here. No more waiting. She groaned and lifted her hips.

Sam's body followed hers back to the bed. He sank into her with one swift thrust that made them both cry out in ecstatic relief.

It took her a minute to open her eyes. When she did, she smiled up at him. "Hey," she murmured.

Sam stayed still, but his look of concentration lifted. "Hey. Sorry, I'm just… Well."

Her smile broadened. "Well, what?"

"Just trying not to explode. I don't want this moment to ever end."

Emotion closed her throat. "I know, Sam."

His cheeks colored. "But if I'm being honest, I also want to fuck you into this mattress."

Her face heated, too, but she laughed. "Then do it, silly. That's what I want, too."

"Goddamn, you are amazing."

With a deep breath, he began to grind against her until he was thrusting harder and harder. His cock filled her as his body bumped her clit. After so much teasing, Eleanor didn't last long. Pleasure pooled in her abdomen and exploded through her bloodstream. She thrashed under him and dug her nails into his shoulders.

"Don't stop, don't stop. Go hard, Sam," she gasped. Eleanor fell back to the bed and gripped the pillow to brace herself.

Sam grunted and obeyed. He thrust hard, his face flushed and his back slick with sweat until the moment he rocked forward and collapsed on her with a shout.

And then, the lights went out.

They both froze. Sam's gasping breaths filled the darkness. He stirred, but she hummed.

"Don't move."

"I'll just—"

"I said, don't move. Just lie on top of me for a while." Her whispered voice was sandpaper.

"Won't you be uncomfortable?"

"Not at all." She craved the idea of his weight holding her down. Holding her steady.

Sam settled between her legs with his head on her heart. He threw the quilt up and around them like a human cannoli. "Are you sure you're comfortable?"

"Sublimely." The sheets smelled like Tide detergent and him. She breathed deeply. "Are you?"

He just hummed.

They lay together, their breath in perfect sync. At last, Sam spoke. "How are you, Elle?"

She hugged him. "I'm *happy*, Sam," she said, then promptly fell asleep.

28

SAM

She's happy. She is happy. She's happy.

Happy had a new definition, and all of it centered around Eleanor Field and what they had just done all over his bed. Sam listened to her rhythmic breathing and replayed the sounds she'd made, every blurry moment he could remember, until his eyelids grew heavy. His foggy brain wondered what time it was and how long the power would stay out, but he drifted off with little concern for anything but her beating heart.

* * *

"I have to know he's safe. Go check his circuit breaker."

Sam hummed, still asleep.

Waking up was very much how he imagined falling off a ledge might be: when he understood what was happening, it was too late to change anything. Sam's consciousness was slow on the draw. A thrill of panic raced through him, but it was too late when he lifted his head at the slash of a flashlight's beam and the sound of his mother's voice.

"Sam?"

"No, um—"

While he struggled to speak, the lights blazed on.

"*Oh*! My god!" Mrs. Greene gasped.

"Oh, my *god*," he groaned.

Ee-uhh-hmm was approximately the noise Eleanor made when she jerked awake underneath him, realized the situation, and buried her face in his shoulder.

"I'm sorry, I'm so sorry." Mom clapped her hand over her eyes. She spun around and walked straight into the wall. "Dammit," she cursed softly.

"I'll—uh—I'll be right out," Sam babbled.

She shut the bedroom door. Sam leapt out of the blanket, tearing at his hair in disoriented terror. He cursed and snatched his boxers and jeans from the floor. When he licked his swollen lips, he cursed again and made a mental note to keep several feet between his mother and his sex-soaked self.

But then he paused as a smirk tugged at him. *I'm a fucking mess. And it is fucking incredible.*

Eleanor's green eyes peeked out of the blanket in pure horror. "I'm dreaming, right?" she whispered in a shaky voice.

He knelt and kissed her forehead. "It's fine. I'll be right back."

Mrs. Green had perched on the edge of the couch, spine straight as a rail. Sam slipped out of the bedroom and immediately realized he'd forgotten a shirt—and that his, along with Elle's dress, were in a pile in the bowl chair.

"What's up, Mom?" Sam hurried to snatch the shirt, then shuffled to the kitchen for water. He offered her a glass.

"No, thank you, son," she said in a voice as rigid as her posture.

Sam took a long drink and leaned against the wall. He met her gaze patiently until she exhaled and sagged.

"I'm so sorry," she whispered.

"I've lived here four years. I lived in your house eighteen before that. I've never known you to enter my space without asking."

She stood up, her palms out as if to stop him. "And I

never did, but you've been gone—"

The front door opened.

"Paul," she said sharply, but the pouring rain had Mr. Greene hurrying inside.

"What?" He shook the rain off his hat and glanced between them.

She looked back at Sam. "I never violated your privacy, son. But between this storm and not knowing if you were back safe, I worried. I saw your car, but your place was dark and I… I worried."

Sam sighed and nodded. "That's fair. Sorry, Mom."

She smiled at a random spot on the carpet. "As a mother, you know your boys are grown men. As a mother, you still don't picture them as grown *men*."

"Probably for the best."

She arched a brow in agreement. Her eyes lifted to his, and they traded a sheepish smile.

Dad cleared his throat.

Mrs. Greene ignored him. "She seems like a lovely girl," she said to Sam.

"She's so great." Sam flashed a grin but then winced. "But I need you to not tell Brian about this. I need you to swear you won't."

"That pretty little thing you were with at the party yesterday? Is that why you look like that?" Dad grumbled. His lips twitched at their answering poker faces. "The storm's supposed to go all night. Y'all want to come stay in the house?"

"Nope," Sam said promptly.

He laughed. "Good. Come on, Claire, let's get out of here."

She rose, flashed her son another apologetic smile, and shut the door. Sam listened to their car start and roll down the drive. Then, he rushed back to his girl.

She had shut off the overhead light but lit the bedside lamp. But Eleanor was completely hidden in the quilt. "I'm not going to survive this day." Her words were muffled but audible.

Sam leaned in the doorway. "Come on, you've got like two hours until midnight. You'll make it."

The quilt rustled around until her eyes peeked out. "Uh-uh. I'm humiliated beyond words. Kill me now." She groaned and hid again.

"Yeah, pretty much," Sam chuckled.

She flipped to sit up, her face finally visible. "No, you're the darling baby boy. I'm some jezebel who—"

Sam jumped on the bed and cradled her cheek to kiss the idea out of her mind. "My mother's words, her exact words, were, 'she seems like a lovely girl.'"

She sucked her lip into her mouth. Sam watched with extreme interest. Her bottom lip rolled out, slick in the low light, and Sam's blood surged. He flicked his tongue out to lick that soft skin. Because he could. Because he'd wanted to every damn time she sucked on that lip over the summer, and now he freaking could.

"You are so great," he said.

"Forget talking," she blurted and lay her hand on the back of his head.

Sam captured her mouth with his own. He lost himself in the thrill of just a kiss. Eleanor whimpered. Her hands slid to his cheeks as she curled toward him until Sam laid her back on the bed.

They were insatiable, all hands and mouths and racing blood—and no regard for the time or the weather. Over the long hours of that night, they found themselves on his bed, in the shower, and finally back in the bowl chair where they'd started.

In between blinding passion, they talked in each other's arms, played their lyric game, and listened to Bowie and The Smiths before the power went out again.

By the time the sun came up, Sam's hands had memorized her body.

They opened heavy eyelids at the sound of birds outside and the first shafts of pink light. Elle stroked his cheek. She rolled off the bed, pulled on his shirt, and drifted out the front door. Sam hurried to follow.

Eleanor stood on the top landing, smiling at the sunrise. "A new day. I feel a little bit in love with everything right now." She rolled her eyes. "I know, I know: science. But still."

Sam wrapped his arms around her. When he opened his mouth, he didn't plan his words. Just said, "Science or not, I think I'm more than a little in love… with everything."

His heart skipped as he tacked on that ending and hated that he did. But it must've been the right thing because in a blink, her arms were around his neck, her ass was in his hands, and he was carrying her right back to bed.

* * *

It was almost noon by the time she was dressed in his t-shirt and sweatpants, eating a bowl of Life cereal on the couch. She'd called her boss yesterday morning in Atlanta, so they had no one to answer to until the afternoon when Monica got off work. Jennifer had called an hour ago to report that she was off to decorate her classroom and that Alex was on his way back to town. Everyone was meeting at the house for dinner.

There was no question about how they'd fill the hours in between.

When it was getting very near time to fetch her car from Mac's Joint, they savored the remaining minutes curled in the bowl chair. The rain had dropped the temperature, and a fresh breeze wafted in from the window just to their left. They gazed at each other, not needing to speak to agree this was the most incredible day.

She broke the silence. "I didn't want you to come to Atlanta. I wished—I wish—that you didn't know all the ugly parts about me. But," she added when he began to protest, "when I heard your voice in that hall… When you held onto me and didn't let go… I thanked God you were there. Alex is amazing, the best brother ever, but it's different."

She lowered her eyes. "Thank you for being there."

He stroked her cheek and realized that touching her was quickly becoming a habit. Before he could speak, Elle rolled to her back and stretched her toes to the windowsill.

"That air is so nice. I feel like I could be anywhere right now. I think I'll be on the French Riviera. After my vagabond week in Paris, I'm in a private bungalow on the beach. What about you? Where would you be if you could be anywhere right now?"

Sam lifted his head and confessed. "Whenever I'm around you, that's exactly where I want to be. I know you don't really need protecting, and I know you'd be perfectly happy on the French Riviera alone. But there is nowhere and no situation where I don't want to be with you, Elle

Field."

Her eyes shut tight. Her cheeks flushed dark red as she gripped his hand. "I'm going to miss you," she whispered.

He exhaled. "We have another weekend before you leave for New York. And we'll both be busy this fall, so… what?"

She smiled one of her Eleanor signatures, the kind where her nose wrinkled and her teeth flashed. Like she was embarrassed to admit the truth but knew she would anyway. That smile never failed to shut Sam up.

"I meant tonight," she said.

She squealed when he climbed on top of her. *This chair is fucking awesome. How did I never realize before how perfect it is for fooling around?*

He tickled her neck with kisses until she ducked and pushed him away. Raising up, he grinned and ran a hand through his permanently rumpled hair. Her eyes sparkled with happiness, and Sam caught his breath.

"Next spring, when we're back, I think we should go on vacation together," he said.

"The French Riviera?"

"Sure. I'll just rob a bank, and we'll go first-class."

"I think we should," she began, but then bit her lips together.

Sam looked deep into her eyes and felt his heart jump. She wouldn't say it, whatever it was, but it didn't matter— she was planning their future. Even if she wasn't ready to do it aloud, that was exactly what she was doing.

"I'm in," he murmured.

"You don't know what I was going to say."

"I know. I'm still in."

"Come here and kiss me again."

"Oh, I am so in for that." He laughed and fell on top of her for one more kiss before they had to go.

29

ELEANOR

Monica smothered her with hugs and concern the second Eleanor entered the house. There was no way to keep her best friend in the dark, so Eleanor filled her in. Yes, Dad was doing okay. Yes, Mother had been Mother. Yes... she'd seen Bobby.

Monica turned into a storm cloud right in the middle of the kitchen. Sam sat quietly at the table with a beer while the ladies whipped up dinner for the group. They'd inventoried the fridge in a mild panic. Now, they were busy browning meat and cooking rice for a makeshift Mexican bowl. Monica gripped the jar of salsa so hard that Eleanor worried the glass would shatter.

"He was... you saw... where? Why? What?" she spluttered.

"Len's okay, Mon. She held her ground just fine."

They all looked up at Alex's tired voice in the doorway. He traded a smile with his sister and a nod with Sam. His arm was around Jen, and he leaned heavily on her. Given the flush on her cheeks and her hand on his chest, Eleanor surmised that she didn't mind bearing his weight in the least.

Eleanor rescued the Old El Paso and gave Monica another hug. "I'm okay, I swear."

She couldn't resist a glance across the room to the navy gaze she knew would find her. She couldn't stare for long—

not if she wanted to keep herself from climbing into his lap—but it was enough.

Monica's fingers dug into her back. "You're amazing," she cried, shaking her head. "I hate this ever happened to you."

"We all have dark days, I guess. Hard choices aren't all that define me."

Echoing Sam's words from last night, plus Nana's, gave Eleanor a sense of peace she hadn't felt in years—maybe ever.

It's okay. It's part of me, but I can still be happy.

Oh, god. I'm home.

That thought flipped her stomach inside out. She grabbed tightly onto Monica and looked around. After the initial thrill of panic, a brilliant warmth broke in her chest and spread through her whole body. Tears rolled down her cheek, but she laughed.

"Sis? You okay?" Alex asked.

"Len?" Monica jumped back with an alarmed frown.

Eleanor shook her head and laughed again. "I'm great. I, uh, I'm glad to be... home." More tears fell when she tested the word, but her smile was radiant.

She barely finished speaking before both Monica and Alex crushed her in a hug. Monica burst into tears, and Alex growled and kissed the top of her head. Jennifer whimpered and threw her arms around the group, decreeing that she had to be in on this moment. All three agreed.

Monica was the one who lifted her head first. "Sam, get over here for the lovefest."

Eleanor froze, her face hidden in Alex's shirt, but Sam cleared his throat. "I think y'all have it covered," he chuckled softly.

Alex caught her eyes. She blinked, stunned at the question she saw on her brother's face, but he looked away and stepped back. "What's for dinner?" he asked.

"Uh," Monica and Eleanor answered in unison.

They assembled the meat, salsa, and rice, added a healthy amount of cheese and a can of chilies they found in the cupboard, then loaded it into bowls. The break in humidity was perfect for dining al fresco, so they ate in the backyard. Eleanor was so famished that her bowl was empty well before anyone else's, so she leapt up and volunteered to fix dessert.

Mixed berry fool was fast and easy. She grabbed the beaters and went to work. Within minutes, she spooned the creamy violet dessert and reached for fresh strawberries to top it.

Two hands slipped onto her hips. She crashed to a stop with the berries in her hand.

"That looks good."

The words were low and languid, almost like his DJ voice. Her body melted at the sound. Without a word, she dipped the strawberry's tip into the cream and held it up. Sam's tongue swiped the pads of her fingers as he accepted the offer.

He hummed and gave her a squeeze. "That is the second sweetest thing I've tasted today."

Her knees and voice both shook. "Behave yourself."

"Oh, I will."

In a flash, he was in the kitchen chair, and she was straddling his lap. His smooth, freshly-shaved face under her fingers made her groan. He tasted like strawberries and smelled, as always, so clean and divine that it blanked her mind.

Sam's hands roved up her legs and under her t-shirt, fast and eager because they both knew this was brief. Eleanor rushed to feel her way to his hair, then over the contours of his shoulders to squeeze his arms. They traded kisses with the same kind of rushed intensity. Whenever they paused for a breath, they traded guilty grins that only made it hotter.

The back door opened. From the den, they heard Jennifer's voice. "Len? You need any help?"

She fell off his lap and flew back to the counter. "No, thanks, I'm just finishing up."

Behind her, Eleanor heard Sam's rustling clothes as he straightened himself out. She took a deep breath and laughed softly. *We're so fucking reckless. Why does that make it even better?*

"There you are, Sam." Jennifer sounded mildly surprised.

"Yeah, uh, well, we were just chatting while she finished up."

"Mm-hmm," Jennifer drawled.

Eleanor spun around with two bowls in her hands and thrust them toward her. She pushed a bowl into Sam's hands, too. "Help me carry, please."

Jennifer gave her a sideways look and laughed. "Sure thing, girl. You're the best, Elle, you know it?"

She pursed her lips and raised a brow. "It's just dessert, Jen."

Jennifer bubbled with giggles as she turned to lead them out. "Oh, is that all?"

Eleanor shot Sam a panicked glance, but he just grinned and shook his head.

Reckless is fun, but cool it. You have one week. Now's not the time to go dropping bombshells. Let this summer end. We'll tell them when the fall settles in. Keep it in your pants, Eleanor Beatrice!

Much, much easier said than done while she sat there and watched him lick that spoon.

30

SAM

"WRVU." A grin already stretched across his face, and the caller hadn't spoken yet.

"This number was scratched in the wall at Mac's Joint, in the third listening booth. Said I should call if I was looking for a good time."

It had been one day since he'd seen her, and yet her voice set off a cocktail of relief and thirst inside him. Sam exaggerated a grunt and played along. "Finally, it worked. I'm desper—uh, I mean, I've got a stacked schedule of hot dates these days. When should I fit you in?"

"As soon as possible, please." Her tone was flirty and eager, but he could also hear her stifling a laugh.

"Hmm. Well, I guess I could tell all my hot dates they have to wait. They'll be disappointed, of course. This better be worth my time."

"Tell them to wait. I'm the kind of trouble you've been waiting for."

The way she teased him with his own words kicked Sam in the heart in the best way. *You're damn right you are, Beautiful.* He opened his mouth to say it, but she spoke again.

"Come over, Sam." All her playfulness had dissolved into pure want.

Sam shifted in his chair to relieve the instant tension in his pants. "Come over? What about the others?"

"We'll be silent."

He breathed a laugh. "Not possible. Come to my place instead. If you leave now, I'll be just a few minutes behind you."

"What song are you going to play for me tonight?"

"You'll have to listen while you drive." This time, he hung up first.

The song block closed out and went to station identification and a handful of commercials while he queued up the last track.

"Another Tuesday, another signoff," he said into the mic right on time. "I'd say I was sorry, but you've got Joey Silver to take you through the night, and I've got someone waiting for me to get home. Let this song be your inspiration if you're driving around, deciding whether or not to make a move, okay? Until next time, Nashville."

He punched play on "I Need You Tonight" by INXS, then jumped up and pulled off his headphones.

Joey walked into the studio to take over. He grinned at Sam. "Hot date?"

"Hell yeah." He laughed. It was the first time he'd gotten to say yes to that question, and yet he was more drunk on the thought of Eleanor than the high-five Joey slapped on him.

How did I get this lucky? How did I meet this woman? She's my best friend. She loves music, quoting random movies, and joking about nerdy topics. And, on top of all that, she makes me hot as hell. What the fuck did I do so right that day in the record store? He'd asked himself these questions all summer. He suspected he would continue for a long time to come.

But not while she was waiting for him. He jogged to his car and sped home.

The white VW sat silently in the driveway when he arrived, but Eleanor wasn't in it. He stepped out and looked around in the pitch dark.

"This is not what nice girls do."

He turned to her voice drifting down from the staircase, then climbed two at a time to find her seated at the top landing. He stopped when they were at eye level. "Nope, it's probably not. This is scandalous, clandestine, and about to get very wicked indeed."

"Mmm. Mm-hm."

"Aren't you glad you came over then?" he added softly.

She leaned forward and touched his hair. "Yeah. Yeah, I've been missing you."

"You saw me yesterday."

"Yep."

He leaned into his hands planted by her hips. Finding her lips in the darkness was easy, and she answered right away. She inhaled, then exhaled in a gentle groan that ignited his blood with its implication. Their lips fused together while her fingers dug deeper into his hair and her strawberries-and-champagne scent went straight to his brain. Her tongue teased him, licking lightly until his elbows shook and he groaned.

He felt her smile into the kiss before her tongue slipped between his lips again. Holding his shoulders, Eleanor got to her feet without breaking away. Immediately, his palms were on her waist, under her shirt and up her ribs. She laughed and ducked so that their foreheads touched.

"You and those hands," she murmured. "From the start."

"Tell me to stop, and I'll stop."

"No one said stop, Sam."

"Good because I can't help it. You're so damn soft, it makes me—"

"I'm skinny these days. I got too thin in Peru."

He shook his head and caressed her sides. "You're perfect, Elle. You're *perfect*."

She whimpered and buried her face in his shoulder. "I'm out of my mind for you," she muttered into his shirt. "I told myself I'd wait until you called me, but I couldn't resist."

"I don't want you to resist. I want you to do what you want, whenever you want. Especially if it has to do with me."

"Like this?" She reached between them and slid a hand into his shorts to glide her fingers along his hips, just below his aching cock.

"Oh, my god, yes."

He expected her to giggle and keep teasing, but Eleanor lifted her head and gazed at him in the dark. Her voice dropped to an urgent rasp.

"Sam, I'm crazy about you."

He stilled. "Oh, yeah?"

Her hand retreated as she nodded.

"Eleanor, I-I…" Sam spluttered, but then took a long breath and smiled.

"You what?"

But instead of talking, he lifted her into his arms and carried her inside, straight to the bed.

"You what, Sam?" she insisted when he began removing clothes, kissing every inch of skin as it appeared.

"Beautiful," he murmured against her neck. "There aren't words for what I am about you. That's why I'm about to show you."

When she was naked and sprawled out on the bed, Sam sat back and gazed down in reverence. His mind flashed back to that hazy, drunken night when he'd first seen her. She'd looked like an angel through the muck of his addled brain.

Raging anticipation and complete satisfaction—for all they were about to do, for all they could be together—gripped him.

"What is it?" Her whispered question took him from his thoughts.

Her hand drifted to cover her breasts, but Sam fell forward to swat her arm away and suck the soft pink tip into his mouth. Eleanor moaned and arched her back. Sam let his mind go blank as he kissed and touched her everywhere. Finally, when she was squirming and tugging his hair, he reached between her legs and found her clit.

She went off within moments.

When she stopped shuddering and opened her eyes again, he flashed a brilliant grin. "Was it nice?"

"I'll show you nice."

With a little growl, she shoved him backward and took him in her mouth. Her tongue pressed against his throbbing dick, and light exploded behind his eyes. *No, no, not yet—*

"Oh, fuck, Elle, wait."

His fingers touched her jaw, a physical request to hold still. Eleanor glanced at him through her golden hair cascading around her face.

Sam sucked in a breath. "Beautiful, your mouth... I don't know if I can stop if you..."

She smiled. "Don't stop. I want to taste you."

His cheeks flooded with heat. Sam held his breath.

She nodded and flicked her tongue across his tip. Then she closed her lips around him and flattened her tongue along his smooth, warm skin again. Sam cursed, unable to stop the thrust of his hips. *I can't hold on, Elle, oh fuck, oh fuck…*

Her green gaze flitted up. One eyebrow arched like a saucy dare for him to let go. Her mouth on his cock and her eyes locked on his was more than Sam could take.

"Harder," he wheezed.

"Mmm-hmm." Her mouth vibrated as she complied, and he was done.

Sam groaned as he climaxed. He forced himself to keep his eyes open as much as he could—he couldn't get enough of the sight of her, ever, but especially in that moment.

Eleanor threw herself upright and then fell back on the mattress. She swept her hair back with one arm and gasped for breath. "Shit, that was amazing."

He huffed a laugh. "I think that's my line."

She lolled her head to look at him and grinned. But Sam's eyes went dark with lust. His voice was raw when he spoke again.

"I want to do that to you."

Eleanor blinked. She squeezed her knees together. "Really?"

He crawled over her to dust a kiss on her mouth. "Hell yes, really."

She bit her lip, and Sam waited.

Elle wrinkled her nose. "I've, uh, never…"

"Me neither."

They both blushed.

Sam leaned in and kissed her. "I want to know every

part of you, Beautiful. What do you think?"

Her eyes were glassy, cheeks a dark pink. She wet her lips and bobbed her head in a dazed nod, and Sam's lips curled.

He didn't say another word, just kissed her mouth once more, then licked and nipped his way down her body. Eleanor lay back and traced the quilt's pattern with her fingertips. Her eyes fluttered closed, but she tensed and squeezed his head with her thighs when he rubbed his nose between her legs.

Sam chuckled. "Just tell me what you like and what you don't. And remember—I would do anything for you. Don't hold back."

Her skin was hot to his touch, but her gaze melted into pure affection. "Um, kiss me, then. Your tongue, I—I can't get enough of your kiss, so… Oh, Sam."

Her words became a wail when he dragged his tongue across her lips, then sucked lightly on her clit. Eleanor threw her head back and gripped the sheets. She tried to hold still while he explored her, but it was too much. Her legs wrapped around his back as her body arched and squirmed. Desperate moans and whimpers fell from her mouth until Sam reached up and laid a hand on her heart.

As always, his touch seemed to soothe her.

She gripped the quilt but relaxed her legs a little. Her breath came in gasped huffs and hums, so Sam kept it up. He dragged his tongue from back to front, relishing how she tasted, how her juices rolled down his chin. *This is pure heaven.*

Elle opened her eyes as he gazed up at her. His eyes crinkled in a smile. *Tell me what you want, Beautiful.*

Skye McDonald

She wet her lips and seemed to understand his silent message. "Um, I like when your tongue kind of… plays with me. Like that, but higher—*yes, Sam*."

He hummed, and she moaned.

"Do that again. Yes. And, um, um, your fingers? Yes, two, oh please yes."

"Mmhmm."

Eleanor's hips were rocking rhythmically against his face; she'd let go of all inhibitions. Sam was hard again at the sight and taste of her. He realized he was rocking his own hips into the bed in time with her movements, but his need didn't matter. Her walls began to tense, and the taste on his tongue intensified. *Fuck, she's close. Come for me, Elle.*

He didn't let up. Didn't dare change a single damn thing. His fingers pumped inside her. She pulsed right back.

"Suck on me, Sam, I can't—"

She didn't have to finish the thought. His lips closed around her clit, and she shattered with a wail, all over his bed and mouth.

When she quieted, Sam reared up with a gasping groan. "Fuck yes."

Elle breathed a single laugh. "My line."

She circled her hand to invite him up. Sam crawled over her and found her lips parted and waiting for his kiss. She didn't seem to care that his mouth was saturated with her flavor. She kissed him deeply and sank her nails into his back, legs wrapping around his hips. He couldn't resist the invitation. She was so soaked from her orgasm and his mouth that he drove hard inside her.

"Sam."

"Elle."

"I want this to last, Sam. I want…"

He shushed her with a kiss that promised her everything she wanted. Sam knew that his body and his heart would give her absolutely anything. He fucked slow and steady until she looked up at him and whispered a command to come.

And he obeyed that, too.

Afterwards, lying wrapped in her arms, Sam thought for a second about saying it, the three words that he suspected she knew already. But their breaths were slowing with each moment, and his eyelids were so heavy. Besides, they had time for all that. He was certain.

"Stay all night," he whispered instead, then turned his head and kissed her temple.

She hummed and squeezed him. "I've got work at nine. I can't be late."

"You won't be. But stay."

She stayed.

* * *

When it was barely 6am, just shy of four hours from when they went to sleep, Eleanor stumbled out of bed and stepped into her clothes. Sam yawned and watched from the sheets, then rolled out once she was dressed. He followed her to the front door and pressed her into it for a goodbye kiss. His morning-wood against her hip made her laugh.

"I'm so jealous of you right now. Go back to bed and take care of this," she teased, stroking him.

Sam saw stars at her touch, but he shook his head. "I have a better idea. You come back and spend the night tonight after the concert."

Echo & the Bunnymen had almost been forgotten in the jumble of the weekend. But those tickets were sitting on his bookshelf. The show was at seven.

"Again?"

Sam wiggled his brows. "Problem?"

But she frowned. "No, I can't. I don't know how I could and keep the girls from knowing. Jennifer already almost caught us."

"Would it be the worst if they knew?"

Guilt flashed in her eyes. Sam braced himself to hear a yes, but Eleanor said, "No. No, I didn't mean that. I just thought we should let this week be our last with the group. Maybe we tell them at Christmas or something."

He exhaled and nodded. "It's a fair point. There's a lot of change just a few days away."

And besides, you're planning the future again. There was nothing like the relief that came with that.

He grinned and rolled his hips against her. "Fine, I'll save this for you."

She laughed and grabbed him again. "Aw, but I like the idea of picturing you in bed, jerking off while I work today."

Sam blinked, suddenly wide awake. "Uh, yeah, that's— you can picture that for sure."

Her eyes lowered as her strokes slowed. A blush colored her cheeks. "I like to do it when I listen to your radio show," she blurted, then kissed his cheek and darted out the door.

Sam was behind her as soon as he could breathe. He gave not one damn that he was stark naked and hard as hell.

"Are you serious?" he shouted just before she got in her car.

Even from a distance, the flash of green kicked his heart. "Have a nice day, Sam."

He'd planned to go right back to sleep, but with her

confession on his mind, there was business to attend to first.

31

ELEANOR

You are definitely the kind of girl your mother warned you about, Eleanor thought as she drove through the quiet morning. This time, though, the idea made her smile. Ever since she'd left Buckhead, she'd felt more at peace with memories of her mother. Finally voicing her heart on the porch had given her some resolution. The guilt she'd carried wasn't so great anymore. She knew she disappointed her mother, but there was simply nothing to be done about it. In declaring it, Eleanor felt free.

But her peaceful dreaminess shattered before she got off Sam's street. Eleanor clenched the steering wheel when she spotted Mrs. Greene. Sam's mother sported Jane Fonda leg warmers over tights and a neon pink tank top. She pumped her arms on a power walk.

A brief urge to gun the engine and roar past winked through her, but Eleanor made herself brake instead. Mrs. Greene squinted, shaded her eyes, and…

Smiled.

"Eleanor, it's good to see you again!" She bent toward the VW's rolled-down window.

Is it? Eleanor put the car in park and stepped out to greet her. "Um, nice to see you too, Mrs. Greene."

She wiped her brow and smiled deeper. "Claire. It's Claire. I thought I'd take a walk before it gets too hot. I didn't realize you and Sam had been… on a date."

"Oh, um, yes." Eleanor appreciated the genteel lie. Claire certainly knew that Sam had been at the station until late, but she wasn't about to contradict the older woman. "We, uh, we've been trying to see each other since we're both leaving town so soon."

"Of course," she agreed, but then dropped the farce and laid a hand on Eleanor's arm. "I'm so sorry about the last time you were here. I felt horrible that I intruded."

Eleanor's shoulders slumped. She squeezed her hand where it rested on her arm. "Oh, no, Mrs. Greene-uh, Claire. I'm the one who's sorry. It's—I'm so embarrassed to—and now, again."

With a sigh, Eleanor forced a brave smile. "I hate to think what you must think of me," she whispered.

Claire cupped Eleanor's face with both hands. It was a move Eleanor's mother had never gotten quite right. She'd never found it comforting until Gran had done it when she'd first arrived in Nashville, shaken to the core and barely verbal around anyone but Monica and Alex.

But this touch was reassuring. Claire looked Eleanor square in the eye to say, "No more of that, you hear? I watched him walk you around that party on Saturday, and I knew—I *knew*—how much he cares about you. You'll understand when you're a mother and your child meets someone special. It's the way he looks at you. The way you look right back at him. You have nothing to be sorry about."

Eleanor almost hugged her. Emotion choked her throat. "Thank you," she croaked.

Claire gave her a gentle pat, then stepped back. "I've kept you long enough. We'll have coffee soon. For now, have a lovely day, dear."

Eleanor took off, deep in thought. She marveled at how comfortable Sam's family made her. A vision flashed in her head of getting off work that afternoon and going right back to his apartment. He'd be waiting on the stairs, grinning down at her. Maybe he wouldn't be able to wait for her to get to him, and they'd meet halfway to kiss hello and race inside. He'd ask what she'd created at work while carrying her to the shower. "I'm glad you're home," he'd say between kisses and soaping her back.

It could be like that. The thought made her smile.

The week just got better. They had a blast at the concert. The next night, Sam's entire final show was laced with messages to her. She suspected that every track he played had to do with them, and all his commentary seemed to be for her benefit. She didn't call, though, just grabbed her keys and snuck out the door. His farewell song to Nashville—to her, she liked to think—was "I Melt With You."

He found her on the stairs again that night.

"Was that last song for me?" she asked.

"It was all for you."

She smiled. "I thought so."

And that was that.

* * *

Wild. Wild, wild, wild. That was the only way Eleanor could describe her and Sam over that perfect week. They were reckless, stoned on desire. Sam set her on fire. He burned away all the fears she carried and torched her doubts about whether she deserved this happiness. Eleanor heard herself more than once mentioning their future, and when she did, it didn't scare her. She knew for sure that they wouldn't end once they left town. She knew there was so much more they could be, and god, did she want it.

It was easily the happiest week of her life.

But it wasn't just him changing her. Eleanor noticed how he was affected by their passion as well. Where she felt grounded, their connection seemed to set him free. Every ounce of hesitation or reservation he had was gone. He touched her with confidence and talked so filthy that she blushed to her toes—then came even harder when he commanded her to. It was clear that together, they were becoming something entirely new.

It was pretty clear, to Eleanor at least, that they were falling very hard in love.

Too soon, it was the last Friday together. The gang had big plans for the weekend. A marathon lovefest would start with a fancy dinner that night at Irelands, a local spot known for their steak biscuits. The weather forecast held rain, so they decided to skip another boat adventure. Monica planned for Saturday to be a day of movies and a dinner party. After the bootleg meal the week before, she declared that hosting a proper dinner was something they needed to master.

"I'm good at chocolate and buttercream," Eleanor said while they strolled the aisles of H.G. Hills grocery Friday afternoon. "Why can't we just go out to eat?"

Monica shook her head and grinned. "Come on. After next year, when we're all living in Nashville, we've got to grow up. There will be, like, Thanksgivings with the families and everything. We have to learn someday."

Eleanor rolled her eyes and muttered about not having time for that kind of thing. But she let Monica pick out a chicken to roast while she and Jennifer bagged potatoes and green beans.

Friday night, they glammed up. The ladies spent the afternoon laughing and creating a cloud of hairspray so heavy that it required a fan in the bathroom to dissipate. They'd gone to the mall and gotten new clothes. Monica sported a hot pink minidress that looked incredible on her tiny figure. Jennifer went with an off-the-shoulder blue dress and a wide leopard-print belt. Eleanor wore a baby-pink chiffon dress with a denim jacket and white Keds. The guys arrived spiffed-up as well in khakis and blazers.

They feasted at dinner, then decided their sharp clothes meant they should go dancing. At the Zebra Lounge, Brian took Eleanor out for a spin on the dance floor. While they danced to The Police, he grinned at her and shook his head.

"What?" she shouted over the music.

"Ah, nothin'." He laughed. When the song ended, he cocked his head. "There's a redhead at the bar who looks lonely."

"God forbid I stop a good deed." Eleanor rolled her eyes.

"I meant you should go talk to her, actually," he replied with a wink.

They laughed, but then he straightened his collar. "Alright, sweets, I'll see you later… maybe tomorrow."

He started to stroll away but turned suddenly and pointed behind her. "Take care of Sam, will ya?"

Eleanor blinked, but he just laughed again and was gone.

She was alone for less than ten seconds. "God, that was the longest song of my life," Sam grumbled.

She threw her arms around his neck as they found the

beat, then lost themselves in it for ages. The night melted away into a blur of thumping bass and Sam's body swaying against hers on the dance floor. Sometimes they bumped into their friends and traded shouts of hello, but Eleanor needed nothing more than his hands on her waist.

When they were sweaty and exhausted, the crew collected to return to the girls' house. Everyone's cars were there, so they all walked back together, Brian included, in a haze of laughter and chat.

Sam and Eleanor trailed behind as always. When they got to the house, their footsteps slowed as they crossed the lawn.

"Monica asked me to make one more caramel batch, and I'm making a triple recipe of coffee cake that I promised to freeze for them. Will you be over for cartoons?" she asked.

Sam shook his head. "Mom wants me to spend the morning with them, and I need to pack. I'll be over before dinner."

"Hmm, well, Monica says if it's raining, we're playing games inside. You'd better be here if we get into a round of Twister." She cut her eyes to him, smiling at his grin.

"I won't miss it," he whispered.

They turned and faced each other. In her periphery, Eleanor could see the others on the porch. But she couldn't stop gazing at the face of the man she was going to miss so, so much.

"I'm looking forward to the day," he murmured softly, "when what happens next is that we get in the car and leave together."

Her brows lifted. "How scandalous."

"It won't be." Sam took a quick breath. "You're beautiful, Beautiful. In case I didn't say it already."

She broke into a grin. "You're pretty spiffy too, Sam Greene."

Sam smiled and opened his mouth to speak, but a wolf-whistle stopped them.

"Would you just kiss him already, Len?" Brian shouted from the porch.

She squeaked and spun to see them all leaning on the rails, grinning at them. "What?" she blurted, hands on hips. "What are you—"

Brian laughed. "You heard me. Kiss him. He's wanted you to all summer."

Sam and Eleanor turned about sixteen shades of red. Meanwhile, Monica giggled and swatted Brian's arm.

"Oh, so generous now, are you?" Monica teased.

"What?" Brian whipped his head to her.

"You put the moves on her on the porch that night, and now you're passing my BFF to your brother? Len is a lady, you jerk."

She laughed, clearly enjoying the joke, but Brian's eyes went wide. "The hell are you talking about, tiny woman? I haven't made a pass at Eleanor! Well," he amended with a grin, "I haven't made a serious move, I mean. What night on the porch?"

"Shit," Sam breathed, and Eleanor bit her tongue so hard she tasted blood.

Monica's brows furrowed. "You came over in the middle of the night. You kissed her on the porch. I busted you. How do you not remember?"

Shit indeed. The entire group ping-ponged their attention from Monica to Brian to Eleanor.

Brian saved the day. He snorted and shook his head. "I never kissed Len, goofy. You must've dreamed that."

Monica's jaw dropped. She clapped a hand over her mouth. "Oh, my god—did I?" She turned to Eleanor for answers.

She held up open palms and shrugged. "You must have. I never kissed Brian on the porch—or anywhere."

Damn, I can't believe I said that with a straight face.

Brian burst out laughing. "Holy shit, what would Freud say about that, Dr. Huang? Projecting fantasies about me onto your best friend, hmm?"

Now Monica turned bright red. She protested loudly against the echo of laughter all around. Dylan hugged her tight, laughing louder than the rest of them. Sam and Eleanor traded a look while they were distracted.

"And this is where I escape," he said, then shouted goodbye to the porch and jogged for his car.

Eleanor joined the crew. She laughed and high-fived Brian as he took his leave as well. The night closed fast, Monica muttering until the last moment about not having a thing for Brian and wondering how the hell she'd made that up. A tiny part of Eleanor thought about confessing, but she figured no harm, no foul. They could finish the weekend and work the details out later.

She'd regret the decision for a long time to come.

33

ELEANOR

The rain that was supposed to last all day cleared up by midmorning Saturday. Eleanor happily worked in the kitchen to the soundtrack of laughter and cartoons. They feasted on coffee cake and decided to take the party to the park for some sunshine.

They strolled the grounds of Centennial Park and played around on the giant replica of the Parthenon. Jennifer brought her Pentax, so lots of photos were taken before an intense game of Frisbee began. Dylan and Brian wound up muddy, thanks to their dogged determination to catch everything thrown their way. Eleanor joined in and found herself mucked up as well. Her days of volleyball in high school made it impossible for her to skip a diving catch when needed. Monica and Jennifer weren't nearly as dedicated to the sport. They were happy to cheer her on from the sidelines.

Afterward, the guys decided to go to their place for lunch and showers. They promised to be over well before dinner for Jennifer's mojitos. The ladies cruised back to the house in Monica's car, belting the *Grease* soundtrack at the top of their lungs. At a light, Monica threw her arms around Eleanor and kissed her cheek.

"Ew, cooties," Eleanor laughed, pushing her away like they'd done all through high school when one of them got sentimental.

"Yep, riddled with happy cooties over the idea of you living here. Infected, even."

Jennifer sighed and reached from the back seat to squeeze Eleanor's arm. "I agree. This has been the best summer. You're a good luck charm, Len."

Eleanor flashed her a grin as Monica upped the stereo.

They were still singing when they pulled into the driveway. Monica smashed on the brakes. John Travolta and Eleanor kept crooning, but the other two went silent.

Eleanor finally noticed the girl on the porch.

"Um," Jennifer muttered when Monica killed the engine.

"What the hell?" Monica hissed.

They climbed out, and the girl stood up. She wore cuffed denim shorts and a baggy pink t-shirt knotted at her hip. It was air-brushed with a sunset and the word España scrawled in black. Her honey brown hair was crimped, pulled up into a side ponytail with a pink scrunchie.

Eleanor didn't have to ask. She knew who it was.

"Hey, gals," she called, grinning big and cracking her gum.

"Hey, Trish," Jennifer and Monica replied.

She glanced at Eleanor as her brows arched. "What have y'all been doing?"

"Just messing around in the park. This is Eleanor. Len, meet Trish," Monica said.

They nodded at each other. Trish turned her attention to Monica. "Doc, I need a chat," she teased. "Are y'all busy?"

"Uh, no. Let's sit on the porch."

Monica, Jen, and Trish took chairs while Eleanor went for a shower. She rushed through with lightning speed but made damn sure to scrub all the dirt off her skin. Wrapped in a towel, she slunk down the hall to her bedroom, softly shut the door, and crouched down by the window to shamelessly eavesdrop.

"You've got to go to Spain, ladies. I'm just saying."

"Sounds great," Monica and Jennifer murmured, and Eleanor got the sense they'd been repeating it.

Monica cleared her throat. "So, what are you up to now that you're home? And you said you wanted a chat?"

"I can leave," Jennifer volunteered.

"Nah, Jenny, stay. I just wanted to say this out loud." Trish took a dramatic pause, then said in a rush, "I'm getting back with Sam."

Dead silence. Dead silence outside. Dead silence in Eleanor's ribcage where her heart should've been beating.

At last, she heard Monica mutter, "Oh?" before Trish spoke again.

"I went to see him before I came here, just to surprise him. He was with Claire and Paul, but we went to his place—not like that! I see your face, Monica," she interrupted herself with a giggle. "Just to talk. Actually, we didn't even go inside, just sat on the stairs—"

The stairs where he kissed me. The stairs where I waited. The stairs she probably walked every day for five years. Who did you think you were, Eleanor?

"He was busy, but I told him I needed to *talk*."

"And… what did he say?" Monica asked.

"He's taking me to Houston's tonight! It always was my favorite, so he said we could go."

Houston's. Where he was going to take me. It was their place. I see. Eleanor's heart turned over, just once, and then was silent again.

"You asked him back just like that?"

Trish popped her gum. "Nu-uh. I didn't want it to be all casual. I'm gonna wait until tonight so it can be serious. Girls… I'm going to ask for him to propose again."

Eleanor's ass hit the floor. Outside, she heard the metal lawn chair scrape and Jennifer's voice, far louder and harsher than Eleanor had ever heard her before: "*What?*"

"Geez, Jenny, what's with you?" Trish cried. "You look like I just spit in your soda."

"I-I," Jennifer fumbled, and it seemed as if she sat back down. "Sorry, Trish. You're going to…"

"I want the ring. I'm sure he had one. He'd never have mentioned it otherwise back in May. It's time, ladies. Oh, my god!" She squealed.

He wasn't going to propose. He did propose. Because of course he did. Five years together. Going back every time. Of course. Eleanor bit her lip to hold the tears at bay.

Finally, Monica spoke. "Are you sure about this? Because, Trish, y'all have broken up so many times, and the last time you said it was over for good. Why do you think—"

Trish pshawed. "Oh, Mon, come on. I couldn't go to Spain with a commitment here. I had to sow my last wild oats, you know? But now this'll be perfect. We can get engaged. I'll spend the fall planning a June wedding. Then, I can go do the internship in the spring, and boom. A wedding right after we graduate. Ooh! Or maybe we could just do it at Christmas! A big thing at Opryland with all the lights, and then I'd be able to introduce myself as Mrs. Greene at the internship." She giggled with glee.

Monica's voice was delicate, very unusual for her, as

she said, "This will sound harsh, but do you think Sam still wants to marry you?"

"As if! What a question! Sam and I have history. Why wouldn't he?"

"Honestly, Trish? Y'all never seemed very… in love… to me. Certainly not passionate."

Her laugh was airy. "What do you think flings are for? Marriages aren't for passion—gah, what a romantic for a shrink! That's why it was important we take breaks. We got all that stuff out of our systems with other people. But come on, Mon. Everyone knows marriages are about stability and making a family. Now that we've done our college years, it's time to settle down. Sam will be a good provider, and I'll be a good wife and never wonder what I'm missing out on. It just makes sense."

Eleanor looked around her room. At the transistor radio she'd used all summer to listen to Sam's shows. At the pile of albums in the corner, Red Hot Chili Peppers stacked on the bottom—the start of her summer. The start of something that, she realized now, was just a summer of movies, baking, and fun. Of trivialities. A summer that would turn into recollections of good times and youth as the crew got older and settled in their careers. She'd thought she was building a home, and they'd all just been making cool memories.

You are a fool, Elle Field.

It was as if every root she had let grow underneath her had been planted in sand. She realized she was trembling all over, freezing to death on an 80-degree August day. A breeze swirled around her naked shoulders and shook her even more. She gripped the bedspread behind her just to have an anchor while she desperately tried to deny Trish's words and silently begged her girlfriends to do it for her.

But then Monica sighed. "Well, if it's what you both want... if you both know what you're agreeing to, and you really are ready to commit to him forever... then, yeah. Tell him."

"Trish," Jennifer burst out. "Sam—he's the best. He's such a great guy. Please, please don't..."

"Aw, Jenny. I'll take good care of my Sammy, I promise. And you girls already know you're bridesmaids! Look, I've gotta go. I want to buy a new dress for tonight. Underwear, too. See you later, okay? Oh, uh, tell your other friend it was nice to meet her. Peace out!"

Eleanor was curled in a ball, staring into space, when the phone rang. She didn't move, just listened to feet hurry down the hall, then the announcement she knew was coming:

"That was Sam. He said he's not coming to dinner." Why Jennifer sounded like she was crying, Eleanor wasn't sure. She couldn't inquire, though—she couldn't do anything but lie there for the longest time.

* * *

Eleanor didn't remember when she climbed off the floor and huddled into the sheets, but she woke up in bed when the shadows were long. The smell of food crept under the door. Staring at the ceiling, she realized she was numb. Totally, totally numb. No panic, no worry. What would be the point? What was there to worry about? Her silly fantasy of a life had just fallen away. She was back to square one, adrift, and about to be on the move again.

She wandered into the kitchen to find a party. Jennifer was making mojitos while Monica laid out bread and dip.

Everyone cheered when they saw her, but Jennifer didn't meet her eyes when she handed Eleanor a drink.

They all made dinner. There was a lot of talking, but none of it was about the afternoon. Eleanor wondered if Monica was nervous to tell the boys. She bet that she was. Only when they were all crammed around the little kitchen table with a surprisingly well-done meal in front of them did Brian grumble, "Where the hell did Sam disappear to? He called and said he'd catch up later."

Monica stabbed a green bean. "He, uh, had something come up."

"Trish came home." The three words burst from Jennifer's mouth, vile and angry.

A pair of masculine shouts answered back. Eleanor peeked up to see Jennifer's brown eyes flashing.

"They're having dinner." Jennifer practically spat the words.

"What the fuck?" Brian bellowed. He banged his fist on the table. "What is that tart up to?"

Jennifer didn't seem to have the nerve to answer that.

Monica took a long drink of water and reached out to touch Brian's and Dylan's arms. "They're adults, guys. Sam can handle himself."

Dinner wasn't so fun after that. The guys sulked, the ladies didn't speak, and Alex glanced at Eleanor anytime she moved. Luckily, that wasn't much. She didn't eat more than a single green bean.

Games weren't even a question. Everyone was pissed or worried—well, except Eleanor. She was still numb. *Eleanor Novocain. That'll be my new identity when I get to NYC.*

Once the dishes were clean, they filed into the den like it

was a funeral processional and took their usual places for a movie. Alex and Jennifer snuggled onto the couch, his arm tight around her, while Brian sprawled on the end opposite. Dylan kicked back the recliner for him and Monica. But Eleanor didn't drop to the bean bag right away. She just stood in the doorway and gazed at her friends. Bile started to coat her tongue.

"What should we watch?" Monica's voice was forced cheery.

Brian motioned Eleanor over. She went to snuggle into the couch beside him. He threw an arm around her, but she knew that this was protective, reassuring, and not a bit flirty. His warmth contrasted with her cold skin. That sour taste in her mouth got worse.

"Lenny? Want to watch *Pretty in Pink*? I know that's one of your favorites."

"Huh?" Eleanor blinked.

Monica grinned at her. "How the hell did we never find Blane this summer? This city's not that big."

Brian snorted. "Andrew McCarthy? The dude from *St. Elmo's Fire*?"

Monica nodded.

"That guy looks like Sam, with the way he cuts his hair."

The ice in Eleanor's veins cracked.

Monica barked a laugh. "He does not."

"Yeah, he does," Brian retorted. "Look at the picture."

Jennifer gasped and sat up straight. "Oh, gosh, he really does!"

Monica studied the VHS case and laughed again. "Huh, maybe so. Whatcha think, Len? Was it Sam you met at Mac's that first weekend?"

"Yep!"

The word burst out of her. She leapt to her feet, out of her mind. "Yeah, sure was. It was totally Sam I met at Mac's. I never told you because—I don't know—but hell yes, it was."

She realized she was pacing. She realized everyone was staring. She couldn't stop now. "Met him, made out with him in a listening booth, fell… fell in… all this summer, and you didn't even know. None of you knew."

"I knew," Alex murmured.

"Me too," Jennifer and Brian chorused.

"Well, what the fuck ever. It doesn't matter now, huh? Fling time is over. Time to settle down and marry his good little wife, Trish. Who needs passion? Time to grow up and get on with life."

She choked, doubling in half and covering her mouth, afraid she was about to be physically ill. No one moved or spoke.

Eleanor forced herself back upright and turned toward Monica, but tears blurred her vision. "You told her to. You said she should…" She winced and squeezed her eyes shut.

Monica's voice was as pale as her face. "Oh, Len, I didn't know."

"I know you didn't."

She wept then and dug her hands into her hair. Ragged, panicked breaths tore from her lungs. Finally, she sucked in enough air to gasp, "I gotta go. I-I can't be here to see when she… when they—oh, god, I have to go. Now. Al… Al, take me to the bus station. I can't be here anymore."

"No, Lenny, wait, we'll figure it out. We'll talk to Sam—I can call Houston's and ask—" Monica rushed toward her in a jumble of desperate pleas.

But Eleanor held up one hand, suddenly stoic. "No."

She glanced around and tried to lift her lips into a smile. The stricken looks trained on her didn't help. "No, it's time. Guys, I love you. Take care, okay? Thank you, really, for everything. Alex, please, let's just go."

He nodded once and stood. Eleanor looked at Monica. Her friend was as broken as she'd ever seen her, and she pulled her close, hugging her fiercely. "I love you most. Always," she whispered into her hair.

But she didn't look back when she walked out of that room.

On her bedroom floor—on the floor of the room she'd been staying in, *This is not your home*—was her suitcase, already filled with clothes and essentials. It startled her to realize she must've packed this afternoon before she slept because she absolutely didn't remember doing so. Nevertheless, she snapped the case shut and barely broke stride out to Alex's car. Her purse held the bus ticket she'd bought ages ago, but she checked it anyway while he started the engine.

"Eleanor." His tone was soft, too gentle.

She sniffled. "Look, if you'll just take any crap I left behind and put it in my car, it can all stay at Gran's until I decide what to do with it."

"You're coming back in the spring. And Monica almost certainly won't let me move your stuff out."

Eleanor took a shaky breath, but her throat closed. "Oh, Al, how can I come back here? How can I look at him—look at them—and keep myself together? Years will pass. She'll have his babies, little auburn-haired kids. She'll sit around complaining about how he never puts his socks in the hamper or some shit, oblivious to how good she has it, never seeing how she... how much I..."

"Love him," he whispered, and she broke down. "Holy shit, you *really* love him."

Eleanor wept into her palms as they drove through the streets. Abruptly Alex pulled to the shoulder and parked.

"Eleanor," he said urgently. He fished in the glove compartment for a paper towel she could use as tissue. "Elle, maybe he refused her. Have you thought of that?"

"Why the hell would he? She was right. They have history, and it's time to settle down. Why would he refuse her after all these years?"

He laughed and squeezed her shoulder. "Because for as in love as you are, Sam is even worse off for you."

"No," she bawled. The scratchy blue towel in her fist was already soaked.

"Oh, yeah, sis. If you need proof—and you don't beyond the way he looks at you—then Atlanta is it. And I think you know that."

She had known it. But that didn't stand up to: "Five years, Alexander. He had a ring. Maybe he still does. Maybe he kept it."

Alex didn't have an answer for that.

They got to the bus station in silence, and he helped her into the waiting room. She had half an hour before departure. She tried to shoo him away, but he shot her a look and sat down on the bench, elbows on thighs, head hung low.

"Goddammit, sis, please come back," he mumbled finally. "I can't lose you again. I love you too much. You're my damn hero."

She whipped to him. "I am not. You've got that backwards."

He twisted his lips, the male version of her own skeptical face. "Nah, not really. You and Monica were always so damn cool. I loathed how cool you were. It wasn't fair for my baby sister to be my model of hip, with your music and your smartass jokes. There I was, plodding along, trying to be Greg Field's son respectably despite zero interest in football, and you… ugh."

Eleanor finally smiled.

Alex chuckled. "Anyway, I hated how much I admired your coolness. But then you endured that hell year and came out of it still cool."

"I was a mess. I would've fallen apart without you. You saved me."

His eyes flickered over her face. "I did what I could. Getting you to Nashville is one of my greatest accomplishments. It was the first moment I felt like my own man. Like I could make a call to do the right thing even if it wasn't the 'proper' thing. Like I could stand up and take care of my people."

She wiped a single tear away. "I take care of myself now because you helped me when I couldn't. Because you looked out for me. You did right, Al. I was a wreck."

He bit his lips and swallowed hard. Alex's green eyes were bright as he shook his head and continued. "If I helped, you took it and fucking ran with it. You got yourself a life. And then, god, you went to fucking Peru, and I just had to admit that I never met anyone as incredible as you are. Dammit," he added gruffly.

Eleanor quit battling the tears leaking out of her eyes.

"You've been my hero since I was old enough to understand the word. I'm going to miss you, brother."

"Then come home. Time will fade this hurt if that's what's meant to happen. Your friends adore you. This is where you should be."

She exhaled and dropped her head. "I can't think about it now. I need space and time. I need to throw myself into this thing and forget him. I'll… I'll know better in the spring, okay? And Al? Don't expect to hear from me for a while. I'll have to get some paychecks before I can get a phone line. But do know I love you. And I'll miss you every day—just like I did in Peru."

He crushed her into a hug just as they called her bus number. "I'll see you in the spring, sis."

Tears slipped down her cheeks and soaked her shirt through a long, sleepless night. She didn't even bother with her Walkman. When dawn lit the hills of West Virginia, she sighed and whispered,

"A new day."

34

SAM

Sam handled the GTO like he was at the Indy 500. Damn Trish's insistence that he pick her up at her parent's house in the boonies. It took him 45 minutes to make it back to town after their clusterfuck dinner.

He practically did a hockey-stop park in front of the girls' place and almost forgot to take the keys out of the ignition in his race to the door. He skidded straight down the hall to the den, narrowly catching himself from falling face-first into the room thanks to a last-second grab on the doorjamb.

Three pairs of eyes looked up. Monica, Dylan, and Brian fixed dulled stares on him.

It was then that Sam realized two things. One, he had passed Alex's car at the end of their block. Jennifer had been beside him. And, two, Eleanor's room had been empty when he ran down the hall.

"She's gone."

His voice echoed in the silent room. It wasn't a question. Three heads bobbed. He looked around, seeing them but not, then turned and went home. Those two words rattled in his chest the whole way. Sam waffled between denial and certainty with every quarter mile. By the time he parked, certainty and nauseous regret had won out.

Brian's El Camino screeched to a stop just behind him in the driveway. Sam glared at the headlights and set his jaw.

He jumped out with his shoulders square, but Brian was already out and storming toward his brother.

"What the fuck, Sam?" he shouted. "The fuck were you thinking, going right back to that—"

"Stop. Stop right there. You don't know shit about this. I never went back. She showed up here this afternoon. She was throwing herself on me in front of Mom and Dad and telling me we needed to talk. She wanted to have dinner—what should I have done?"

"Told her to fuck off," he snarled.

Sam held up both palms and rasped an angry laugh. "Yeah. Guess I should've. Fucked that up pretty good, didn't I? So goddamn nice all the time, putz that I am. I figured… you know how she is. I didn't want her to flip out or go crying to the girls about how I wouldn't see her, making drama here on the last weekend—"

"She did go to the girls."

Sam paled. "She met Elle?"

Brian shrugged, clearly unsure of the details.

Sam wiped his face with his palm and sighed. "I thought, get her out of our hair. Give her one more dinner. Let her tell me whatever she thinks she needs to. Hell, I seriously thought she was going to say she was getting married or something about school. I'm a huge fool, obviously. I just—I never thought she'd—we were over. I was fucking glad, Brian. I was glad from the moment it happened. And then I met Elle, and…"

He wiped his face again. "I had no idea what kind of mess I was walking into. I just wanted to keep her away from the group."

The concrete was warm when Sam dropped to his ass,

head between his knees. His twin came and leaned with his back against his, a pose they'd done since toddlerhood when one of them needed support.

Brian lolled his head back, touching their skulls together. "Sam," he whispered.

"Don't say it."

He didn't.

Sam gazed into the night. Ahead of him, he could envision the autumn. Studying in Knoxville, throwing himself into his classes while the leaves changed and football season began. Coming home for Christmas break, maybe working at the radio station again. Springtime in Tennessee as the flowers bloomed and the weather warmed, promising summer and his future.

His future. Which now held no Elle.

The first time in my life I got it right. And I let it go. For what? Politeness? Being nice?

"Forget fuck Trish, man. Fuck *me*."

"Yep," Brian replied.

35

ELEANOR

She shivered in the phone booth and toyed with the stack of quarters on top of the black box. Even though this phone was just down from her apartment in a quiet Brooklyn neighborhood, Eleanor had still brought a towel soaked in bleach to sanitize the receiver. Public phones in NYC were gross in her opinion. Eating lunch caked in Peruvian mud was one thing. Putting a piece of plastic to her mouth that god-knows-who else had breathed on was another.

He answered on the second ring.

Eleanor's face split into a grin. "Merry Christmas."

"Len? Sis, is that you?" Alex's pitch rose two octaves before he laughed. "God, it's good to hear your voice."

Eleanor hadn't bothered to get a phone. She figured it was an easy cost-saver, and New York was expensive. She'd written Alex a letter every week since leaving, but this was the first time they'd spoken since August.

After the shock of hearing her voice, Alex bombarded her with questions about how things were going.

Things were great. The internship was great, and Eleanor was good. She talked about living in downtown Brooklyn, a tiny sublet in Brooklyn Heights, and her job on the Upper East Side. Alex listened and hummed in understanding, thanks to a map she'd sent in an early letter. Explaining the boroughs to someone who'd never been there was difficult without context, but it was clear he'd studied up. He wanted to know how taking the subway was. She laughed and promised him it wasn't as scary as the movies made it seem.

"Are you working today?" he asked.

"Al, it's Christmas. The interns have the week off until New Year."

He laughed and put on a deep Georgia drawl to say, "I didn't even know those Yankees celebrated Christmas."

She giggled but then said, "Oh, no. Christmas is amazing here!"

She rambled on about how beautiful the city was in the fall and at the holidays, gushed about the Rockefeller tree and all the storefronts, and finished with, "You really will have to see it someday. I could talk about it for hours and still not describe it well enough."

"I guess I will."

"Anyway, tell me about you." She fed another quarter into the box. Her emphasis on you was pointed. Their correspondence had deliberately featured no questions about anyone outside of him and their grandparents. Not even Jennifer had been mentioned because Alex understood what she needed.

Alex recapped what she already knew: he'd left the firm he'd clerked for and joined a smaller one committed to environmental law. It was far less money than a climbing partner would make, but it also wasn't as cutthroat and didn't require 80-hour workweeks. Already Eleanor could hear by the tone of his voice that it had been a good decision.

Alex finished reporting on work and cleared his throat. "So."

Eleanor plunked in another quarter, forgot about her

frozen nose, and listened carefully. "So?" she echoed when he didn't speak.

"So, I've got some news. I'm, ha, getting married."

Eleanor suspected she caused one of the many cracks in the glass of the phone booth with her shout of excitement. She burst into frenzied babble, demanding details and shrieking congratulations all in one mess.

Alex laughed through her noise until she quieted. Then, he said, "I asked her this morning when we were, um…"

"In bed?" Eleanor grinned even harder at his inability to say that to her. Always the gentleman.

"Well, yeah," he said gruffly, then told her about asking for Jen's father's blessing last week. Eleanor was about to ask if they'd thought about a date when there was a scuffle on his end.

"Len?" came Jennifer's breathless voice.

Hearing her stopped Eleanor's heart in a way that talking with Alex hadn't. Jennifer's sweetness rocketed her back to summertime and all that came with it.

Her throat closed up. "Hey, Jennifer. Congratulations, girl!"

"Oh, Eleanor, I'm so happy," she gushed, near tears. "I can't believe I'm going to get married."

Eleanor's eyes stung with a weird mix of joy and raw jealousy. She heard the subtext of Jennifer's words: *Someone promised to love me forever.* How could the selfish part of her not ache? How could she not burn, even just for one second, with desperate, yawning loneliness?

How could she not wonder if another wedding had taken place that season?

The joy, of course, won out. Eleanor laughed and

scratched at the wool cap on her head. "I knew y'all would get married the night you met," she teased, an obvious embellishment but not too farfetched. "So, when are you doing it?"

"Depends on when you're coming home."

Silence stretched over the line until the operator asked for more money. Eleanor clinked the quarter in and cleared her throat. "Oh, uh."

"Eleanor, you are totally my first bridesmaid behind my sister. You're going to be my sister! And if it weren't for you, well. Do I need to explain it further?"

Eleanor smiled as her heart warmed to the idea. "I'm going to be your sister. Holy crap, that's awesome! Um, so, but—"

Jennifer squealed, then said, "This is what I'm thinking. God, it's so fast to think about dates, but whatever. The school year's done in early May, and June won't work."

Eleanor cringed. She braced to hear, "We don't want to overlap Sam and Trish's wedding."

But Jennifer threw a curve. "I'm going to England—oh, shoot, I didn't tell you that either! I'm going to study Shakespeare for a month."

"That's amazing!"

"I know! But anyway, I guess all that means that ideally, we'd do the wedding in late May. You finish your internship—when? First of May?"

She swallowed hard. "I do, but I'm… I'm hoping something works out for June, so…" Eleanor bit her tongue and blew out a breath. "Sure, Jen. I can be in Nashville in late May."

"Perfect. I'll let you know the exact date later, but let's

definitely say May. Ahh, how exciting!"

"So excited for you, girl." Even though no one could see, Eleanor forced a smile with her words. *You deserve this happiness, Jen. But I deserve happiness, too. I'll figure it out one day.*

Eleanor kept them both on the line for another dollar's worth of time, then said her goodbyes. It was snowing while she walked through the silent streets, looking into the windows at the Christmas trees and warm lights and families spending the day together.

She'd never felt more alone in her life.

36

ELEANOR

Since she arrived in New York, Eleanor had thrown herself into the work. She knew it was a desperate attempt to keep her thoughts off what she'd left behind in Nashville. It also made her internship extremely successful. She had always had a knack for working with sweets. Chocolate most of all. It was as if she innately understood the science of them. But she'd never thought of herself as anything remarkable, and yet her bosses saw her as a star pupil. When she "graduated" from the program, she was offered two jobs on the same day. One was in New York and one in Chicago. Of course, Dianne at Sweetie's was practically planning on her return. Eleanor promised to consider her options, but there was no rush because she had won *another* internship that would start in June. This one made her heart flutter every time she thought of it.

Paris. Six weeks at a chocolate shop in Paris, France, learning the trade. An apartment on the Left Bank of the Seine. A dream come true.

If only she didn't have to go to Nashville first. That knowledge made her heart flutter, too. In a far less pleasant way.

She stuck around New York for a couple weeks after graduation to play tourist in the slightly warmer springtime. Finally, she put herself on a bus that got her to Tennessee the Wednesday before the wedding.

Jennifer picked her up since Alex was working. Eleanor didn't expect to see her and Monica get out of the car. As soon as she did, tears choked her. They crushed her in a screaming hug. But when they pulled back, Monica leveled her with a serious expression.

"Hey," she whispered.

Eleanor pursed my lips. "Who are you hey-ing?"

She grabbed Eleanor's suitcase. "My best friend. My best friend who I…"

"Missed? Love? Yep, cool, hey, back at you." Eleanor refused to let her open the topic.

The ladies didn't talk much until they were at the house. Eleanor sat at the kitchen table with a glass of tea and the taste of nostalgia strong on her tongue. "God, was it a year ago?" she muttered, almost not realizing she'd said it aloud. "I feel so much older."

Monica and Jennifer traded a look. "Elle, I think you should know," Jennifer began hesitantly.

But Eleanor jumped up. "I've been on a bus for a literal twenty-four hours, ladies. Can we cut the heavy news and gossip, please? I don't want to hear about anything but what Jennifer needs to have the best damn day of her life. I don't care about anything but that. I'm not here to hang out or make caramels or watch cartoons. I'm not here to catch up with the gang. I'm here for you, Jen, and Alex. I don't want to know anything but where I should stand, what I should wear, and how I can help. And then I'm off again on Monday morning."

That final declaration was decided in the moment. Her Paris internship didn't start for two weeks, but she could easily go back to New York and find a short-term lease.

Monica hid her face with a moan, but Eleanor couldn't comfort her. Jennifer's eyes sparkled with unshed tears. "But Eleanor," she whispered.

Eleanor set her jaw and crossed her arms. "No, Jen."

She nodded and swallowed. "Are you still making my cake?"

That made her smile. "Heck yeah, I am. I've got the plans all ready. You're going to swoon. I, uh, thought I'd go over to Gran and Gramp's house tomorrow. They have a fridge in their garage that I can store it in. I'll probably spend the night there and meet you for the rehearsal Friday night."

"You don't want to stay here." Monica's voice was dead, her eyes cast to the floor.

Eleanor touched her shoulder, and she looked up. "Yes, I do, actually. I'll be here Friday night until I leave Monday if that's cool."

They gazed at each other. "You hate me," Monica whispered.

"I never did, and I never could," Eleanor said honestly. "I'm just… I want to think about the wedding."

Jennifer took her to her grandparents' house. Eleanor's car had been stored in their garage. But as Alex had predicted, all her leftover belongings were still at Monica's place. She spent Wednesday night letting her grandmother stuff her with tuna casserole and strawberry shortcake. Then, she slept like a log in the cool, crisp sheets of their guest bedroom.

Thursday, Gran was adorably curious as Eleanor set to work. They took Gran's Lincoln town car across town to a specialty bakeshop. Gran's awe at her expertise had Eleanor hiding a cheesy smile. Then, Gran watched her comman-deer her kitchen with the same kind of wonder. When Elea-nor caught her wide eyes, she laughed shyly.

"Good gracious, sweetheart. You have grown up so much."

"It's just what I learned to do." Eleanor shrugged as she tied her apron.

"It's just that you've found a calling."

She bit her lip. "Maybe so. Thanks, Gran."

"Tell me how to help."

When the cake came out, perfect tiers iced in fondant with detail of roses and strawberries ringing each layer, El-eanor had to admit that she had outdone herself. She and Gran cleared out the racks in the fridge and stored her cre-ation with utmost care. By then, it was late. They fetched Gramps from the yard and had dinner out.

* * *

After breakfast Friday morning, she reminded her grand-parents that she'd return the next day for the cake, then kissed them goodbye and took off. The morning was her own, so she went to the mall to buy some new makeup and pantyhose. She wound up getting her nails done at the sa-lon, just for fun. When she was done, she jumped back in the car. Butterflies began to beat in her stomach because she knew damn well where she was headed.

"Woof!"

"I know exactly why you're here."

Patchouli, weed, and vinyl filled her nose as she stepped inside the dimly lit record store. Affection and memories flooded her. This was truly one of her most favorite places in the world. She strolled down the aisle with Myrtle at her heels.

"Oh, do you? And why, exactly, am I here?"

Mac had a new stool. This one had a back and swiveled. He spun it around and crossed his arms. "*Kiss Me, Kiss Me, Kiss Me.*"

She snorted as she leaned on the counter in her usual pose. "Won't your wife object?"

He chuckled and scratched his beard. "Hey, you know what I always say: love a lot a little, not a little a lot."

Eleanor pursed her lips and arched a brow. "You always say that, huh?"

"Yep, sure do. It's total bullshit, of course, but still."

They laughed.

"So, Miss Len, did you bring your cash, or will you be buying this in magic treats?"

"I have cash." Eleanor whipped out her wallet. She paused for a second as she unsnapped the trifold. *Maybe it's time to get something new, something classy. I've had this thing since I first came to Nashville. It's me, but maybe it's time to change.*

She shook herself out of her thoughts and paid him. Mac slid The Cure's newest album, released just that week, over to her. The cover was an extreme close-up of a woman's mouth with red lipstick.

"How is it?" she asked.

"It's strong if you like The Cure. Go have a listen."

Eleanor loved him for not batting an eye at her presence, even though she'd been gone so long. She loved that she could walk in and be herself and that that didn't change. With a grin, she jogged to the row of booths.

A new album from her favorite band was so what she needed to chill out before the weekend. She put her feet on the bench and floated with the music. Afterward, she had to go see Jennifer and get her bridesmaid's dress. Jennifer had had her send measurements of every conceivable part of her body back in March, so she knew it would fit. Once she had the dress, she'd have to hurry to the rehearsal, then dinner and toasts and the start of the flurry of a wedding.

But there, for the hour or so of the album, Eleanor existed solely inside the music.

With a happy sigh, she lifted the needle after the last song and sheathed the disc. She gave the lips a little kiss of her own. "You're my new favorite," she said firmly.

She flipped out the lights and stepped out of the booth— then froze where she stood.

At the end of the hall was a silhouette she'd know anywhere. That he was there at the exact time she was both stopped her heart and made her think, *Of course he is.*

"Oh, might've forgotten to mention Len was here." Mac's shout broke the frozen moment.

Sam's head snapped up from the album, then swiveled toward her while Mac chuckled. She tried to grab a breath, but he strode forward. He didn't stop walking until she had backed into the booth.

Eleanor tilted her head to look up at him. He was the same. So the same, except— "You cut your hair."

Why was that the first thing I said? Why did I speak first? Dammit.

But she was right. His shaggy hair had been cropped close on the neck, and he now wore a side part, sleeker but still plenty thick. It looked as soft and as tuggable as ever.

"I did. For the wedding. You, uh, you don't have bangs anymore."

The sound of his voice sent shivers down her spine, but Eleanor nodded. She touched the layers of hair that started on her shoulder and feathered down to the middle of her back.

"What are you doing here?" he asked after a beat.

They held up the album at the same time.

His lips tilted up in a completely unsurprised expression. So did hers. He looked at her copy, held proudly to her chest, and smiled a little more. "Your nails are pretty," he murmured.

Eleanor flashed back to their first time in that booth, to her chocolate-caked fingers. She refused to make a comment to recall that moment, but she was certain that was the implication in his words.

"Thanks," she whispered.

They traded a cautious glance. Eleanor shuffled backward and hit her calves on the bench. Sam stepped back, too, and bumped the record stand. "Smooth," he muttered as he rubbed his hip.

"You always were."

They traded another look. This one stretched on and on.

Their first night together, through the long hours of the thunderstorm, they had lain in each other's arms, listened to the rain, and talked. It was then that Eleanor had begun to understand what he meant when he said he and Brian could talk without speaking. It was then that she'd started to hear him through his looks, too.

Maybe she didn't share DNA with Sam. Maybe she'd never be able to appreciate the deep connection between him and his twin. But standing there in that tiny booth, Eleanor and Sam absolutely talked with their eyes. And what they said was the same exact thing: *I fucked up. I'm sorry.*

Eleanor shifted and looked away, unable to take any more unshielded truth. Unable, too, to stand in that tiny space with him anymore. "Excuse me."

He let her walk past. He let her push the door open and step out. But before she reached the end of the hallway, he stopped her with these words: "So, what next?"

Her skin flushed with irritation. *I'm in town for a few days to help my beloved brother get married. Why do I have to be the one to answer that question?* Her shoulders bunched up. She didn't turn around as she snipped, "Guess that depends on if you're married already. Or did y'all decide to wait until June?"

His warm hand rested on her shoulder, and her knees almost buckled. Sam turned her around slowly to meet the bemused smirk on his beautiful mouth. He chuckled. "Oh, Elle. You know the answer to that."

About a week after she arrived in New York, Eleanor had woken in the middle of the night with the unshakable idea that Alex had been right, that Sam had refused Trish. It had felt so certain in her gut, and yet she'd been too afraid to ask or even think on it.

But now, she refused to admit a single thing she didn't know for sure. "Do I? She wanted her ring, Sam. She said you'd want to get back together."

That smirk got worse. It was wickedly delicious. "Come on. After us, there's no going back. Really, I thought you knew me better."

Target: hit. Eleanor felt the impact of his words in the center of her chest.

His hand on her shoulder squeezed gently. His tone softened a little. "If you needed to hear me say it out loud, why didn't you just call?"

"I don't know. I guess I had to go through the pointless forest." It was a reference to *The Point*, the album Mac had given her on that dark day. Her voice was barely audible, but a burst of applause from the front of the store startled them both.

"That's my girl!" Mac shouted.

Shit. You're not here for this. This is too messy. Get out! Warning bells blared in her brain. Sam's shoulders lowered, and his smile deepened. She inhaled sharply and fixed an unsmiling look on him. "I've got to go. I can't be late for the rehearsal."

And with that, she ran out of the store.

Even as she started the car and motored away, Eleanor knew for sure that this was the last time she could run from Sam Greene. She had just burned up the last of her strength—her stubbornness—and, no matter what happened, she could never again find it in her to walk away from him.

But that doesn't mean he won't walk away from you after all your running, Eleanor.

37

SAM

Well, screw listening to the new album. Sam wandered back to Mac and leaned on the counter. He shook his head at Mac's gleeful grin.

"What did that mean, the Pointless Forest?"

"Shit, man, you need to watch that movie. It means she had to go on the journey, pointless though it might've been, to discover her truths."

"What do you think she discovered?"

He looked at his nails. "Probably nothing she didn't know already," he muttered, then looked over at Sam.

"I'll see you around, man."

"Stay cool, Sammy."

Brian's car was in the driveway when he got home. It was family dinner night. Instead of going to the apartment first, Sam parked by his parents' house and let himself in the back door. His brother was opening a jar of spaghetti sauce for Mom in the kitchen. Sam waved to them both and wandered into the living room to collapse on the couch.

"Are you tired, love?"

He opened his eyes at Nana's gentle drawl. She'd been staying with his parents for the past month after having cataract surgery in Nashville. Sam had returned home from Knoxville two weeks ago. Having Nana around had been one of the few bright spots in that time. Everything else reminded him of last summer.

"Not really, Nana. I'm just thinking." He sat up as she settled her tiny frame in the armchair. Sinking his face into both his hands, he sighed deeply and peeked at her.

She narrowed her eyes, then smiled. "You just saw Eleanor," she murmured.

Sam's hands dropped hard. "How-how could you know that?"

She shrugged one shoulder. The cheeky little move was so out of character, but her tone was as casual as if they were talking about a chance of rain. "I had a feeling you were going to see her today."

Nana knew Sam hadn't spoken to Elle since last summer. She knew it had torn him up and chewed at every waking moment that he didn't devote to study in Knoxville. That he had no idea where they stood. She *didn't* know about Mac's, or the fact that the wedding tomorrow was Elle's brother's. She didn't even know Elle was in town. Sam himself hadn't been entirely sure until he saw her.

To say he was surprised was an understatement.

Nana smiled again and picked up her knitting. "That's very good news."

Sam shook his head. He couldn't stop analyzing how the hell she could have guessed—known? — such a thing. Finally, he said, "I wouldn't call it good news. It didn't go great. Certainly no big revelations."

Nana shook her head. "What revelation would you expect, honey? You already know all that you need to." She put down the knitting and smiled. "Tell you what. You take me for a drive in your car—a real drive, I want you to go fast—and after that, we'll sort everything out."

"Nana, I'm not driving fast with you in the car," Sam

grumbled. She had asked him for this regularly since he got home. At first, he thought she was joking, but she wouldn't let it go.

Brian popped into the room and tossed Sam a breadstick. "What's up?"

"I want Sam to take me on a fast drive," Nana said.

His brows shot up. "Nan, that's not safe."

She tittered. "At my age, do you think that matters? I've lived long enough." She pinned her gaze on Sam. "Come on, Sam."

Sam conferred silently with Brian, who laughed. "I'm in."

They snuck her out the front, yelling to Mom that they were just running to the grocery. The Greenes lived on a quiet street. One road over was a straight lane, not very long but a dead-end that would work nicely. Nana buckled into the front seat, Bry took the back, and Sam turned them onto the lane.

He frowned at her and got a bright smile back. Brian slapped his shoulder and told him to go for it. Sam took a deep breath, dumped the clutch, and floored it.

They only hit 60, but that was quite enough for Sam. He eased on the brake and stopped a few feet from the end of the road.

The car was silent. Nana's hand fluttered to her heart, and Sam's blood ran cold. But then she turned huge, dazzled eyes on both of them.

"Oh, my, I haven't drag-raced in forty years. How wonderful!"

Brian howled while Nana laughed. Sam at least exhaled. Back at the house, she waved Sam into the guest bedroom and shooed Brian away. Nana went to the dresser and fussed around while he waited, unsure what they were doing. When she turned back to him, she wore another one of those placid, all-knowing smiles.

"You already know where you're headed, Sam. This is all you need now, sweetheart." She pressed a little velvet bag into his palm and had him bend down so she could kiss his cheek.

"Sweet boy," she whispered affectionately.

When Sam opened the bag back at his apartment that night, his pulse stopped, then burst into a gallop. But then he cinched the drawstring tight and set his jaw.

"You're right, Nana. I know exactly where I'm headed."

He peeked in the bag again and swallowed hard.

"Fuck. I hope I do, at least."

38

ELEANOR

"Oh, my god, this dress."

Monica and Eleanor took one look at each other and dissolved into helpless laughter. They collapsed on the bed, exactly like they did when they used to get high before society parties.

Monica kicked her legs in the air. The thigh-high slit in her gown gave Eleanor a full view of her underwear, which only made her laugh harder. But when the lace hem of the peach satin dress rustled, Eleanor squealed for her not to let it rip.

"Shit, you're right," Monica gasped. They struggled to their feet and caught their breaths.

Monica examined herself in the mirror. The bodices were tightly fitted. Ruffled lace created an off-the-shoulder neckline. "It's like, half eighties glam thanks to the peach satin, and half *Gone With the Wind* with the lace and swishy ankle-length skirt."

Eleanor exploded into giggles again. "Moonwalking in hoop skirts. Fantastic. Oh, but wait. You forgot the best part."

She set Monica's floppy peach hat on her head, then placed her own on. The girls stepped into peach-colored satin-heeled sandals and looked in the mirror again.

"At least she didn't require an updo," Monica muttered. "Jesus, our kids are going to love these photos."

"If it makes Jennifer happy, we're happy," Eleanor reminded her best friend.

The day was bright and sunny, perfect for a spring wedding. Jennifer was a doll in her big white dress and veil. Every few minutes, she held a handkerchief to her eyes and sniffled, no matter what was going on. Everything was a rush of instructions and flurried motion once they got to the church. Before Eleanor knew it, she was clutching a bouquet of peach roses and baby blue hydrangea, step-stepping up the aisle to organ music.

Of course she spotted Sam right away. He might as well have been the only person in the church for the way she picked him out. Dressed in a sharp gray suit and black tie, he was seated near the front with Brian, who mouthed a welcome home when he saw her. Beside him, Dylan grinned and waved, too, and Eleanor smiled.

Her brother, so serious, so handsome in his tuxedo, made tears sting her eyes as soon as she got to the front of the church. He twisted his lips when he caught her eye, but otherwise, he didn't crack his stoic stance.

When the doors opened and "Here Comes the Bride" began to play, the whole church turned to watch. But Eleanor watched Alex. She saw the way his lips disappeared, then fell open with a gentle sigh. The way his entire face softened at the sight of his bride. An adoring, dazed smile curled his lips. He nervously straightened his tie, and Eleanor's heart melted.

Will someone look at me like that one day?

She couldn't resist a glance at Sam. He was watching Jennifer and her father, but he turned as soon as her gaze landed on him. Navy eyes darkened even as one brow lifted.

Eleanor looked away fast.

The ceremony was beautiful but short. The crew posed for pictures, then finally made their way to the reception at a nearby hotel.

The wedding party was seated at a long banquet table for dinner, so Monica and Eleanor spent the meal catching up and laughing together. Monica shot a pointed look at her parents, and Eleanor nodded. Alex had made it clear that their mother's job was to stay out of the way. He'd told Eleanor via letter that he'd almost not invited them. It had been a lot of discussion with Jennifer, soul-searching, and explicit instructions before he made his decision.

Mrs. Field seemed to be content, though. Eleanor had said hello to her at the rehearsal the day before, but no more had been exchanged. Her dad was the one who was shining. He laughed joyfully and toasted the couple with kind, beautiful words. It was an interesting change. Her whole life, Eleanor's dad had stepped aside to his wife's desires. She appreciated the new dynamic.

But dinner dragged out too long. One course followed another, with pauses for toasting in between. Over an hour had passed before the entrée was served. Eleanor itched in her seat, tired of smiling and posing all afternoon. Tired of being among so much joy when her heart just wasn't in it. She'd known joy, and she'd run away. Eleanor accepted her choice, but it didn't mean she wanted to revel it.

She picked at a few bites of chicken, then tossed her napkin on the table and told Monica she'd be back before they served fruit.

She couldn't be sure if she looked at Sam, or if he was looking at her and drew her attention. Either way, as she strode to exit the ballroom, their eyes connected—and he stood up. She turned away quickly but didn't hurry. If anything, her strides slowed.

He was behind her before she got to the hallway to the bathroom. His fingertips touched her spine to steer her to the right, into the nearest door. She didn't argue.

There were no lights on in the room they slipped into. The only illumination was the glowing orange sunset through open French doors at one end. A fresh spring breeze snuck in and brought the scent of sweetgrass and roses. When Eleanor's eyes adjusted, she could see that the space was smaller than the dining room they were eating in. A hardwood floor clacked under her sandals.

They walked across half the floor, closer to the terrace, before Sam stopped. She turned to face him.

Eleanor cursed the audible hitch in her breath as she gazed at him. She knew he heard it by the glint in his gaze and the way his attention darted to her lips. *Just once, just freaking once, could I not be so fucking obvious about what you do to me?*

"Dammit, why can't I be cool around you?" she asked bitterly.

"Are chicks supposed to be cool?"

She huffed to keep from laughing. "They definitely are. They're supposed to be cool as cucumbers, aloof and mysterious."

"You, Beautiful, are quite a mystery."

Beautiful. That moniker turned her insides to jelly, but she set her jaw. "I am not. I'm obvious as hell and have been since go."

He hummed. "And what are you so obvious about?"

"How… how much I…"

Sam hooked her chin and tilted her face up to his. With his other hand, he lifted her hat and tossed it away. It floated to the floor, and she smiled as she watched its landing. The brief, whimsical distraction gave her a tiny relief from the heart-pounding angst running through her veins.

"Say it, Elle," he murmured.

"No."

His hand cupped her cheek. Like always, his touch stilled her from hair to toes. A warm, liquid security blanket wrapped itself around her heart. Her eyes fluttered shut. She knew her breath sounded like a thoroughbred after the Kentucky Derby.

"Eleanor," Sam urged, so she reluctantly opened her eyes. "Eleanor, you already know this, but I want it said aloud: nothing has come between us. Nothing *will* come between us as far as I'm concerned. You know that, don't you Beautiful?"

Both hands held her face now. She sucked on her lip and watched him watch her. Finally, she nodded. "I know that."

He exhaled more air than Eleanor thought lungs could hold. Sam rested his forehead on hers and opened his eyes. "Say it, then," he dared, then pressed his lips to her cheek.

His mouth seared her skin, so hot that she gasped. Sam hummed and kissed the other cheek.

"Sam," she croaked, and somehow, they were closer. She stood between his feet. He slipped his hands from her face to the back of her head to cradle her. Eleanor lifted her mouth and found his waiting for a chaste kiss.

"Wait, wait." Eleanor opened her eyes and leaned away from him. "Wait, no, I…"

"You what?"

"I'm leaving again. Monday—maybe. Definitely before the end of the month."

He froze all over. "You aren't." Abruptly, he stepped away. Sam groaned a sigh and rubbed his face. "Oh, Eleanor, you're not."

Silence was her answer.

He finally looked up. His brows ticked together in a self-loathing look of pain. "It's never going to be enough, is it? I'm not enough. Of course I'm not. God, so foolish, thinking you could ever..."

He rubbed his face, pressing the heels of his palms into his eyes with another groaning sigh.

"I love you, Sam Greene."

The words caught on the wind and swirled around them in that empty room, not a whisper but not a shout. Just her voice, clear, and even, and sure—so, so sure.

Eleanor wet her lips. "I love you," she repeated, just to feel the breeze thicken with it.

But Sam didn't move. "Finish the thought. Give me the but."

It cut deep, the knowledge that this was her moment. If this was a movie, it would feature music swelling and her in his arms. This wasn't a movie, though. This was Eleanor Field's life. And since it was, the only thing swelling to crescendo was that one word:

But.

It was a long road to this moment. Until those wild, passionate weeks last summer, Eleanor never thought a moment like this would come for her. But she'd suspected all along that if it did come, it would be as twisted as the rest of her heart. One thing she learned over the long bus ride and equally lonely months in the city was that fretting and trying to change reality was useless. She'd been dealt a hand in life, and she would play it. Eleanor could've let everything that brought her to this moment crush her. She could've let Bobby crush her so long ago. She could've let her mother crush her into a life of misery.

She could've let her own doubts crush her last fall.

But what would be the point? It was all still her. Still her life that had to keep going. She could find a way. She could still find things to call a life. She had learned that lesson over and over, but it took falling in love to make it stick.

How ironic. Surrendering my heart taught me to protect it most.

Eleanor looked at the ceiling as tears burned her eyes. "Right. The but."

She walked toward the doors and breathed in the heady spring scent. "But it won't matter. I'll never be wife material—girlfriend material, either, for that matter. I'll never be the nice girl. I'll always be weird. Trish said it that day: stability. That's what you need. I can't promise you that. I can't promise you steadiness or routines. Hell, I'm going to Paris for six weeks. No suitable girl would tell you she loves you and then wing to Paris to make chocolates for a month and a half. That, Sam, is the but."

He'd followed a few paces behind as she wandered around, but he stepped right behind her when she stopped walking. Her name fanned warm on her neck when he murmured, "Elle."

She lifted her head and choked, "All I can promise is that when I say I love you, I mean that you completely hold my heart in your hands. There's no mystery, Sam. I'm a geek for you."

His mouth pressed against the curve of her neck and shoulder. "Elle," he groaned.

"Don't, Sam, I—"

But she couldn't finish. Her breath hitched as his arms circled her waist and pulled her tightly against his chest. His passionate words hissed in her ear. "Don't give me that don't unless you know for damn sure you don't want whatever you're going to say. I'm sick of holding back on the things we both want because we're worried about shoulds. So, if you say don't, say it to me. Say don't when I've displeased you, crossed a line, or generally need to hear it to keep my ego in check. I'm not sure I had an ego before you. But with the way you make me feel and act, I'm sure it'll be needed now and then. Just don't say don't to yourself."

Her voice shook as her pulse exploded. "Now and then?"

"Mm-hmm. Over time. Time where we're together because I don't know how else I'm supposed to live. Because I can stand you traveling to chase your dreams, but after last summer and these past ten months, I'm not embarrassed or shy to admit that I don't have any concept of how my life means something without you in it. Go chase your dreams, Eleanor. Just let me come with you—or come back to me when you're able. It doesn't matter. I love you so much. All I want is for you to be happy. And I know I make you happy, too."

"Sam... come with me."

"To Paris?"

No, everywhere. She nodded.

He squeezed the sips of remaining oxygen from her

lungs. "Yes. Hell yes. I will."

A jumble of joy and logic erupted inside her. "Really? But what will you do while I make chocolate all day? You'll be bored, and—"

"I'll take up photography or read. I'll walk around and wait for you to finish work. Doesn't matter. I'll be with you."

"You'd really come?"

"Of course. Jesus, Elle, I'd follow you anywhere. Didn't I already say that? If you love me like you say, let me prove it."

Her knees buckled, but he held her firmly. "Sam, you—"

"I adore you, Beautiful. I—god, I told you this already, too. There aren't words for what I am about you. I…" he buried his face in her shoulder again, breath fast and ragged. "Elle, you're my—"

"Home."

They said it together and went completely still. Slowly, infinitely slowly, he lifted his head, and she turned to meet his eyes. Except for her blazing hot cheeks, Eleanor was cold all over. Another full-body shake racked her hard. She felt his arms tremble.

"Home," she whispered again.

"Home," he growled.

She spun around. Her hands flew to the slick skin of his shaved jaw. Sam leaned her backward as they melted together. His kiss started wild and new, like slaking a thirst he'd—they'd—held so many months. But it quickly morphed into a continuation of where they'd left off last August. He sucked her lower lip, exactly like he'd done the last time they kissed. Eleanor smiled, then gave it right back.

"I love you," he mumbled with his lip between her teeth.

He dug his fingers into her back. "And, fuck, I want you."

"It's the dress. It turns you on."

He hummed. "It's cute. The hat especially."

She giggled as he kissed down her neck. "It fades my coloring so bad that I look like a natural sponge."

"Come on. It has some merits." His laugh rumbled against her body while his fingers teased at the slit on her thigh.

Eleanor gripped his suit coat as a wave of heat broke between her legs. "No, Sam," she stuttered.

Navy eyes looked up, blazing. "What was that?"

Heat flooded her face. "I-I meant, oh, Sam, I love how you touch me. Don't stop."

His beautiful mouth curled. "Don't worry, I don't intend to."

She smoothed his lapels. "This suit is majorly sexy, by the way."

His bashful, pleased smile stole her breath in the second before his lips were on hers again. "I'd like to think it compliments your… pink," he rasped as his lips trailed along her neckline.

"Peach, silly,"

"What fucking ever."

Eleanor laughed, but her humor died when he kissed her neck once more—and then dropped to his knees.

Goosebumps broke all over her thighs as he kissed her hip and worked down the skirt's slit. Meanwhile, his hand slid up and in. Eleanor moaned. She scrabbled to hold his shoulders so that she didn't collapse. "If you tell me to take off my panties, I am definitely saying don't tempt me."

Sam just laughed and ran his knuckle against the damp

fabric between her legs. His voice was dark and languid. "Are you really?"

She sucked on her lip and met his daring stare. "Well… maybe more like not yet."

"Not yet, huh? Not yet, implying later? Implying that you will say yes to coming home with me? To spending the night in my bed, against the wall of my shower, and—"

"In your bowl chair," she sighed with a grin. Eleanor stepped her feet apart a little wider, and his palm slid up her inner thigh. She forgot all about where they were as she pictured that bowl chair by the window.

"Yes," she groaned. "Please, oh, god, yes."

"You want me to make you come right here on this dance floor, Beautiful? Say the word, and we're doing this."

Dance floor…

Eleanor hummed. Her face was close to melting at his teasing strokes and feathery kisses. "Sam, Sam, just—"

"…and gentlemen, it's almost time for dancing and cake!"

A loud click, followed by a crackling sound and a blazing ray of light, stopped them cold. The wall between their room and the wedding reception was being pulled back. The accordion panels folded fast as chandeliers blazed to life.

"Eleanor? What on Earth are you doing?" Her mother's voice rose over the din of people ignoring them. Thanks to her booming volume, that din died fast.

Sam's hands were gone, but too late. Attention was on them like a magnet. Eleanor stood in the middle of that dance floor with Sam on his knees. Her vision blurred with humiliation.

Oh, god. Ohgod. Kill me now.

She flashed back to the horror of when Mrs. Greene walked into Sam's bedroom that night. *Kind of like that. No, not like that. Like that times a thousand. A million, maybe.*

But Sam didn't flinch. He sat back on his heels and grinned up at her. Clearing his throat, he reached into his pocket and turned his head to the now-silent room.

"Here goes nothing," he said, and then turned back to her.

"Eleanor Field, will you be my wife?"

Someone gasped. Eleanor assumed it was Jennifer, but she wasn't sure. All she could do was gaze down at the gold band with a brilliant teardrop emerald perched on top. Her eyes drifted in slow motion from the gorgeous jewelry to his gorgeous face. She read nervous tension and unfiltered hope in his eyes.

"Don't say no now, Beautiful," he breathed. The right side of his mouth curled as he nodded backward to their audience.

Eleanor whimpered and dropped to her knees. She couldn't speak, but she nodded her head like a Pez dispenser. She held out her arms and collapsed against his chest. Sam caught her and held on tight as applause bounced off the walls.

"Why do you have a ring in your pocket?" she asked into his ear.

"Nana knew I was going to see you today. I'll tell you everything later."

She pushed back enough to look him in the eye. "Are you serious? Did you just ask me to marry you? That wasn't a joke?"

He shook his head. "It wasn't how I had planned to ask. I just had the ring for luck. But hell yes, I'm serious. Be my wife, Eleanor. Be my *home*, Eleanor. And never doubt again what you're worth to me."

Eleanor gazed at him as a stampede of people headed their way. Suddenly, she began to laugh. "Smooth, Greene. Extremely smooth."

"Are husbands supposed to be smooth?"

"Yes, absolutely."

When the crowd circled around them, Eleanor and Sam were too busy laughing. Their foreheads pressed together, and they didn't give a damn about anything else.

EPILOGUE

SAM

A few years later.

Jennifer frowned. "I never realized how violent this show is. Why are these cute little animals always trying to kill each other? Anvils on the head? Bazookas? Why is that funny? What are we teaching our children? Elle, what do you think?"

Elle frowned, too. She rubbed her belly. "I'd never thought about it before, but you're right. It's pretty horrific."

Jennifer beamed and rubbed her own midsection. "Thank you. I'm glad I'm not the only one who thinks so!"

Brian chuckled and stood from the recliner. "Protective moms already. Chill out a little, ladies. *Pee Wee's Playhouse* starts in ten minutes. Nothing nefarious about a manic man-child and his talking furniture, right? Fun for the kiddos and perfect for…" He grabbed the bong off the coffee table and headed toward the back door.

Jennifer stuffed a pillow behind her back and put her head on Alex's shoulder. "It feels weird to watch cartoons without the whole gang. I hope Monica gets home early today. And I hope Dylan remembers my chocolate glazed donut." She giggled.

When they married last year, Monica and Dylan turned the hangout house into their home. It was still the gathering spot. But now that Monica had her Ph.D. in psychology, she

Skye McDonald

worked every other Saturday. Dylan had volunteered to do the donut run since Elle wasn't baking these days.

Sam glanced over at his wife. As ever, just the sight of her made him smile. *My wife. Damn, that doesn't get old.*

Sam and Elle went to Paris and never looked back. No more doubting if their friends would be cool with them together. No more shame or regret over past decisions. No more ifs or should. Just the two of them in deep, total love. They were married in the fall after Paris. Married life had come with the usual growing pains, but they worked through them. Sam's job at the Tennessee Bureau of Investigations had a lot of upward mobility, and Elle had taken over as manager of Sweetie's. Eventually, she would be part owner in the business, too.

When she told him she was pregnant eight and a half months ago, they were drunk with excitement. Sam worried like it was his job and had read every book and article on childbirth he could find. Elle was calmer, but Sam could see how seriously she took the idea of being a mom. She had worked until last week, but since then, she had been more tired than usual. When Sam worried about her napping at 9am, Elle simply laughed and joked about charging the baby rent if it didn't hurry up and come into the world.

Now, he pushed a strand of blonde hair off her face. "How're you doing, Beautiful? Is Sam Junior kicking again?"

Elle smiled and rolled her eyes like he knew she would. "Little Elle is quiet right now. I'm okay. Just tired of being tired."

"I know. We're almost there. And you know I'm kidding about Sam Junior, right?"

She huffed a little laugh. "Of course I do, silly."

"But seriously, David Bowie Greene would be a hella rad name, right?" He grinned.

She put her chin in her hand. "I like the sound of Pat Benatar Greene better. That could be for a boy or girl, to be fair."

They had tossed around names for weeks. Sam had read an article about the growing use of ultrasound to determine a baby's gender in utero. But Dr. Walsh, their OB, had waved that off. "We reserve that for high-risk situations. No reason to think that's you," she'd said.

So, Sam and Elle had decided to wait on a name. Instead, they teased each other with silly ideas. Everything from Spaghetti Greene to homages to their favorite singers and movies had been lobbed between them.

Elle groaned. "Whatever we call it, this kiddo is pressing on all my organs. I'd better go pee before the show starts."

Elle braced her hand on the loveseat's arm to stand. But, as soon as she was on her feet, she staggered. Sam leapt up just as her knees buckled. He caught her under both arms before she collapsed.

"Shit," Elle wheezed while he eased her back to sit. A sheen of sweat made her forehead sparkle.

"What's going on, Elle? I'm right here." Sam palmed her forehead.

"I—my water broke. Call Doctor Walsh. It's time."

Sam was up and running to the kitchen before she finished speaking. He stabbed the phone's buttons with jittery fingers and held his breath as the call rang through. Because it was Saturday morning, their OB/GYN's answering service picked up. He puffed out a hard breath and blurted, "This is Sam Greene. My wife is in labor. I need Dr. Walsh to meet us at the hospital now."

"Yes, sir, we'll contact the doctor. Dr. Walsh's standard instructions are to freshen up, pack your bag, and try to be at the hospital within the hour. No need to panic."

Jennifer flew in, filled a cup with ice water, and disappeared. Sam stretched the phone cord as far as it would go, but he could only peer out into the hallway and down to the den. The back door was open, so he assumed the others were taking care of her.

Before the receptionist could hang up, he said, "Okay, but, um, can you send a message to the doctor? Elle said she felt kind of weird. She looks pale. Are you sure we're okay?"

The receptionist hummed. "I understand. I'll send the message to the doctor. But, Mr. Greene, please remember that nerves are normal at a time like this."

He bit his lip. "Alright, thanks."

Back in the den, Brian was leaning on the wall next to the open back door. He gently swung it open and closed to create a breeze. Alex was on the edge of the sofa cushion. Dylan stood in the room with a box of Krispy Kreme donuts in his hand—Sam hadn't even heard him come in.

Jennifer sat with Elle on the little loveseat while she sipped water. He noticed vaguely that, instead of her maternity pants, she had a towel wrapped around her like a skirt. *Jennifer must've helped her to the bathroom.* The simple thought made his heart swell in gratitude for their friends.

His wife's green eyes locked on him, and Sam flashed back to the first time he saw her in this den. Seated with Brian's arm around her shoulder, just a day after rocking his world in that listening booth. He'd been hit with dread at the thought she'd mistaken him for his twin.

Now, a very different kind of dread coated his throat with a bitter taste. *Why? Nerves are normal. We're fine.*

But Elle's face was still waxy, and pain radiated in her gaze.

Jennifer stood up so Sam could sit again. He reported on their instructions.

Elle's eyebrows knitted, but then her forehead cleared. "Right, the overnight bag. I don't know. I just feel kind of woozy. But I guess that's normal, right?"

Sam nodded. "She said jitters are normal. But if you have any doubts, we can go right now."

She hesitated, then shook her head and flashed a watery smile. "I hate interrupting *Pee Wee's Playhouse*, but we need to go. Tell me what Cowboy Curtis and Miss Yvonne are up to this week, okay?"

Jennifer snorted. "As if. As if we're about to sit around and veg over TV while you're giving birth." She jumped up and pulled Alex with her. "We'll be in the waiting room before you even get there. I'll call Monica and have her meet us."

Elle breathed a laugh. "Love you guys," she said while Sam helped her stand.

She clutched the towel around her swollen waist with one hand and Sam's fingers with the other until Jennifer took over towel duty. They formed a little processional out to the GTO, with Brian, Dylan, and Alex taking up the rear.

When she got to the car, Elle looked around and giggled. "The neighbors must think we've finally lost it completely with a little parade like this. Seriously, guys, thanks—*ughh*."

Everyone jumped as her face contorted with pain. Sam's fingers went numb where she squeezed them as she bent forward, hissing for breath. "Oh, god, that hurts," she panted.

"Elle? Should I—" Sam started.

"Just hang on. Hang on, I'm… okay… okay." She stood up and blinked in surprise. "Holy shit, that's painful. Uh, I mean, it's magical and doesn't hurt at all," she said with a sly grin at Jennifer.

Jennifer's eyes were wide, but she smiled back. "Yeah, it looks super fun. Now, y'all better hurry up and go!"

Sam helped Elle into the car and slid across the hood to the driver's side. He and Brian mastered the move two summers ago just for fun. Nana had cackled with laughter while they practiced in their parents' driveway on the old El Camino.

Elle rolled her eyes when he got in. Sam flashed her an innocent expression. "What? I've got to get it out of my system now. I don't think dads are supposed to have sick moves like that."

"With you as a dad, this kid'll be changing oil and drag racing before they're out of diapers."

"That's the plan. Gotta teach him early."

Elle's laugh was a salve on his nerves. Her humor told him that they were okay. That having a baby was totally normal, and there was no reason for the tingly adrenaline that wouldn't stop coursing through him.

Sam was glad it was a relatively short trip to their house. Six months ago, they signed their first mortgage on a tiny home in East Nashville. When traffic was light, it was less than 20 minutes to Monica and Dylan's spot near campus. Sam pulled into the drive and killed the engine.

"Can you pack for me? I don't want to move," Elle murmured. Her eyes were closed, and that sheen had returned to her forehead.

"Of course. I'll be back in ten minutes, and we'll be on the way, okay?"

She nodded, so he ran inside. Sam threw Elle's clothes and toiletries into a bag, forgot about packing for himself, and ran out without locking the door. He skidded back to jam the key in the door, then sprinted to the car.

Elle had slumped down, seemingly asleep. Her head lolled against her seat.

The adrenaline in Sam's system went cold. "Elle? Wake up. Wake up." He reached over and patted her cheek until her eyes fluttered open. She blinked and sat up, but all the color was gone from her face.

"Hmm? I'm tired. I don't feel right. I... I think we need to hurry."

He didn't answer. He tossed the bag in the backseat and threw the car into reverse. No drag racer would've stepped to Sam that morning. He zoomed through the quiet streets of Nashville with his fingers wrapped around the steering wheel, obeying only the most necessary of traffic laws until—

"*Dammit*," he hissed, slamming on the brakes so hard that the tires squealed. The railroad crossing arm dinged as it lowered. An old freight train came crawling across their path.

Elle laid a clammy hand on his forearm. Sam turned and forgot his anger. Her lips curved in a little smile. "Tell me a story, Sam. I feel so tired. I... need something to focus on."

He stared at her for a beat. The train was eternally long,

with no caboose in sight. So, Sam opened his mouth and blurted, "I lied to you, Elle."

Her brows knitted. "Hmm?"

He leaned over and pressed his lips to her forehead. Sam realized he was shaking, but he continued. "I lied to you, Beautiful. I—I knew when you walked into Mac's that first day that you were friends with Monica. I knew we'd see each other again, that we had the same friends."

She didn't speak, but her eyes did. *Oh, really?* they said.

He nodded.

"How?" she breathed.

Sam swallowed the lump in his throat. "I saw you at Monica's two weeks before we met. You were asleep on her couch, and I was drunk off my ass. I fell through that front door, and there you were. The most beautiful thing I'd ever seen. You were like… some kind of… celestial dream. I think I fell in love with you even then."

She cocked her head, but the crossing arm finally lifted. Sam kissed her once more and floored the accelerator. They swung up to the ER minutes later. By then, there was no question that Elle couldn't walk into the hospital, so he put his flashers on and ran inside. Sam explained the situation to the admissions desk and pleaded for help. The nurse nodded and promised they would be right out.

Elle had opened her car door and gotten her feet on the ground. She was bent over, panting through another contraction, when he returned. Sam dropped to his knees in front of her and let her grip his hands as she rode it out.

When she relaxed, those green eyes kicked his heart again. Like always.

"Celestial. That's a pretty word. You don't hear it a lot,

do you?"

It took Sam a full beat to realize he was the one who'd said it. He crooked his lips. "Guess not."

Her lips curved, too. "Sam?"

"Yeah, Beautiful?"

"It's a girl."

He blinked. "How do you know that?"

She shrugged. "Just a feeling, I guess. I don't know. But Sam? Let's name her Celeste, okay? No more jokes. For real."

Two nurses appeared, so Sam stepped aside and let them help Elle into the wheelchair. He pressed her knuckles to his lips as they jogged inside together. "Totally. It's perfect. I'm just relieved you're not pissed that I lied to you."

"Oh, I am. I just figured we'd talk about that later."

He laughed, even with his heart in his throat.

They rode the elevator to the 10th floor, where Dr. Walsh met them. As soon as Elle was hooked up to monitors, the doctor's mouth set in a line. She turned to Sam. "Eleanor's heart rate is dangerously low. So is the baby's. I don't think we can wait for her to progress any further. I'm recommending an emergency C-section immediately."

Sam swallowed hard. "Whatever you have to do," he rasped.

She put her hand on his shoulder. "We'll take good care of your wife and child, Sam. But I'm afraid you'll have to wait. Limited staff only for surgery."

He floated out to the waiting room to find that, true to their word, all his friends were already there. Even his parents and Nana had arrived. He mumbled an update on what was going on, then looked around and croaked, "Excuse me."

In the restroom, Sam gripped the porcelain sink and struggled to breathe. Sobs racked his body even though no tears came at first. *What is going on? Why am I not with her? Why can't I be there? She's my whole life. She needs me, and I'm standing here like a helpless dork.*

Two strong hands clapped onto his shoulders and spun him around. Sam stared into his twin's face, only then realizing that tears had begun to flow down his cheeks. He clenched his teeth. "I can't handle this," he choked.

"Of fucking course you can because everything is fine," Brian barked. His words radiated authority, but Sam saw the fear in his eyes. "Pull it together. Your wife is strong as hell. You gotta be strong for her, too."

Sam's angst ebbed. He gulped several deep breaths. "You're right. I can do that."

"Damn right. Put some water on your face, and let's go."

Sam splashed his cheeks, then turned around again. He didn't speak, but he told Brian with his stare how grateful he was.

Brian smirked. "Always glad to tell you to get your shit together, bro."

The restroom door had just closed behind them when the door across the waiting room opened. A nurse popped her head in and scanned the crowd. She did a double take on Sam and Brian. "Mr. Greene?" she asked hesitantly.

They chuckled. "Me this time," Sam said, but then he stopped and turned to his brother. "Will you come with me?"

Brian rolled his eyes. "Dweeb." But then he twisted his

lips. "Hell yeah, I will."

They followed the nurse down the hallway and into an anteroom to the nursery. The brothers stared through a window at rows of clear plastic isolettes. Most of them were filled with babies.

"Holy shit," they breathed at the same time.

Brian laughed. "I'm not getting married until I'm thirty-five. Even then, I doubt I'll be father material. But, wow, this is wild. You're a *dad*, dude."

"And you're an uncle," Sam replied.

"And I'm Nurse Alice, and you'll both need to put these on," the nurse said as she offered them green surgical scrubs. She flashed a little smile that told them she saw this reaction all the time.

"But what about Elle?" Sam asked as he fumbled into the gear. As soon as he asked it, fear began to claw at him again.

Nurse Alice paused. "She did great," she said quietly.

"She did indeed." They all turned as Dr. Walsh entered the room. Her eyes were tired behind a surgical mask. She pulled it off and smiled. "It's a good thing we got into surgery when we did, though."

Sam's brain buzzed. "Wait. But is she—?"

Dr. Walsh smiled and touched his arm. "A champ, Sam. She's a champ. She's resting now and should be mostly out of anesthesia in an hour or so. The three of us can discuss details later. For now, go meet your daughter."

"I'd like my brother to come with me, if that's alright." Sam gestured to Brian as if anyone wondered who he meant.

"That's just fine," Dr. Walsh said with another smile before walking out.

They followed Alice into the room, where Sam sat in a rocking chair. Alice disappeared and returned with a bundle swaddled in a green blanket with a little cap on her head.

His daughter. Sam could only stare.

Brian leaned over the back of the chair to peer over Sam's shoulder. "Oh, my god," he muttered. "I can't believe this."

"She's beautiful, isn't she?"

"She's fucking perfect."

"Don't say fuck in front of my daughter," Sam grumbled. "We have to be grownups and shit."

They traded a smile.

"Dude, we gotta go introduce her."

Sam glanced at Alice, who nodded and motioned toward the door. They walked back to the waiting room.

He squeezed Celeste, and she cooed. "Sorry," he whispered with a sheepish smile.

She opened her eyes. Already they were bluish-green.

Blink, went Celeste.

Sam cocked his head. *Can we talk like this too?* He asked with his gaze. *Your mom is good at it. Want to have a go? I'm Sam. I'm your dad. I'll spend the rest of my life doing all I can to make sure you're happy, but your mom is the cool parent. You'll figure that out pretty quick, I'm sure. I'm the biggest geek, but I'll try not to embarrass you too much. I don't know how I got this lucky, how I got her and you. But I'm here for whatever you need, okay? All in, Celeste. I promise.*

"Guys?" Brian's prideful voice took Sam out of his hazy reverie. "It's a girl."

"Nah, it's Celeste freaking Greene," Sam corrected as he held her high.

The whole room melted.

He flashed a grin at Jennifer. "You think they'll be friends?" he asked.

Jennifer scoffed. Her hand automatically drifted to her abdomen again. She'd declared after her first OB visit that it was a boy. The nursery was already blue and yellow, even though she was barely out of her first trimester. "No doubt they will. Nick had better look out for his cousin Celeste."

Sam rolled his eyes. "Please. Celeste will be the one looking out for him."

Jennifer laughed at that, but Alice reappeared before they could say more. "Sam? Eleanor is awake."

Sam didn't even glance backward, but then he knew he didn't need to. They would understand. He power-walked as fast as possible without jostling the precious bundle in his arms. Alice stopped at the end of the hall. She pushed a door open for him. Sam mouthed, "Thank you," as he stepped through, and she winked.

"We're closed."

Elle's exhausted, dusty voice closed Sam's throat when he walked into the room. She opened one eye and kicked his heart with that sideways gaze.

"You're definitely open," he whispered, echoing their first exchange in the record store long ago. "And anyway, I've got someone for you to meet."

He walked over to her bedside, and Elle leaned forward, the haze of anesthesia receding quickly.

Celeste squirmed as she was transferred from her father to her mother. Sam sat on the side of the bed and put his arms around his family. He watched the instant it took for his wife to fall in love with their daughter, and his heart burst. His whole world, right there in a hospital bed.

Finally, Elle looked up at him. Tears brimmed in her eyes. "Oh, my god. My heart, Sam. I... I've never felt this way before. Is it the drugs?"

He laughed and pressed his lips to her forehead, covering Celeste's head with his palm. "Nah, it's just science."

Elle's tears spilled down her cheeks even as she laughed. "Let's raise her to be anything but a nice girl. She can be cool, smart, nerdy—whatever. She can even be a freaking debutante if she wants. But I want her to be herself. And I don't want her to ever doubt that that's not good enough. I want her to know that she'll never disappoint us by doing things her way. I want her to love herself. To be free to be exactly who she wants to be."

Sam grinned. "Absolutely, Beautiful. Absofreakingloutely."

ACKNOWLEDGEMENTS

First and foremost, thank you to the real Mac. For teaching me that we don't pay no attention to kangaroos. For *The Point!* For being my lifelong buddy.

Thank you to Alyssa for encouraging me to share my sparkle. Thank you to the pastry crew for bringing light, love, and romance to my life. Sarah, Sandy, Stef, & Sonia, you all are true friends of the first rank. Thank you Nathaly for technical advice on Elle's baking journey. Thank you Brian for absolutely everything.

And thank you to my mom. You are not Eleanor, but you are my constant inspiration for a strong woman who made her way no matter what. And, you were my technical advisor on the medical bits, so thank you as well for that!

In memory of my own 'Nana,' aka Mimi. I love you forever.

Thank you to all the Anti-Belles who keep reading and loving these stories. Y'all mean the world.

ABOUT THE AUTHOR

Skye McDonald writes contemporary romance novels that will make you laugh, cry, and swoon. Skye's Anti-Belle Series features Nashville GRITS (Girls Raised In the South) learning to love themselves before they can claim their happily ever after. Spoiler: they always do! She has been featured in anthologies and podcasts. Skye also co-authors the Unlikely Pairings novels with Sarah Smith. Writing as Sarah Skye, this duo took a friendship and shared love of romance and turned it into a bestselling series.

When not publishing novels, Skye is a wellness coach, assisting women in becoming the heroes of their own lives via fitness, habit changes, and self-love. The happily ever after in real life is all about loving yourself. Skye's "A Bit Much" newsletter on Substack chronicles her own self-love journey.

Skye lives in Montclair, NJ. In her free time, she hikes with her dog, leads a women's networking group, runs Spartan races, travels, Scuba dives, and is learning to ski. Someday she'll take a break and chill out, preferably on a beach. But not yet. There's so much life to live first.

9 781960 226013